Looking Glass

Miranda Renae'

IMMORTAL WORKS
SALT LAKE CITY

Immortal Works LLC
1505 Glenrose Drive
Salt Lake City, Utah 84104
Tel: (385) 202-0116

© 2023 Miranda Renae'
mirandarenae.com

Cover Art by Ashley Literski
strangedevotion.wixsite.com/strangedesigns

All rights reserved, including the right to reproduce this book or portions thereof in any form whatsoever. For more information visit immortalworks.press/contact.

This book is a work of fiction. Names, characters, businesses, organizations, places, events and incidents either are the product of the author's imagination or are used fictitiously. Any resemblance to actual persons, living or dead, events, or locales is entirely coincidental.

ISBN 978-1-953491-72-5 (Paperback)
ASIN B0CPWM3DGQ (Kindle Edition)

You are seen
You are loved
You will be missed

Prologue

"If I survive, tell him not to look for me. To live a normal life. He deserves that."

Markus clasped her hand. "It won't stop him from looking, and you know it. He won't stop looking until he finds you."

"He won't find me." A sad smile crossed her lips. "Marci's too good." *Not Kaleb or even Reid Redding herself will be able to find me.*

She moved to stand next to the bed and pulled his car keys from her pocket. As she did, Turtle's bracelet fell to the floor at her feet. Alice picked up the unusual piece of jewelry she had thought was in the car with her blood-soaked clothes and slipped it onto her wrist. She wasn't sure what was so important about it, but if Turtle wanted it, she planned to hold on to it.

Alice laid the keys next to the note she had agonized over for the last hour. The letter would explain her disappearance and encourage Kaleb not to look for her, to move on with his life. She pushed Kaleb's blond curls from his forehead, leaned in and kissed him. A tear trickled down her cheek. "I thought I might have loved you, but... I'm sorry."

Markus met Alice at the door and handed her two blue and two red pills and the instructions on where to meet Marci. "If you do this and it works, there's no going back."

She looked back at the room Kaleb slept in and hoped one day he would forgive her. Then she tossed the pills into her mouth and waited for them to dissolve on her tongue, leaving a minty aftertaste.

It wouldn't matter much longer if he did forgive her. If everything went how she hoped, in ten minutes, she'd have no memory of anything from the past four years. Not even him.

Chapter 1

Marci looked down at the bright white numbers of the dashboard clock. Alice was late.

To be fair, so was Marci. Getting her twin sister Kit somewhere safe had taken longer than planned. Marci pulled out her phone, scrolling to the messages from Kaleb's brother, Markus.

Alice is on her way to you.
ETA 5 minutes.

He'd sent that ten minutes ago.

Marci looked toward the automatic doors of the hospital entrance. The reflection of the low-hanging evening sun twinkled on the clean glass. *I knew I should have gone inside to get her.* Alice wanted to leave on her own for some reason, and Marci wanted to respect that. *Something must have gone wrong. Who knows what those pills from Dr. Turtle really do?* Marci growled. *Alice's erased memories might be the least of our problems.*

Alice was surprisingly stubborn for someone who lived life in the moment, letting things happen to her instead of taking action.

She pulled out her phone, debating calling Markus to get some idea of what direction Alice might have gone. If she was lucky and Markus was smart, he discreetly followed her. She hit dial and held the phone to her ear, listening to the ring as she shuffled through the documents she'd put together to help Alice disappear.

There was a spelling error on the new birth certificate. Marci sighed as she pulled a notebook out of the backpack from the floor. She turned to a blankish page, noting the error under an old grocery list before shoving everything back into the bag.

Markus's deep voice came on the line. "Hello, Hello... Why are you calling when you can text?"

His voicemail message was the worst, and Markus never answered his text. With a tight jaw and a held-back curse, Marci dialed his work phone.

She was helping Alice disappear against her better judgment. Kaleb was going to freak out when he woke up, and Alice was gone. He wouldn't care if she didn't remember who he was, only that Alice wasn't safe on her own.

Straight to voicemail. Marci slammed her fist on the steering wheel. Something was definitely wrong. She got out of the car, scanning the parking lot for Alice. Marci didn't want to leave the car empty in case Alice came here. If Alice's memories had already faded, the note Marci had her write would lead her to this spot and this car.

A dark van sped past Marci. The Red Queen Inc. logo plastered on its side. It pulled into the ambulance bay moments before two men dressed in scrubs rushed out the hospital doors. Each one held a body over their shoulder, one in jeans and sneakers and the other in a hospital gown, his messy blond curls sticking up in every direction.

She knew before the words left her mouth. "Alice and Kaleb."

Marci ran toward the van, dialing Markus as she went. Her heart sped up with each ring.

Come on, pick up.

Don't be dead.

Marci knew better than most what happened to someone who got in the Redding's way. Alice and Kaleb were in their way.

The men yanked open the van's back doors, tossing Alice and

Kaleb inside before climbing in themselves. She needed to act fast; if Kaleb and Alice disappeared now, she might never find them.

Marci pounded on the closed door before it could speed off. The door swung open, and one of the men loomed over her. A surprised look etched on his pockmarked face. She pushed her long, dark hair behind her ears and made eye contact, using the unusual violet color contacts she'd worn today to her advantage. Like so many others had in the past, this man tried to look away.

"Miss Lewis," he gulped. "What are you doing here?"

What am I doing here? Marci had no idea what to tell them, but she couldn't let them take Alice and Kaleb. *If I go with them, will Kit know how to find me?* She knew her sister would start looking if she missed their daily check-in call. *Would she know to call Ryan or even Markus—if he's alive, that is—for backup?* They hadn't been working with them for very long.

Marci stepped forward, close enough to hear her speak but not so close he could grab her easily. The inside of the van had been turned into a makeshift ambulance. Tubes and wires hung above Alice, who lay on a wooden bench bolted to the van's floor. The beep, beep, beep of two heart monitors echoed through the small cab. Marci couldn't see Kaleb, but she assumed the second beep belonged to him.

They're alive, but she wasn't sure for how long.

She fought down the shaking in her voice. "Ms. Redding sent me. I'm to escort you." It wasn't the best plan, but at least she'd know where they were.

"Stop," someone screamed behind them.

Marci turned around to see Markus stumble out the hospital door, blood trailing down his cheek, his dark hair matted to a cut on his head. She was relieved these goons hadn't killed him, but they must have knocked him out. Her relief was short-lived when she saw the gun in his hand pointed at the men in the van.

No, no.

Her plan may not be good or fully formed, but it was better than pointing a gun at two guys in a van.

What is he thinking? There is no guarantee he won't shoot Alice or Kaleb by mistake.

Before Markus could get another word out, the pockmarked man pushed Marci to the ground, his weapon drawn. A shot sounded above her, followed by the shattering of glass. The van door slammed shut moments before it sped off, tires screeching.

She watched as Markus ran past her, kicking up dirt and rocks with his quick steps. She thought about going after him, but there was no point. Markus was never going to catch up to them.

Marci's fingers brushed against a strange-looking bracelet made up of small liquid beads on the ground and wondered if Alice dropped it. She shoved it into her pocket before checking herself for any injuries. She let the relief of seeing Markus alive settle around her, waiting for him to pull himself together.

It didn't take long.

Markus turned toward her, his shoulders stooped, defeat shown in every inch of his body. His eyes met hers before his large frame crumbled to the ground in front of her. Marci ran across the parking lot, kneeling in front of Markus, forcing him to meet her eyes.

"They took them." He wiped away the blood that dripped from a gash on his forehead. "They took Kaleb and Alice."

But the men who took Kaleb and Alice had screwed up.

They left witnesses.

Chapter 2

Six months later

Kaleb looked at the neon blue sign for his oldest brother's coffee shop. The words Button Up, a clever play on the last name he shared with their mother, Button, gave the street an unearthly glow.

Alice would have loved this place. Today was her twenty-second birthday.

The French cafe-style chairs, vintage cups, and local art covering the walls created a Bohemian style she would've found charming. *I'm not supposed to be doing this alone. You should be here, living our dream, having a normal life.* It had been six months since Alice's funeral, and Kaleb still wasn't sure how to live without her. He knocked on the glass door to get his brother Jake's attention.

Jake walked across the store, leaning on his cane harder than normal. *The old injury must be giving him trouble today.* Kaleb smiled at his brother as he approached the glass door.

Until six months ago, Kaleb hadn't seen Jake since the incident that caused him to walk with a limp. Jake had shut out everyone after that day three years ago, and if it weren't for Jake, Kaleb would have done the same now. Not that he talked to anyone other than Jake and the people that worked at Button Up these days.

He hadn't realized how much he missed his brother until Jake showed up at his door shortly after Alice died, offering Kaleb a job and a place to live. It was a chance for Kaleb to get away from their father and Red Queen. A clean break. Sorta. Ohio with his mom might have been a better choice since everyone thought she was dead and had no idea how to find her. It would have been quieter, at least.

Here gave him a chance to get to know an older brother he'd always looked up to and who had been there for Kaleb in his way until he couldn't.

The door swung open. "Forget your key again?" Jake asked.

"Nah, just making sure you get your exercise for the day." Kaleb walked past him into the darkened store. "Getting a bit flabby in your old age."

Jake chuckled. "Who needs exercise when I'm always picking up after your lazy butt?"

Kaleb grabbed a black apron from behind the counter, pulling the thin strap over his head before washing his hands. "Me lazy? You must be confused. Who left the half-eaten pizza on the counter last night?"

Jake laughed. "Right next to your advanced chemistry book. Are you even taking that class?"

He shrugged. "Thinking about it." He wasn't, but he didn't want Jake asking too many questions. No, Kaleb was still trying to understand what had happened inside Red Queen Headquaters and why Alice had died.

Jake smiled at him but didn't say anything else about the book.

Kaleb was relieved. It was an easy lie since he'd only been two classes away from graduation when he'd dropped out. Well, not dropped out, but he'd stopped going to classes, too caught up in the guilt and grief of losing Alice.

Jake walked around the counter, filling the dessert case. On a typical day, Kaleb would do this; it was part of his routine. The only time Jake did it was if he wanted to talk. Kaleb grabbed a donut from the large rolling rack next to Jake, placing it in the case as he waited for Jake to say what he needed.

It took him five minutes of sighs and false starts before Kaleb finally turned to him. "Spit it out." Jake's face scrunched up in a way that meant whatever he was going to say wasn't going to be good.

"Markus stopped by yesterday."

Kaleb dropped the last pastry into the case and shrugged. "And this is new? Markus comes by or calls at least once a week." Not that Kaleb ever talked to him. He hadn't spoken to Markus since he'd told Kaleb about Alice's death. He knew it wasn't fair to blame Markus for what happened, but he did.

Jake leaned against the wall. "He asked me to give you this." He pulled a crumbled, coffee-stained envelope from his back pocket. "You know, since you're acting like a jerk with this whole silent treatment thing."

Kaleb rolled his eyes but took the envelope from his brother. *It's probably another update on his investigation into Red Queen and the fake Task Force.* He was about to tear it up, but Jake's words stopped him.

"I debated giving that to you. You've been doing so well in the last few weeks. Going to classes. Showering." Jake rubbed the back of his neck. "Then I thought about what I wouldn't give to have one last thing from Ruby. Anyway, it's not my place to keep it from you."

Kaleb turned the envelope over in his hands, studying the thick black letters of his name scrawled across it. He knew that handwriting.

The way the 'A' connected to the 'l' and the first line of the 'K' was thicker than the rest of his name.

Alice.

The letter was from Alice.

But how?

Jake kept talking as Kaleb only half-listened, his heart racing as he ran his shaky finger under the seal.

"They shouldn't have kept it from you. You deserve to know what Alice had to say at the end. Even if it turns out to be nonsense."

Kaleb could feel Jake's gaze creep up his back as he pulled the lined paper from its envelope, staring at the black letters without seeing the words on the page. Dread turned inside his stomach. *When did she write this?* Kaleb ran his fingers over the words. "How long?"

"Markus told me this morning." Jake limped away, mumbling under his breath. "Maybe if you'd had that letter, you wouldn't have felt so lost."

Maybe.

He sunk into a nearby chair, the oversized brown cushions releasing the scent of dark roast coffee trapped in its confines. Kaleb laid the letter on the table in front of him, tracing the mixture of print and cursive that was Alice's handwriting. Too scared to read it. If it weren't for one word, CURE, that caught his eye, Kaleb would have shoved the thing into his pocket, forgetting about it until he was in a dark place looking for pain.

He took a deep, grounding breath and started to read.

Kaleb,

If you're reading this, it means the cure worked. I'm glad you don't have memories of the things that happened inside Red Queen during those hours you were infected. No one should have to see the things we've seen.

Kaleb sighed. He wished he'd forgotten. Maybe it wouldn't hurt so much if he forgot Alice and everything that happened inside Red Queen that day. Especially the short time that WonderLand ran through him, taking over his every thought, driving him to the brink of insanity. He hated himself for every thought and action he took that day.

If I hadn't let myself get exposed, Alice wouldn't have taken those pills.

He never understood why she'd taken Turtle's pills. They were a distraction from what was really happening. One that cost Alice her life.

Kaleb shook away the memory. He wasn't ready to think about that day. About Marci finding Alice dead. He considered putting the letter away but needed to read Alice's last words.

Kaleb, if you hadn't found me in the coffee shop that day, I don't know where I would have ended up. Without you, I would never have become the person I am today. If you take one thing from all of this, know that you are important. You made a difference. Never stop fighting for what you believe is right.

Don't let what happened to me stop you from finishing what you started all those years ago.

Stop Reid Redding.

Alice

Hoping for more, Kaleb turned the paper over in his hand, looking for something he knew wasn't there. A sentence, a stupid drawing, anything to spend more time with her. He needed answers. He only had questions. The biggest one—why had she gone back into Red Queen after getting him out?

Pain and anger radiated through him. He thought about calling Markus, even pulled his phone out, thumbing through his contacts, but then he thought better of it. *The only reason Markus gave me this now is because he needs something from me.* Kaleb wouldn't do it. The cost would be too much. It didn't matter that Alice had asked him to keep fighting. He had nothing left to fight for, not anymore.

He did the only thing he could; he shoved the letter in his pocket and got to work, pushing his past into the knot that took up residence in his stomach six months ago. He thanked whatever higher power that it was not only a Monday but a holiday: the shop would be extra busy today.

Chapter 3

Six hours later, Kaleb finally slowed down enough to think about the growling in his stomach. As he made his way to the break room, an older man with salt-and-pepper hair walked in the door and called out to him. Kaleb thought about pretending he didn't hear Hank. But Kaleb knew Hank would wait until Kaleb would help him, bothering the other patrons.

He grabbed his apron, pulling it over his head once again. "Good afternoon, Hank. The usual?"

Hank smiled with his whole face and asked in the graveled voice of a lifelong smoker. "Did you see the news today?"

"I haven't, but everyone's been talking about it." He'd spent the last three months trying to avoid it. Pretend like it wasn't happening. Even now, the radio behind him chirped in with the headlines that had flooded every other information outlet since the cloud appeared over the city three weeks ago.

A mysterious pink cloud is still covering Salt City. City quarantine restrictions tighten.

Hank coughed. "The CDC asked Red Queen Inc. to help contain the health crisis."

Kaleb nodded.

He wasn't surprised.

Reid Redding had friends in high places.

They'd make it look like some freak thing, and Red Queen—ever the compassionate organization—would sweep in and save the people. Of course, there were losses, but the great Reid Redding wasn't to blame. All the while, they would experiment on the sick and dying. He suspected something else had happened, something that changed everything. *Why else would Markus give me that letter now? He wanted me to come back to help. It's never going to happen.* Kaleb filled Hank's cup with black coffee. *That part of my life is over.*

Kaleb handed Hank his cup. "Huh, hopefully, they find a way to help the people in Salt City."

Hank leaned in close to Kaleb. "What do you think is really going on? 'Health Crisis' has to be code for something."

That money ruled the world, and Reid Redding thinks nothing more of people beyond what they can do for her. "I don't know," Kaleb said, shrugging.

"Oh, come on, how could you not know? You worked for the government."

Kaleb rolled his eyes. "Once again, Hank, I never worked for the government." *Just an evil CEO bent on world domination.*

Hank winked at him. "Sure, and I've never smoked a day in my life."

He wasn't sure where Hank got the idea that he worked for the government. All he knew was that the more he tried to persuade Hank otherwise, the more Hank seemed convinced that Kaleb was lying.

The new girl, Mandy, handed Kaleb an empty cup—"decaf soy latte w/extra shot and cream"—written on the side. He held back a groan at the absurdity of the order. *Soy with cream; what's the point?*

"Sorry, Hank, I need to get back to work."

Hank picked up his cup from the counter, looking around the shop. "Of course, busy day." He turned around and walked across the room to a table in the corner and pulled out his usual book about conspiracy theories.

Once Hank sat down, Kaleb turned to Mandy mouthing the words, thank you. He liked the man, but he could talk, and it was always about something in the news or some crazy theory he'd read about in one of his books. A few months ago, he spent an hour telling Kaleb that nothing was real, and they were trapped in some elaborate dream world, and if someone focused on just one thing for too long, they would see computer code. He insisted that a shadowy organization was doing experiments on everyone while they slept. Kaleb had seen and heard some crazy things, but that was up there.

Kaleb finished making the drink Mandy had given him, thinking of the leftover pizza in the fridge as he worked. He turned the cup around, reading the name "Linqu" in permanent marker.

Maybe it was because the name was spelled unusually, one of Mandy's specialties, or that he hadn't seen him since the funeral. Still, Kaleb was surprised to see Linc Sanchez stroll to the counter sporting a teal t-shirt under a black leather jacket. His dark hair was pulled into a haphazard ponytail on the wrong side of a haircut.

Kaleb's heart rate increased at the sight of him. *First, the pink cloud over Salt City, then Markus leaves Alice's letter, and now Linc arrives.* It was too much of a coincidence.

"Hey." Linc leaned against the counter. "Do you have a minute to talk?"

Kaleb wanted to scream, NO, but knew it wouldn't do any good. If it weren't Linc, it would be someone else. There was no way his friends would leave him be, not with what was going on in Salt City. Not when he was the one who pulled them all into this life. *At least Linc will respect my decision. I think.*

"Sure, give me a minute."

Instead of hanging his apron on one of the pegs on the wall behind him, Kaleb folded it into a tiny square, took it to the backroom, and placed it in his locker. On the way back up front, he considered grabbing a cold piece of pizza and scarfing it down before meeting Linc, but his stomach rolled with the thought. Instead, Kaleb walked to Jake's office. He told himself it was to let his brother know he was going on break, something he'd never done before. Kaleb wasn't prepared for the wave of emotions that churned in his stomach at the sight of his friend.

Jake's office was empty.

Of course, the one time I need an out, he's not here.

He couldn't think of anything to keep him in the back and knew the longer he put this off, the worse the feelings fighting to get out would be. Repeating Alice's mantra of "I'm fine" three times, something he started doing after her funeral, Kaleb walked out of the backroom to find Linc.

He sat alone in the back corner, sliding his drink from one hand to the other, his eyes focused on its movements. Kaleb sat in the chair across from Linc, arms crossed over his chest.

"Before you ask, no, I'm not coming back."

Linc flinched at Kaleb's words, or maybe it was his tone. Either way, he didn't look up. "So, you've heard about Salt City."

Of course, who hasn't? "Just what's on the news. A health crisis? Who came up with that?"

Linc took a sip of his drink. "Marci. She's been suppressing the media from inside the city."

"Of course she is." *That explains why she missed their weekly call. He never picked up, but it was nice to have someone from his old life checking up on him.* "I bet she hates that."

Linc looked up from his drink, a smile on his lips. "She's driving Markus crazy. Keeping this a secret is killing her. Last week I heard them argue over her releasing a video of people tearing each other apart while people in lab coats watch." Linc looked back down at his coffee. "I think she's the first person I've seen get under your brother's skin. Other than you, of course."

Kaleb tried not to focus on what was happening in Salt City. He knew firsthand what those people were going through. Instead, he focused on the sadness mixed with a bit of jealousy that threatened to take hold of him. *Markus can have a happy ending with Marci, while I have to live without Alice because of him.*

"I'm glad Markus has someone," he lied, attempting to hide his jealousy of Markus and Marci.

Linc ran his hands through his dark hair. "Look."

Here comes the speech about why I should come back.

"I'm supposed to try and convince you to come back. To finish what you started." He sighed. "I'm not going to do that."

"Wait, what?" His stomach knotted. "Why not?"

What kind of game is he playing?

"You have a life here, and Kaleb, more than any of us, you deserve a normal life." Linc started moving the cup between his hands again, the black wristband catching on the table with each pass. "But I need a favor."

There it was. "What kind of favor?" he grumbled.

"Tom found something; it could be nothing, but he thinks it might be a cure for WonderLand, a way out of this mess."

Kaleb opened his mouth to remind Linc that Tom had tried to kill him, but before he could say anything, Linc raised his hand, stopping him. "Before you say anything, I've seen—"

Kaleb cut him off. "I don't know what you saw, but—"

"Are you telling me that you're living this nice, normal life while being infected, Kaleb? Because I was there when Alice pulled you out. We all knew you were infected, but Alice insisted on taking you to the hospital."

Kaleb ground his teeth. "Linc, WonderLand is—"

Linc interrupted him again. "Whatever." He threw a piece of paper across the table. "I'm not arguing with you. Tell me, is there anyone on that list I can trust?"

"I..." Kaleb pinched the bridge of his nose and sighed.

Linc stood up, pushing the chair in with more force than necessary. "Don't help. Just know if something happens to me, it's your fault."

Rolling his eyes at Linc's dramatics, Kaleb reached for the crumpled paper on the table. "Sit down."

"Why?"

Kaleb scanned the list of names. "You wanted my help, didn't you?" All the names were people who had been inside Red Queen during the so-called outbreak. They'd only be available for Linc's mission if they'd bought or traded something for their freedom.

"Seriously, Linc, every single name on this list is someone who either worked for Red Queen or the Task Force. We went over this. Don't trust anyone who has worked for either of them. We have no way of knowing if Gryff and Joseph were lying about the Task Force being a sham."

Linc sat back down with a huff. "Marci said the same thing."

Then why ask me? "If you're done wasting my time," Kaleb stood up, "I need to get back to work."

"Just one more question." Linc rubbed the back of his neck. "Did he give it to you?"

"Did who give me what?"

Kaleb's stomach sank. He *can't know about the letter. He would have given it to me while I was still in the hospital if he did.*

"Markus. He didn't give it to you. I'm going to..." he grumbled something under his breath. "I voted to give it to you when you woke up, but no one listened."

Unable to believe what he was hearing, Kaleb sat back down. "What are you talking about?"

"The letter Alice wrote before she–anyways, it's how I know there's a cure. Alice took it. You both did."

"Linc, I don't know what we took, but..." He rubbed his temples. "WonderLand is a distraction from what's going on. Whatever it was we took, Turtle has it. He disappeared with it and all of his notes. No one has been able to find him since that day. Not even Marci." *If there were anything to find, Marci would have found it on the flash drive he gave her after finding Alice in the creepy rotunda thing months ago.*

Linc took a long sip of his drink, his eyes unfocused. Kaleb wondered if he heard him or was so desperate to help Tom that he heard what he wanted to hear.

"What about the side effects? There were supposed to be side effects." Linc rambled. "Though yours wouldn't be as bad since you'd been exposed to the virus for a short time. Alice, on the other hand..."

A heavy weight settled inside Kaleb, gluing his feet to the floor. "Side effects?"

"Umm, well." Linc looked around the room, scanning it as if he thought someone was listening to them. "Memory loss for one."

Kaleb growled. "Linc!"

"Alice, she's..." He pulled at the thick, black, rubber-looking band on his wrist.

Kaleb stood up, hands on the table, looming over Linc. "She's what?"

Linc kept his eyes trained on the table and spoke in an almost whisper.

"Alice is alive."

Chapter 4

The room went sideways. Kaleb didn't want to believe what Linc had told him. If it was true, everyone he'd ever trusted had lied to him. Linc snapped his fingers in front of Kaleb's face.

"Kaleb, you there?"

He shook his head, clearing away the thoughts that raced through his mind. "Yeah." Kaleb ran his fingers through his hair. " I need to text Marci."

Kaleb grabbed his phone, his fingers rushing over the letters as he typed.

Alice is alive!

Quicker than should have been possible, a text from Marci popped up with a quiet ding. With shaking fingers, Kaleb opened it: an image of a sleeping Alice lit up his phone. Her dark hair matted to her face; wires and tubes attached to her arms.

She's in Salt City.

Kaleb started to type out a response, but before he could get two letters out, a new message from Marci came through, pinging both his and Linc's phones.

Be out front in 15.

Linc started to fidget with the black band on his right wrist. "What are you going to do?"

"I don't know." Kaleb stood up. "I need a minute."

He stormed into the back room, not waiting to see what Linc would do. Kaleb needed to untangle the mess of what his life had become before Marci arrived. The quickest way to do that was to talk it out. He made his way past the lockers to his brother's office, hoping he was back from wherever he had disappeared.

Jake still wasn't there. Kaleb tried to call him. Jake's phone vibrated across the desk. Kaleb fought the urge to throw his phone across the room. *Now what?* It wasn't unusual for Jake to disappear for a few hours a couple of times a week. He needed to talk to his brother, plus something about this time made Kaleb uneasy. *Why now?*

Not wanting to focus on it too much, Kaleb pushed the feelings down, writing it off as nothing more than his new normal life imploding around him. Like it always did.

He paced the office, reviewing everything that had happened in the last hour, but he kept returning to the same thing. *Alice is alive. If they are pulling me back in, then I have to assume she's in trouble.* He grabbed a blank piece of paper from the printer and a pen from the desk and jotted down a quick note, letting Jake know what had happened. He was going to do what needed to be done to save Alice.

Jake will understand.

Kaleb laid the key to the coffee shop that he hadn't "forgotten" this morning on top of the note. He looked around the office, knowing it could be the last time he would be there, and let the possibility of this life drift away. Before leaving, he grabbed a Thanksgiving card someone had sent to his brother to change into an impromptu birthday card for Alice. He walked to the front of the shop. "Mandy, you're in charge until Jake gets back."

Kaleb stepped out into the cool fall air that stung his cheeks as he waited for Marci. He ignored Linc, who pretended to scroll through his phone. Instead, Kaleb focused on the sunset rolling across the snow-covered street. A single black sedan pulled up to the curb, blocking what little light was left in this barren world.

Linc climbed into the front seat, leaving Kaleb to take the empty seat next to Marci. Her long hair, streaked with purple, was pulled into a complicated braid. Kaleb slid into the cold leather seat next to her, pulling the seatbelt across his chest. He took a deep breath to clear his mind before turning to Marci.

Before he could speak, Markus turned in the driver's seat to face Kaleb. His dark green eyes brimmed with emotions Kaleb didn't want to see. The harsh, yellow interior light of the car highlighted the curves of a face that took care of Kaleb when the world had fallen apart. Now it reminded him of the secrets that changed his world.

"Kaleb, I—"

Kaleb cut him off. "Don't," he snapped. "I can't, not right now." *Maybe not ever.* He looked at the other passengers. Linc sunk down in the seat in front of Kaleb. Marci sat next to him in the back and never looked up from her phone.

He shook his head. "I just... I need time."

Markus nodded. Kaleb sank into the seat, waiting for the next thing to implode. Markus turned around and pulled the car onto the empty street, heading toward Salt City without saying a word.

Kaleb waited for Marci to say something, but she didn't. Her eyes focused on the phone screen in her hand, like when she worked as Reid Redding's assistant. Kaleb grumbled under his breath. *Okay, maybe the car isn't the best place to talk, but she could at least look up long enough to acknowledge I'm here.*

He looked out the window and watched the city turn from strip malls to row houses, trying to let the silence that hung in the car drown out his frustration. It didn't work.

It had taken three words for him to go back on the promise he made to himself. *Alice is alive. And less than a day's drive away the entire time.* He looked over at Marci, who still had her head down, staring at her phone, fingers moving across the screen. Anger coursed through him. He wanted to scream at her.

Do you still have the flash drive I gave you? Is this why Alice is in Salt City? Why let me think she was dead? What else are you and Markus keeping from me?

But he didn't. He couldn't. He was too afraid of what would happen if he lost control. So, he did what he'd done since escaping Red Queen. He buried those feelings and looked for an explanation.

If Alice's last words to me happened and weren't a WonderLand-induced hallucination, then maybe Alice convinced them it was best to let me live a normal life.

He'd played those words over in his mind a million times. "*I thought I might have loved you, but...*" He couldn't remember the rest, maybe something like *I wish we lived a different life—one where we could have a happily ever after.*

Chapter 5

Kaleb only planned on closing his eyes for a minute, but the early morning and the day's stress pulled at him, and the itch of sleep scratched at his brain.

Marci's shaky voice moved through the car, "Kaleb, wake up."

They were parked in an empty parking lot, lit by a single streetlight. A warehouse covered in dark swirls and harsh lines of graffiti stood in front of them, the grayish-pink skyline of Salt City in the distance. A broken shopping cart lay in the middle of the cracked pavement.

He turned to face Marci. "Where are we?"

Her eyes, a natural gray, missing the bright color contacts she favored, were wide with fear. "Look, Kaleb, we don't have a lot of time. Listen carefully. Don't trust anyone, not even me."

He swallowed down the rising fear. "Marci, what's going on?" This wasn't like her.

She pushed the sleeve of her shirt up, showing him a black band like the one he saw on Linc's wrist. The band looked like the ones used to track steps, only there wasn't a bulky section where a small screen with the time should have been. It was all the same thickness and color.

"Kaleb, this is important. If this band is anything other than black, the person is compromised," Marci said.

Markus tapped on the window, and Marci flinched.

What is going on? Why would she be scared of Markus? I've never seen Marci scared of anyone or anything.

"You two coming?" he asked.

She took a deep breath before turning to face him. "Be right there." Marci smiled, and she waved him away. Once Markus was out of sight, she said, "Nod if you understand."

He didn't understand why the band was important, why she was so jumpy, or what would happen inside that warehouse. But he trusted her; if Marci said it was necessary, it was.

He gave a slight nod.

"Good, we're going to go in there." She pointed to the door Markus stood by. "The person running this mission's name is Bobbins, code name FG. You can trust her, but only if her band is what?"

"Black."

"Right. FG wants nothing more than to get everyone out safely. Got it?"

He nodded.

"Okay." She opened the door, letting herself out, and she met Markus at the door with a bounce in her step. Taking his hand in hers, Marci dragged him into the warehouse.

Kaleb reviewed Marci's information, focusing on the few facts he knew. *Marci wasn't telling him everything for some reason. She's scared.* He pushed the car door closed behind him and made his way into the warehouse. *Whatever's happening here will come out eventually. Everything always does.* He hoped she had a chance to tell him before too much damage was done.

He stepped into the building, letting his eyes adjust to the harsh lights from the humming fluorescent bulbs that hung high above. A single box fan stood in the far corner, its uneven blades ticking the seconds. Four light-gray tables sat in the center of the room facing a large screen, reminding Kaleb of his days at Red Queen. If he closed his eyes, Kaleb could swear he heard the *click, click, click* of Reid Redding's shoes.

Kaleb took a deep breath pulling in the smell of dust and...*bubblegum?*

That didn't make sense.

Memories of the theater pushed their way to the surface. A chill moved through him, causing his stomach to turn. He tried to focus his breathing and not the guilt of what he'd done to protect himself and Alice that still haunted him at every turn. Keeping him away from a memory he couldn't quite grasp.

A warm hand clasped his shoulder, sending frantic images of large blood-soaked hands pulling at him and tearing away the parts of him that made him. His skin burned with each touch; muscles tightened with the urge to fight his way to freedom. Spots swarmed his vision. Kaleb clenched his fist, ready to strike his attacker.

Markus's voice broke through the panic. "Breathe," he whispered. "One, two, three."

Kaleb didn't acknowledge his brother, but he did take a few calming breaths looking around the room in an attempt to ground himself. He focused on the people in the room and not the setup. Besides Markus, there was only Marci and Linc, who sat at a table arguing about something. And Tom. Who stood in a corner glaring at Kaleb.

Kaleb ground his teeth. Tom had been the reason Alice went back in. He was the reason Alice was dead. *No, that's not right.* Kaleb shook his head. *Alice going into Red Queen headquarters to get Tom was just a rumor. You looked into it yourself. Tom had done some terrible things, but he hadn't been the reason Alice went back into Red Queen.* He ran his fingers through his hair. *Besides, Alice is alive.*

He still didn't know why they had lied to him. Sure, Linc had said something about protecting him or giving him a chance at a normal life, which was the stupidest thing he'd ever heard. Anger brewed inside him. It wasn't a lie when he'd told Markus he didn't want to talk about it. Turning to face his brother, Kaleb closed his fist, ready to hit Markus.

The door behind them slammed open, revealing the imposing figure of a woman who knew she was in charge. Her long silver locks and bright makeup looked out of place with the dark business suit she wore. She scanned the room as if she were hunting prey. Her footfalls made no sound as they moved across the concrete floor toward Kaleb.

"FG, I'm glad you made it." Markus moved to meet the woman. "Let me—"

FG waved him away. "Kaleb, I'm glad you're here." Her violet eyes focused on him, a twinge of familiarity swimming beneath their depths. She pulled him close, wrapping him in a bone-crushing hug, surrounding him with the scent of sunscreen and cookies. It was the kind of hug that made him miss his mom.

Before he could let that thought sink in, FG let him go. As quickly as she'd pulled him in, she acted as if nothing had happened and turned to face the rest of the room. "Okay, let's get started."

Sitting in a chair at the back of the room, Kaleb resisted the urge to rub his now sore arms where the tight pull of FG's hug still tingled. He couldn't remember the last time someone had hugged him. It would have been weird no matter who it came from. This stranger with the familiar touch was uncomfortable in an entirely different way.

Markus moved to the front of the room to sit next to Marci, leaving Kaleb alone with his thoughts. Tom and Linc sat at the table next to them.

FG stood in front of the room, watching them before speaking loudly. "The plan is simple. Give the people inside Red Queen's Salt City location a reason to move Alice. Once she is out of the building, it will be easier to get her to a safe place."

Marci turned to face the room. "Since my cover inside Red Queen is still intact, I'll stay with Alice, gauging the memory loss until I can bring her to the rendezvous point inside the city."

"Sounds like you have it all worked out," Kaleb said. "So why am I here?"

The others exchanged the kind of looks parents give each other when a child asks something they aren't prepared to explain. Kaleb knew that whatever they said would only be a version of the truth.

Tom turned to him. "It's been made clear to anyone who works inside the building that we are to keep you and Alice apart at all costs."

"Why?"

Marci and Markus cast knowing glances at one another before Marci answered with a sigh. "The two of you together tend to ruin their plans."

"Who are "they"?" he asked.

FG cleared her throat. "It doesn't matter. Not right now."

Huh, so they don't want Alice and me to find each other? Interesting.

The rest of the meeting was spent going over what they could expect once they got into the city. Much of it he'd already known because of his time spent at Red Queen, thanks to the coffee house ramblings of Hank. However, he did learn a few things.

The Task Force had started a group that rivaled the Red Queen's Knights. They called themselves the Bishops. They weren't the same groups, but Kaleb was told both should be avoided at all costs.

It didn't matter whether they had a Knight or Bishop stitched on their uniform—if one of them picked you up, it would result in the same thing: death.

The pink dust that littered much of the city was WonderLand. Get enough on your skin, and you'll go mad.

Once they were behind the quarantine zone, there would be no one to help them but each other.

With that, the meeting ended.

Kaleb watched his brother talk to Tom and Linc as they armed themselves for the mission. Thankfully, he didn't need to be armed for this. Kaleb being in the building should be enough distraction to get the guards to alert the Reddings, who would have no choice but to move Alice.

The last thing Red Queen wanted was for the two of them to reconnect.

But why?

Why keep Alice and me apart? It doesn't make sense, and no one here seems to know or even care why. Just that they can use it to their advantage to get Alice out. What has she gotten us into?

He pulled out the card he'd taken from his brother's office, scribbled out Happy Turkey Day printed on the front of the card, and replaced it with Happy Birthday. Opening the card, he silently thanked whoever had sent it for only writing sincerely and their names. Kaleb scribbled out the names and started a message to Alice that she might never get.

Ace,

I'm sorry that I can't be there when you wake up. There is so much I need to tell you. You have been gone for a long time, and a lot has happened.

I...

Kaleb ran his fingers through his hair, unsure of what to say. *Is this how you felt when you wrote your goodbye letter?* There was a good chance she wouldn't remember anything since the last time they saw each other. According to Marci it was a side effect of the drug Red Queen used to keep her asleep.

I don't know what happened to you that would make you think it was okay to disappear. Leaving those of us who cared about you to believe you were dead. Did you know what was coming and thought you could stop it on your own? Or did they lie to you, too?

You know what? It doesn't even matter. Look, I have a way to remove Red Queen and the Task Force from our lives. To do that, though, I need you to find me. You need to ditch whoever is with you. I don't care how but they can't know we've talked.

He hoped he was doing the right thing, getting her away from everyone. Marci said he shouldn't trust anyone, not even her.

Remember the last time we were in Salt City? We spent hours walking around and missed our show, never finishing the scavenger hunt.
   Meet me at the place where we watched the sunset.

He signed the card and put it back in his pocket until he could find a way to get it to her. Marci sat beside him, sliding a black band like Linc's across the table. "You'll need this to blend in."

Kaleb slipped it around his wrist. "Does this mean WonderLand won't affect me?"

Marci nodded. "Yep."

"It will though."

She shrugged. "Maybe it will, maybe it won't. I'm honestly not sure what will happen if you're exposed to WonderLand again. Either way, the band gets you where you need to go without being harassed by the Guard."

"Okay?" She was trying to tell him something without saying it like she used to back when she was Redding's assistant. This time he couldn't figure out what the message was. Of course, he could ask her. But if she was talking in code, there had to be a reason. He'd have to figure it out on his own or wait until they were alone.

"Do you have a card for Alice?"

How did she know?

"I can get it to her."

He thought back to her warning in the car. *Was this too convenient, or does Marci know me that well?*

"Alice is going to be pretty confused when she wakes up. As you know, the drugs they are giving her may even erase parts of her memory. Did you add something about how the world works now?"

"Not yet."

Marci was right, and he had no choice but to trust her. Kaleb pulled out the card, scribbling a PS about the bands and the Guard. They are basically the same thing, the only difference being how they treat the afflicted. No matter who they claimed to work for, either the Task Force or Red Queen, they were still the same opportunists who wanted nothing more than to watch the world burn.

Watching Marci, he sealed the card, remembering what she'd said about the bands. She reached out to show the black strip of plastic on her wrist, giving him the confidence to give it to her.

Markus slapped him on the back. "Time to go."

Chapter 6

Marci swiped through the screens, keeping track of anyone trapped inside Salt City. They were the unknowns–people stuck inside with no idea what was really going on–the one thing that could compromise the mission. This had to go perfectly, not like last time. Too many people had died.

Her phone pinged with an incoming message.

They made it to the wall.

ETA 5 minutes.

Time to go back.

Fiddling with the black band on her wrist, Marci relaxed into the chair, watching the clock count down the minutes. It will have to be fast. There was no one to watch her back. Ryan was still MIA. She needed to get in, get Alice out, and away from DeeDee.

Marci counted backward 5, 4, 3...she was in.

Chapter 7

The warm rays of the sun heated Kaleb's skin under the black T-shirt he'd borrowed from Markus. Everything had happened so fast. He was filling the display case at Jake's coffee shop only yesterday. Now he sat in the back of an old, pickup truck on his way to Salt City.

Kaleb laid his head back against the cab window, leaning into the sharp turn of the truck. He listened to Tom and Linc bickering in the front seat like old times and watched Markus, who sat across from him. He tapped out something on his black wristband moments before the truck abruptly stopped, its engine stuttering before shutting off.

"We're here," Markus called out, jumping out of the truck.

They'd arrived at a weaker part of the wall that surrounded Salt City. Kaleb followed his brother out, their boots echoing off the barricade, breaking up an eerie silence that settled in around them.

Kaleb looked up at the white brick wall that would become their entrance once Tom worked his magic. His vision flickered like it had when he was on WonderLand, only this time, nothing changed red. For a moment, he saw the thick glass wall of the boxes Dr. Turtle used to keep his test subjects contained. Bright fluorescent lights lit the black-lettered labels on each box of the drug being tested.

A cold sweat settled on his back, and the trapped feeling that plagued him for months pulled at him.

This isn't real.

Tom's voice echoed through his earpiece. "Stand back." It tugged at Kaleb, dragging him back to this reality.

Kaleb moved away from the wall that hadn't changed, fighting back the fear that burned inside him. This place had been picked because of the proximity to where Alice was being held. Plus, it was in a part of the city that was abandoned. The hole should open into an empty alley between two large buildings.

Tom rushed past him, pulling a long white blade from his vest, and with a flip of a switch on the hilt, it began to glow.

This doesn't make sense. Why would Tom use a blade? This can't be real, he tried to remind himself. *You got out of Turtles lab.*

Pink dust fell to the ground around Tom as he cut through the wall. Drumming worked its way through Kaleb's mind as he fought to understand what was reality and fiction.

Markus's voice boomed in Kaleb's earpiece. "How's Jake?"

Confused, Kaleb turned to face his brother, who stood next to him watching Tom. He shrugged. "Fine, I guess."

"Never thought I'd see a day when he wasn't chasing bad guys."

Kaleb hadn't either, but death had a funny way of changing how you viewed the world. Things that were once important weren't anymore. "It was his and Ruby's dream to open that shop together."

Markus nodded but didn't say anything. Jake found Ruby in their house, dead, murdered by someone he'd been hunting. Their brother hadn't been the same since.

Kaleb turned to face the wall. As he watched the red-hot blade in Tom's hand sink into the glass that should be brick, Kaleb accepted that he didn't see the truth of things. Even with Markus trying to distract him, part of his mind was still trapped inside Red Queen and might always be.

Kaleb watched as shiny, melted, amber-colored globs of glass slid down the wall's surface, puddling onto the asphalt below. He knew it wasn't real but couldn't stop seeing it. To pull himself back to reality, he replayed the list of reasons why he was angry with the people he should have been able to trust.

They lied to me.

Let me think Alice was dead for six months.

He glared at the people around him. People he'd once called friends.

Tom, who had told Reid about his plan to flee with Alice. For what? A fix?

Linc, who'd sent Alice into Red Queen to find a cure that didn't exist.

Markus kept her letter for months and let him believe Alice was dead.

Watching Tom and Linc clear the rubble away from the entrance, Kaleb considered how he could hurt them. Holding back the growl that sat on his lips, he stepped back, pushing the anger down. The anger had done the trick. He was no longer seeing Turtle's lab.

He took a deep breath. *Now is not the time to lose control.* He calmed himself enough to keep going, but not so much that he would be lost in his trauma.

"Ready?" Markus nudged Kaleb.

Kaleb took another cleansing breath before nodding. *The sooner we do this, the sooner I can get Alice out and away from this world.*

Kaleb watched as Tom tried to slip off his thick, gray gloves, his hands shaking. So, he was still using Turtle's drugs to escape. Kaleb heard *Thavasi* was a hard drug to quit. Actually, anything that came from Turtle's lab was. *Hopefully, Tom won't sell us out again.*

Linc stepped in front of Tom in what Kaleb guessed was an attempt to hide the symptoms from the others, helping his brother with the gloves. Markus had warned Linc that bringing Tom on this mission was a bad idea. Kaleb agreed. They couldn't afford Tom compromising things, but Linc wouldn't go without his brother. He claimed they needed him. For what? Kaleb had no idea.

"Are you sure about this?" Markus asked Kaleb.

Linc helped Tom through the circular hole they'd cut into the brick wall. He looked back towards them, meeting Kaleb's eyes before following his brother inside.

He wasn't. "I'll be fine," Kaleb lied. "Now go."

Markus shrugged but didn't say anything more before crawling through the opening. Kaleb looked around the sun-bleached world one last time, saying goodbye to the life he'd built without Alice. Kaleb crawled through the tunnel of thick concrete, leaving his new life behind. The air cooled with each scrape of his knees toward the city.

No longer confined by the small opening, Kaleb stood up, wiping pink dust from his black gloves. He then looked up at the pink cloud that hovered above the city, trapping it in the grips of the new norm: a never-ending winter.

Markus moved past him and pushed a large, green dumpster in front of the hole to hide their exit. They had to keep WonderLand mostly contained until they could find a way to neutralize its effects.

"Let's go over the plan one more time." Markus looked at the Sanchez brothers. "Tom?"

Tom grumbled but reviewed the plan. "We go in the back, using Kaleb's computer gadget to get past the keypad."

This is why they needed Kaleb: he was the only one who had found a way to beat the games Turtle used as security without playing them.

Tom went on. "Once inside, Linc and I will go one way while you and Kaleb go the other."

Markus pulled his earpiece into place. "While we distract the Guard, Marci will take Alice out the front." He motioned toward a nearby door. "Ready?"

Kaleb didn't say anything; he just turned and walked to the whitish door, a dark red heart painted in the center. He pulled out the handheld device he built last night from his pocket, hoping it would work. Turtle wasn't one to change his patterns, but the person who programmed it for him might have. The keypad that unlocked the door lit up at his approach, and bright numbers began to form the entrance code.

He hated to admit it, but he'd missed this. Not just the computer stuff but using the skills he'd worked so hard to perfect over the years. Even if he hated the plan and knew he could get it done faster by himself. *How is Marci going to get Alice to the meeting place without help?*

The door clicked open, and Kaleb motioned the others to go in front of him. Not only because that was how it was supposed to be but because he was unarmed. He didn't want to get shot before the mission even started.

The gun thing was his choice, kind of. Kaleb had tried to pick up a weapon before they left for Salt City. Still, like every other time before, the touch of the cold steel brought overwhelming memories of when WonderLand coursed through his veins, and his irrational thoughts while trapped inside Red Queen. He'd come close to acting on them and would have if Alice hadn't been there. He didn't want to think about what he might have done.

Markus entered first, and Kaleb followed close behind. Tom and Linc split off toward the elevators. It was a risk, but unlike any other mission he'd been on, the point was to be seen by the camera. This went against all their training.

I'm doing this for Alice.

He could feel eyes watching them as they walked across the room to a set of doors that led upstairs. Every muscle screamed in protest, telling him to hide.

They moved through the empty, gray room, making their way toward the stairwell door. Markus pushed the door open, stopping on the small square landing long enough to ensure they were alone before motioning for Kaleb to go ahead of him. They needed to go up, giving Marci time to get Alice out of the basement, but when he saw the steps leading down, he froze. *Alice is down there. I could get her out myself. Just a few steps in the wrong direction.*

Markus shoved him. "Rabbit, move."

Kaleb turned around to glare at his brother, a smart remark on his lips left unsaid. The look Markus gave him mirrored his own, full of both regret and understanding. Kaleb took a heavy step forward, his boots hitting the concrete with a thud.

I have to trust Marci will get Alice out.

They were halfway up the last set of stairs when Kaleb started to wonder why no one had come for them yet. They'd ensured they were seen by every camera on the way in and the way up. He'd done everything but wave hello.

Kaleb stopped, turning to his brother. "Don't you think it's weird we haven't seen anyone?"

"Yeah." Markus looked around the stairwell. "Let's just get to the top floor." "Then I'll—"

The door attached to the landing above them opened, and a single security guard moved toward them. Kaleb froze. He knew the man coming toward them was Madison, the guard who'd been stationed at the checkpoint inside Red Queen headquarters. They'd been friends, sort of, gone out after work to grab a drink kind of friends, and now he had a gun pointed at Kaleb's chest.

"You're going the wrong way," Madison growled. "They have her."

Marci or Alice?

"Drop your weapon," Markus demanded in a cold, commanding voice.

Madison didn't move, his gun still pointed at Kaleb's chest.

Kaleb was trapped. His heart pounded in his chest, causing it to tighten with each breath. He tightened his tingling fingers into a fist before they could go numb. Fighting the panic that had become his constant companion since being trapped in Red Queen, Kaleb stood frozen.

Madison exchanged a look with Markus. "You didn't tell him?"

The idea of Markus lying about something else snapped Kaleb back to the moment. "Tell me what?" Kaleb demanded. "What is going on?"

Neither of them answered, but Markus motioned to the gun on his hip with his free hand. He knew what Markus wanted. Kaleb tried to swallow, his throat dry, choking the breath from him. Markus wanted Kaleb to use that gun.

His brother was right. This was one time that Kaleb should be armed. They'd fought about it. Not wanting to draw attention to himself, he slowly moved closer to Markus. His hands clasped the hilt of the gun. The feel of it against his palm reminded Kaleb of what he'd done while WonderLand influenced him.

Rabbit took a step closer to his victim, delighting in the feel of the cold steel in his hands and the fear glistening in their eyes. Bright red spots on damaged gray skin. A twisted smile pulled at his lips.

A cold sweat rolled down his back, leaving its icy touch to dance across his nerves. *I can't do this.* Kaleb released the gun, leaving it with his brother.

"You deserve to know what's really going on here." Madison's voice echoed off the concrete walls. "Nothing is what it seems. It's all a lie."

"What's a lie?" Kaleb asked.

"Everything!" With his free hand, Madison motioned to the room. "Turtle did something that trapped us all here in Salt City."

The overhead door swung open, and Linc stepped onto the landing, Tom following close behind. They'd gone around the long way to distract the guards on the other side of the building.

Madison's eyes traveled up the wall, stopping on the tiny blinking light mounted on the ceiling. "The gun is just for show."

Why would he tell us that? Madison looked at the cameras again, studying the slick case. Kaleb remembered installing one of those cameras inside Turtle's office at his father's request. It was one of his first assignments; they didn't pick up sound.

Tom's voice boomed through the stairwell. "Is that why the alarm hasn't gone off? Or is it something else? Maybe you're playing God again. Or was it a good little soldier? I was never quite sure."

The color drained from Madison's face. "That wasn't me." He whipped around to face Tom. "How are you even here? I..."

"Killed me?" Tom finished for him. "That wasn't me you used the ax on." A dark grimace crossed Tom's thin lips. "It was Harrison you killed." He raised his hands, fluorescent light glinting off the silencer attached to his weapon. "And it had nothing to do with WonderLand. It was all you."

The smell of gunpowder hung in the air as Madison crumbled to the ground. An impossibly perfect round hole in the center of his forehead. The black band around his lifeless wrist turned white as life left his eyes.

Kaleb gulped air, his mind racing, unable to hold onto a single thought, incoherent words tumbling out of his mouth. Blue lights started flashing around him as the floor shook below.

Markus yelled into his mic, "We have to go!"

His brother's words bounced around him, but he couldn't move, watching as Tom and Linc pushed past him. All Kaleb could focus on was Madison: honest, loyal Madison. His lifeless body lay on the ground before him, dark eyes staring at him. Accusing him.

This can't be real.
It has to be a dream.
This isn't my life.
Not again.

Markus dragged Kaleb down the stairs. The panic radiated off him, falling with each step away from the carnage above. Bringing Kaleb back to the present and the reality that Tom was a cold-blooded killer.

Kaleb stumbled down the last few steps before crashing into the large room they'd walked through earlier. The door to the outside stood wide open, letting the light of the day seep into the darkest corners.

Why is the door open?

Other than Madison, he hadn't seen anyone else in the building. At the very least, someone should have come when the alarm sounded. That's when he remembered his first days at Red Queen, what the blue lights meant, and why Markus wanted them out of the building. Red Queen was destroying evidence the best way they knew, leaving nothing but a burnt-out pile of rubble.

A rumble moved through the walls around them, and the building shook.

Markus tugged on Kaleb's arm, urging him to move faster while yelling at Linc and Tom to keep the door open. His voice was swallowed by the rumbling that charged past them, bringing the walls down.

I hope Marci got Alice out in time.

Chapter 8

Alice stood beside his bed, pulling the car keys from her pocket. Turtle's bracelet, the one he'd been looking for earlier, fell to the floor at her feet. Alice picked up the unusual piece of jewelry, running the liquid-filled beads through her fingers. She thought it was in the car with her blood-soaked clothes. She wasn't sure what was so important about it, but if Turtle wanted it, she would hold onto it. Alice slipped it onto her wrist.

Someone was poking her side. "Alice, wake up."

She laid the keys next to the note. It would explain her disappearance and hopefully encourage Kaleb not to look for her and move on with his life.

"Ssh..."

. . .

ALICE PUSHED Kaleb's blond curls from his forehead, leaned in, and kissed him. A tear trickled down her cheek. "I thought I might have loved you, but... I'm sorry."

ALICE CLOSED HER EYES TIGHTER, not ready to referee another of her roommates' arguments.

"Leave her be," Marci barked at her sister Kit. "She's fine."

If I fall back asleep, I can finish the dream. It had started out so great, but the ending sucked. It was too real.

"If she doesn't wake up soon, someone is going to have to carry her out, and that someone isn't going to be me," Kit moaned.

Carry me? Alice tried to open her eyes, but they were unnaturally heavy.

Marci sighed next to Alice. "Do you really think anyone will notice?"

Alice screamed inside her mind. *Of course, they would.*

"Not really," Kit murmured. "No one noticed when we carried her in. I doubt they would now. After the last three months stuck behind that stupid wall, nothing seems suspicious anymore."

Three months? Wall? What are they talking about? Alice tried to yell; she needed more information but couldn't move. She was stuck listening to the world around her but unable to do anything. Her mind raced, trying to find a way to free herself.

What is going on? Why can't I move?

A shadow of a memory danced on the edge of her mind, taunting her. The dream she'd been having was only a piece of the puzzle of how she'd gotten here. She tried to focus on the last moments of her dream, and her heartbeat sped up, telling her to forget.

A clink sounded below, and Alice slid across her seat, resting on what felt like cold steel. A voice crackled overhead.

"Hkjs halbroke asjaasf."

Somehow Alice knew that the speaker above was broken, they were on a commuter train in Salt City, and the next stop was Connor

Brooke. How she knew this was a mystery. The last time Alice remembered being in Salt City was two years ago with Kaleb.

How did I get here?

The train moved around a corner, pushing someone closer to her, causing the tingling sensation of waking limbs to run down her right arm. A slight moan escaped her lips without her permission. Then a sharp pain pushed through her, dusting off a memory that bubbled to the surface.

IT WAS RAINING, *and she was lying on the ground. Her hands were covered in blood.* Her skin heated as the images of what happened next flashed through her. *Kaleb was in a hospital bed, tubes connected to his body and a crooked smile on his lips. Lips that moved without sound.*

WITHOUT THINKING, Alice rubbed her shoulder, the static of lost time turning in her stomach. Ignoring her sleep-heavy eyes, Alice forced her sticky lids open, waiting for the world to come into focus. She needed to see where she was and get her bearings.

The train's gray lights hung overhead, giving the car a gloomy glow that matched her mood. Alice looked around. Kit sat on a bench across from her, her long, blond hair covering her face as she focused on a book in her lap. Marci sat next to Alice, her eyes a dark violet, her favorite contacts having their usual eerie effect as she watched Alice.

DeeDee moved down the aisle toward them, her high ponytail bouncing with each step. She had a black phone in her hand, her fingers moving across its screen, and a scowl on her face.

A familiar chill ran down Alice's back, and Kaleb's voice rang in her ears. *Don't trust DeeDee. She's one of them. Nothing she does is real.*

Alice took a deep breath, not sure what to do. Kaleb's words didn't make sense, but they felt right, not because she didn't like DeeDee or even trust her. It was because —she didn't know.

It was weird.

Why can't I remember?

Alice looked around the train car, hoping to see Kaleb. Maybe if she could remember when he'd said not to trust DeeDee, she'd know what happened to him. Warm fingers pressed into her thigh.

Is Kaleb even alive?

She turned to face Marci, the look in her eyes said she was trying to tell Alice something, but she wasn't sure what. Whatever it was, Alice decided it was best to not ask any questions and stay quiet.

For now...

DeeDee plopped down in the empty seat next to Kit, her ponytail brushing the top of the cushioned seat. "Good, you're up. How are you feeling?"

How am I feeling? Alice thought about it. She wasn't sure how to answer. It's not like she and DeeDee were really friends. DeeDee wasn't asking because she cared. No, she wanted something. But Alice wasn't sure what.

Alice closed her eyes, trying to think of what to say. If she was honest, she wasn't really sure how she felt. Only that there was something wrong. Like she was herself and not at the same time. She opened her eyes, and for a moment, the train disappeared, changing into a hospital room, then back to the train car.

DeeDee cleared her throat and continued to stare at Alice, waiting for an answer.

What is going on? Alice tried to ask, but only the whisper of a word came out.

"Foggy?" Marci asked.

That was an understatement.

Alice nodded.

"That's to be expected."

Alice raised an eyebrow. "Why?" she coughed.

"It's a side effect of the Anadormi, one of Dr. Turtle's drugs. Your memory is going to be unclear for a little while."

Alice tried to ask DeeDee how the drug had gotten into her system in the first place, but only a warm breath came out of her mouth.

What's happening to me?
Why can't I control my body?
Is this also a side effect of the drug?

DeeDee didn't seem to notice. She turned to Kit and started talking as if Alice wasn't there. "Kaleb went rogue and destroyed Red Queen headquarters as well as the Salt City branch."

Kit gasped, "Was anyone still inside?"

Alice watched DeeDee, waiting for her answer. Something that resembled fear crossed her face before a sad smile settled on her lips. "It was still in lockdown. Everyone inside is dead. As is our hope of finding the cure."

Kaleb would never do that.
Besides, WonderLand is not the issue. It's a distraction.

Alice wasn't sure how or even why, but she knew this. There was no point in destroying Red Queen, and Kaleb would never take a life. Not like that.

"What are we going to do now?" Kit asked.

Alice watched DeeDee study her hands, her face twisted with deception. DeeDee was playing them. There wasn't a doubt in Alice's mind.

"Linc's keeping an eye on Kaleb for now." DeeDee looked up from her phone, meeting Alice's eyes. "Until Kaleb is back in Task Force custody, it's best to keep moving."

Kaleb's voice echoed in her head. *The Task Force is a lie.* She couldn't remember when he'd told her this but knew with certainty it was true.

Acknowledging Alice's discomfort for the first time, DeeDee grabbed a water bottle from the black bag on the floor in front of her, handing it to Alice. "What is the last thing you remember?"

Alice squeezed the bottle, checking the soft plastic for puncture holes, a habit she'd picked up after Ryan had drugged her. She'd been drugged enough for one lifetime.

What was the last thing I remembered, and should I tell DeeDee?

She twisted the lid off the bottle, the familiar click of the safety seal giving Alice the confidence to take a drink. There were small things, *bright lights above her, people whispering, and a steady beeping. Kaleb called out to her.* She sipped the cool crisp water, a balm to her fractured nerves. *The hospital from her dream, maybe Kaleb was dying.*

Her mind raced. *No, DeeDee said Kaleb's alive, so what happened next?* She couldn't remember. Looking at the three women who sat near her, anxiety and fear turned in her stomach as she tried to decide what to say. *Can I trust any of them? DeeDee already lied.* Taking her time to put the lid back onto the bottle, Alice tried to gather her thoughts.

"I was talking to Kaleb." She gripped the bottle, letting the plastic crackle between them. "We were in my room, I think. He said something about a time not fitting."

Marci looked up, surprised, and something else on her face, panic maybe. "Were you maybe talking about that weird TV show you like? The one about time travel?"

"I think so." Alice nodded. *That had to be it,* but it didn't feel right. *Why would Marci be worried about some TV show?* Alice was missing something.

"Anything else?" DeeDee asked.

Alice studied the metal floor, avoiding eye contact while trying to figure out what DeeDee wanted to hear. That's when Alice remembered the pain she felt in her shoulder when she first woke up. She felt the same pain after Ryan drugged her the first time. "I'm not sure." Alice rubbed her arm. "I think maybe, someone may have injected me with something. Maybe the Anadormi?"

DeeDee nodded, "I suspect that, but it could also be something else. We're not sure what was given to you before that."

Alice opened her mouth to ask more questions. But DeeDee pulled out her phone and effectively ended the conversation.

Confused and a bit relieved, Alice relaxed against the cushioned bench. She knew whatever DeeDee said was most likely going to be a lie. Alice let her mind wander through her scattered memories. She still wasn't sure what was going on, and she wasn't going to ask. Not while DeeDee was close by.

Alice looked out the window and was shocked to see snow-covered streets. Too much snow for it to still be spring. Sure, it snowed in spring, but not this much. This was a middle-of-winter snow.

She remembered Kit saying something earlier about being trapped behind a wall for three months. Turning to face Marci, Alice whispered. "How long has it been since the outbreak at Red Queen?"

"Six months."

Chapter 9

Alice looked down at the floor, trying to find the words to express her shock, but the only thing she could think to ask was, "How?"

"It's a lot, I know. I wish I could help more." Marci patted Alice's knee. "In time, everything will make sense, and your memories should return."

"Should?" *What did she mean should?* "And if they don't?"

Marci shrugged, "We'll figure it out. Like we always do."

Like we always do? Alice had no idea what she meant by that. There had never been a time when they'd dealt with anything like this. Alice rubbed her head. There was too much information to process right now. She let an awkward silence fill the air around them, trying to remember anything that would explain what was going on or how she'd gotten to Salt City.

A frustrated DeeDee moved to the other side of the car, Kit following close behind. Their whispered conversation barely audible over the clink of the train moving over the rails. Alice watched them both, arms moving with angered gestures and lips snarled. She didn't know what they were talking about, but it seemed important.

Marci moved closer, pulling a dark-covered book out of her bag. The white letters "trust nothing" on the cover contrasted the book's deep purple, making them look as if they glowed.

The train horn blew above them, a warning that they were approaching the next stop.

Alice looked out the window again, still trying to wrap her mind around everything that had happened. She thought about how her companions acted like this was just another day. Though it was strange, it gave her a bit of comfort. Their lives had never been normal.

The train came to a stop, and the doors opened, bringing winter air with it. Alice shivered as two men with paper masks and black latex gloves got on the train, sitting a few rows from her and Marci. The words "not immune" popped into her mind. Not that she had any idea what that meant.

Alice rubbed the cold from her arms, noticing for the first time she was wearing her favorite red hoodie. The one with the faded blue university letters stitched across it. The last time Alice remembered seeing it was in Kaleb's car. It was in the bag she'd started to pack before confronting Kaleb at his apartment. She'd pulled it from the dirty laundry, but it smelled freshly washed.

A new memory crept into her peripheral, taunting her. There was no sound, only Marci handing Alice a stack of clothes that were not her style and a driver's license that didn't match her name.

Marci knew more than she was saying. Alice suspected that, however, Marci had gotten into Salt City, and it had something to do with Alice. For some reason, Marci didn't want the others to know about it, not even her sister.

"Marci, how did I get this?" Alice motioned to her outfit.

"I'm not sure." She closed her book, looking toward DeeDee and Kit, and so did Alice. They were still having a heated conversation. DeeDee's eyes focused on her, searching for something. Alice suspected that whatever they were arguing about had to do with her, which wasn't good.

She turned back to Marci, whose face had taken on a vacant look, as if she'd gone somewhere else, leaving the shell of who she was behind. Then as if nothing had happened, she started talking. "You know, when I worked for Reid Redding, I wasn't so much working for her but working against her."

Alice nodded. After Alice had shared her suspicions about Marci, Kaleb told her that Marci could be trusted. She doubted him at first, but as she'd watched Marci around Red Queen during her weekly check-ups with Dr. Turtle, she'd changed her mind. Marci followed the CEO around the building like a good assistant, taking notes of everything going on, but Alice suspected there was more to Marci than meets the eye.

"Part of my job was to look out for you." She looked over at her sister, and Alice thought she saw remorse on her face. "I couldn't do it alone. So, when Kit finally left that jerk of an ex, Kaleb and I brought her in to help. It was a good distraction."

"So, you were assigned to..." *Be my friend.* A nauseous heat moved through her. Marci interrupted her thoughts before she could say them out loud.

"Our assignment was to keep an eye on you. To watch for any unusual behavior. At least, that was what Reid wanted. Not sure why." Marci turned to Alice, trying to communicate something to her. The familiar static Alice started to associate with a memory spike settled in her mind for a moment before it faded away, leaving a trail of disappointment behind.

Marci said, "Our assignment ended six months ago when you disappeared."

"I disappeared?"

Marci nodded. "The Task Force had stopped looking for you, but someone saw you on the street here in Salt City."

"That was three months ago," Alice said.

Marci stiffened next to her. "Are you starting to remember?"

"Yes, no. I'm not sure." Alice twisted a multi-colored bracelet around her wrist. Surprised that the liquid-filled beads were cool to the touch, she knew that whatever was inside had to do with Dr. Turtle's experiments. At some point, he would come for her and the bracelet. "It just feels right. Like...I'm missing some time but not as much or maybe too much." Alice slumped down. "Does that even make sense?"

"Yes." Marci rubbed her temples, scowling at the space in front of them. "Things should be clearer soon. For now, just trust your instincts, and know I'll help where I can."

Kit's high-pitched voice echoed through the train car. "Oh my gosh, Alice, I completely forgot. Happy Birthday!!! November 13th, right?"

Alice nodded.

Kit sat across from Alice, playing with a strand of her long hair. "Sorry I didn't get you anything. You know, the end of the world and all doesn't leave time for much shopping."

Marci smiled and pulled a white envelope from inside her book, handing it to Alice. *Ace* was scrawled in Kaleb's curvy handwriting across the front.

"You got a card." Kit whined, "Why didn't you let me sign it?"

Marci shrugged. "Guess I forgot."

Kit made an annoyed huff but didn't say anything more.

"Thank you." Even though Alice was dying to read the card, she knew Marci kept the fact that it was from Kaleb a secret. She trusted that Marci had her reasons, so she asked, "Do you mind if I wait to read it?"

"Not at all."

DeeDee walked down the aisle toward where they sat, her eyes fixed on her phone. "We need to get off at the next stop. Some of our people set up a temporary communications room."

Our people? If she means the Task Force, they are not my people.

The conductor's deep voice moved through the broken speaker system above them. Alice only understood a few of the garbled words. "Next sksl ashlr Stadium."

DeeDee continued, "We're headed in the wrong direction."

The doors opened, and the women stood, making their way to the platform. The chilled air seeped through Alice's thick sweater and settled in her bones. Her last memories had been of warmth.

Frustrated, Alice stepped out. At the start of summer, play was at the top of her list, not surviving an apocalypse or snow.

Unsure of what to do, Alice followed the others across the platform to wait for the train going in the other direction. She'd stick with them until her memories returned. It was the safest place for her to be, at least for now.

It didn't take long for the train going in the other direction to stop in front of them. The two doors slid open, and a group of men dressed in black Kevlar uniforms stepped onto the platform near them. Marci's hand wrapped around Alice's wrist, stopping any movement she might have made toward the train. "When I tell you to run, run," she whispered to Alice.

Two men broke off from the rest of their group approaching Marci. "Wrist," barked the taller of the two.

Marci pulled up the sleeve of her coat to reveal a black rubber-like band, similar to the one on her wrist.

The other guy grabbed Alice's arm, his fingers tight around her arm. Alice held back a grunt of pain as he forced her sleeve up, revealing the band. The cold air on her exposed skin stung almost as much as the guy's grip. He studied the band for a minute before dropping her arm, frustrated.

Alice rubbed the red marks left by the man's hand, glaring at his back as he made his way over to DeeDee. He wasn't rough with her. He patiently waited for her to reveal the white wristband.

The guy who examined Marci's bracelet moved to stand in front of Kit. A goofy grin on his face. She placed her hand in his outstretched one. He smiled a gentle smile at the bright-eyed girl. Speaking with a hint of flirting, he asked. "Do you mind showing me your arm?"

Kit giggled. Yes, she giggled. The woman could flirt even with the tension that hung in the air. Marci turned to Alice rolling her eyes at her twin sister's antics. Alice was relieved that the sisters hadn't changed in this chaos.

"Of course." Kit chirped as she moved the fabric of her coat up, exposing a centimeter of skin at a snail's pace.

Marci's gasp tipped Alice off that something was wrong.

Kit's band wasn't black or white. It was pink, bright fluorescent pink.

Alice wasn't sure what it meant, but she knew it wasn't good. The guards moved closer, grabbed DeeDee and Kit, then called for backup.

Marci turned to Alice, yelling one word.

"RUN."

Chapter 10

Alice's feet hit the pavement sending vibrating pain to her knees. She ignored it, moving further into the city. The fear on Marci's face when she told Alice to run was pure enough to shake Alice's reality.

She kept running, even after she knew no one followed her, up hills, through alleys, without looking back. Alice didn't know what the pink bracelet meant, but it couldn't be good. She didn't slow down until she knew she was alone.

No Marci.

No men in black.

Just an empty street.

Alice listened to the world around her. The only sound she could hear was snow crunching under her sneakers. Out of breath and unsure what to do next, Alice found a metal park bench nearby and sat down to collect her thoughts and breath. Thinking a bit more rationally, she pulled the hood of her sweater onto her head.

She took a deep breath. *What am I supposed to do now? People are chasing me. I can't remember how I got to Salt City. And it's November. How is it already November?* Alice wasn't sure, but without a doubt, she knew Dr. Turtle had something to do with this.

Alice tightened her fists, a wave of anger pulling at her. Images of things she couldn't remember rushed through her, teasing her. *I'm fine.* She didn't let it take her under, afraid of where it might lead. She needed to stay calm. *One, two, three. Deep breath in. Four, five, six.*

The image of four pills lying in her open palm stilled her mind, the words CONSIDER ANYTHING stamped on them in big black letters. *Nothing is glowing red. Does this mean WonderLand's no longer in my system?* She wasn't sure, but that would have to be enough for now.

Frustrated and confused, Alice looked around, hoping something would spark an idea of what to do next. *Marci had told her to trust her instincts.*

In front of her, a row of swings swayed in the slight breeze. A familiarity tugged at Alice like she'd been here before and not too long ago. She blew warm air onto her fingers. *Why is this place familiar?*

She looked around, searching for answers, hoping something would spark a memory. It was odd. There were no sounds, not even the quiet chatter of critters that normally filled the air.

Now that she was thinking about it, the lack of sound was unnerving. That there wasn't a single person around wasn't helping either. She suspected that Salt City had empty streets for some time. But no animals either? That's too weird.

Something else was happening in Salt City, and the wristbands were essential to whatever was happening. *How can I know something but not remember how I got that information?*

Frustrated, Alice kicked a clump of snow, noticing the color wasn't quite right for the first time. Mixed in with the brilliant white were specks of bright pink. Of course, it was unusual, but Alice assumed it was spray paint or chalk. It was a park, after all. Who knows what people do when nobody's watching?

With nothing else to do and no idea where to go next, Alice looked for the card Marci gave her earlier. *Maybe Kaleb left me some instructions. At the very least, a way to contact him.* Alice slid her finger under the sealed tab of the envelope. The tearing of paper echoed through the crisp air.

She pulled the thick paper card from its confines. A cartoon turkey stared up at her, fall leaves stamped across its tail feathers. The words, Happy Turkey Day, printed in pumpkin-orange across the top were scratched out and replaced with, Happy Birthday, in Kaleb's curly cursive.

Alice smiled. He never got a card that matched the occasions. He always picked a card based on the front picture, not caring about what was on the inside. Once, he'd given her a Christmas card with a teddy bear in a pink tutu because he thought it would make her laugh. Inside he'd left the words printed by the card company. Dance like nobody's watching. It was ridiculous, and she'd loved it.

Opening the card, Alice wondered how Marci got the card from Kaleb. According to DeeDee, Kaleb had gone rogue, not that Alice believed her. Then there was the whole hiding it from Kit thing. Alice thought the twins didn't keep secrets from each other.

With all the secrecy around the card, Alice expected it to be written in code or something unique to her and Kaleb. She was relieved to find it written in plain English. Code had never been something she was good at.

> Ace,
>
> I'm sorry that I can't be there when you wake up. There is so much that I need to tell you. You have been gone for a long time, and a lot has happened.

Figured that out without your letter.

> I don't know what happened to you that would make you think it was okay to disappear. Leaving those of us who cared about you to believe you were dead. Did you know what was coming and think you could stop it on your own? Or did they lie to you too?

They thought I was dead? Why? What did Kaleb mean by 'what was coming'? Though, the statement about being lied to was most likely true. Someone was always keeping things from me to keep me safe—even Kaleb.

> You know what? It doesn't even matter. Look, I have a way to remove Red Queen and the Task Force from our lives. To do that, though, I need you to find me. You need to ditch Marci and anyone else who might be with you. I don't care how, but they can't know about this.

She looked around at the empty park. *Well, that's done, next.*

> Remember the last time we were in Salt City? We spent hours walking around and missed our show, never finishing the scavenger hunt.

Of course, I remember. Who wouldn't remember their long-time crush asking them out? Even if it was the one and only date we'd gone on. It was a big deal to me.

> Meet me at the place where we watched the sunset.
> Be safe, and trust no one.
> Kaleb

Alice stared down at the card in disbelief. *That's it?* She thought there would have been more. At the very least, something about how she'd gotten here. Or why he wasn't there with her.
Be Safe. How am I supposed to be safe? The world has lost its mind.
She turned the card in her hands, trying to decide what her next move would be. *Do I try to find Marci or follow another one of Kaleb's cryptic notes?* She didn't know, and her anger grew with each turn of

the card. *He left me alone. Okay, maybe not alone. There was Marci. Though he said I couldn't trust her. That I need to ditch her.*

Alice crumbled the card, ready to throw it in the garbage bin nearby. Once it was balled up in her fist, she noticed something. There was a PS. on the inside flap of the envelope. She uncrumpled it and began to read.

> PS-Just in case you don't remember, or no one thinks to tell you, the Guards roaming around the city are part of Red Queen or the Task Force. They may or may not be working together. Try to avoid them at all costs. The black band on your wrist tells them you are immune to the effects of WonderLand, but I don't know what will happen if they catch you. Usually, the Bishops/Task Force will kill you, and the Knights/Red Queen will experiment on you until you wish you would die. Death is their only business regardless of who the Guard claims to follow.

She thought about the men who had stopped them on the train platform; they had a white symbol stitched into their uniforms. A symbol that looked like a chess piece.

Is that what he meant?

What symbol was it?

Maybe a Bishop. It was the only explanation for the one checking DeeDee's band. He'd shown her respect. He hadn't been aggressive like the one who had checked Marci's. DeeDee was the head of the Task Force, after all.

I hope Marci was able to get away. Even if Kaleb said not to trust her. He gave her the card, so he must have trusted Marci a little.

Alice stood up, shoving the crumpled card into her back pocket, remembering what happened the last time she ignored one of Kaleb's cryptic notes. The fear she'd felt from the Timore that Ryan had injected into her still haunted Alice. She wasn't sure it was the best idea with the memory loss to wander the streets where one mistake could get her killed, but she didn't have a choice. Alice decided to follow Kaleb's instructions and meet him.

There has to be a street sign nearby.

It had been more than a year since Kaleb rushed off to work during their failed date that ended at Butte Gardens.

Alice didn't take long to find a street sign, but it was still covered in snow from the recent storm, and no matter how much she tried to clear it, the snow would not budge.

She shivered. "I'll just head toward the mountains." *Something will look familiar eventually.*

Alice tried to pull on the string of thoughts that linked this snowy nightmare to Kaleb. All she could think was how much she hated everything about winter. She counted down the months, hours, and sometimes seconds until the snow melted and the sun warmed the world again.

Why am I here?

Because of Kaleb.

Why would I blame Kaleb for this?

Annoyed, Alice kicked at a pile of fluffy white snow, hoping it would scatter in front of her and give the illusion of being trapped in a snow globe. Instead, her foot slipped on the icy sidewalk. The air whooshed from her lungs as her back hit the ground. Stars danced behind her eyes while she stared up at the pink-gray sky.

She lay there, letting snowflakes fall onto her hot face. Blowing at the hair stuck to her eyelids, she cursed her life choices.

What am I doing?

Is there a better plan?

The sound of snow crunching under someone's foot pulled Alice from her musings. Embarrassed that she'd laid in the cold, wet snow for longer than necessary and scared the person nearing her might be the Guard, she pushed herself into a sitting position. "I'm okay," she said, sure that whoever came toward her was checking on her.

A man not much older than her stood above her. He was dressed in boxers and a blue bathrobe. One ratty slipper on his right foot. "The rule... Jam to-morrow."

Alice scrambled to her feet. The way the man's voice sounded reminded her of... No.

Her blood chilled.

Droplets of red moved down the scruff that covered his face.

He moved toward Alice. "And Jam yesterday."

Alice wanted to turn and run but stood frozen in fear.

WonderLand?

Kaleb had said something about it. Alice took a step back, *but I didn't want to believe it.* Keeping her eyes focused on the man in front of her, she glanced sideways, looking for a way out. Two men in black Guard uniforms approached the man from behind. The words from Kaleb's card sent fear down her spine.

What will happen if I run? Will they shoot me, or will this guy in the bathrobe lose his calm and tear me apart?

Against her better judgment and Kaleb's wish, she decided it would be best to stay put.

When I showed my armband to the Guard at the train station earlier, they didn't seem to care until they saw Kit's.

One of the men yelled, "Show us your arm."

Chapter 11

Alice raised her hand to expose the black band on her wrist, hoping their reaction would be the same as the men at the train station: indifferent.

It wasn't.

The guy who yelled at her turned to his partner. "Got ourselves a munie."

What did this guy mean by munie? She lowered her arms and looked around, trying to find an escape. *Is it some kind of slang for immune?*

"Really?" The guard's partner had zip-tied bathrobe guy's arms behind his back and pushed him to his knees. "Don't think I've ever seen one."

Alice shifted as he eyed her from head to toe. She crossed her arms over her chest, holding back the mixture of fear and anger that threatened to come out.

He turned his attention back to his prisoner while talking to his partner. "Heard there's a bunch of them with the Bishops though." He pulled the gun from a holster on his waist and pointed it at the bathrobe guy.

"Never Jam to-day," the guy in the bathrobe muttered, his WonderLand-filled eyes staring at Alice. A small part of the person he once was floating in their depths, pleading for help.

Alice watched, her voice lost in the horror of what she knew was coming. She tried to look away as the Guard pulled the trigger. The sound of the weapon firing echoed through the cold November air. She froze in terror.

They shot him.

A memory overtook her. She was no longer in the cold world she'd found after waking to this nightmare.

KALEB LAY IN A BED, *the shimmer of WonderLand floating in his eyes as he babbled similar nonsense. Markus's deep voice asked her, "Are you sure?"*

ALICE WAS THRUSTED BACK to the present before she could grab onto the memory. Her lungs burned as if she'd been holding her breath.

Gulping down cold air, the past fluttered away as quickly as it came. Alice stared at the guy in the bathrobe, watching the blood trickle from his wound and puddle on the pavement. *They'd actually done it. They'd killed him.*

Kaleb was right.

"Stan." The guy who had shot the bathrobe guy nodded toward Alice.

She didn't respond, stuck on something she'd remembered. It had to do with Kaleb being in a hospital bed. It was off. *It could have easily been inside Red Queen, but...* Alice tried to focus on Kaleb in the bed, forcing the memories to return. It didn't work. Instead, dark spots moved across her vision as she stared at the blood-soaked snow. *Was Kaleb... No, I don't know how I know, but Kaleb is fine. But he was dying. That's why we took those pills.*

The cold of wet concrete seeped through her clothes forcing Alice to focus on the current issue.

The Guard.

Warm arms wrapped around her waist. "Upsy daisy." Stan pulled Alice to her feet.

Somehow, she ended up sitting on the sidewalk again. She tried to stand on her own, but her legs wobbled, forcing her to lean on Stan as he helped her to her feet. *That's why I was sitting on the ground again.*

"I'll call this in," his partner said.

Stan guided her into the front seat of a black sedan. She wanted to protest, still unsure what they planned on doing with her, but the words wouldn't come out. *What if they...* Alice took a deep breath to calm her nerves before she started counting.

One, two, three. Some of the tension released from her chest. *Four, five, six.*

They don't seem to care about me; they're more surprised by seeing—what was it Stan called me—a munie. Their bands are white, so if Kaleb is right, they can't be trusted. But that doesn't mean I can't use them.

A plastic water bottle was shoved at her for the second time today. She reached out with shaky hands. Like she'd done with DeeDee, she checked the bottle for any apparent signs of tampering.

What's happening to me? Why am I shaking? It's not the first time I've seen violence like that, far from it.

Maybe the memory.

"First execution?" Stan asked.

Was that it? Alice appreciated that he'd called it what it was, an execution. *I stood by while an innocent man was murdered.* Alice met Stan's eyes, trying to think of what to say. "No, I just wasn't expecting it, I guess." She knew what she'd said was the truth. Sometime in the last six months, this had become the norm, even if she couldn't remember it.

He looked at Alice, confusion plastering his face, and she knew she'd have to explain, but she wasn't sure what to say. Something sparked her memory about munie's working with the Bishops. Kaleb had mentioned the Bishops did the experiments. "I haven't been out of the lab in a while," she told him.

Alice hoped that was the correct answer.

Stan smiled. "So, you're a Bishop."

"Not anymore." Alice took another sip of water. "I left. I wanted to try something different." *Can someone really leave either of these groups alive?* She held her breath, hoping this answer was correct. It seemed right, but she wasn't sure.

He chuckled. "How's that working out for you?"

"Not great."

His partner came over. "Clean-up crew in five."

"Where're you headed?" Stan asked.

Alice looked at the houses around her and knew she was totally and completely lost. *They might be able to help or could take me there.* She debated telling them where she was really going. *Really anywhere would be better than here right now.* She looked the two over. Nothing about them seemed out of the ordinary, extras in the movie that had become her life. Even though they'd just killed a man and acted like it was nothing, she still felt safer with them than on the streets alone.

Sure, Kaleb had said to avoid the Guard, but was he just being overly protective like always? These two weren't a threat to her. Alice trusted her own instincts more than a note from Kaleb.

"I'm supposed to be meeting a friend at Butte Gardens."

The partner climbed into the back seat. "We're headed that way. We could give you a ride."

She turned around to face him. "That would be great."

"I'm Ian, by the way."

"Donna." *Where did that name come from?* The name was only a little foreign on her tongue but not new. Like she'd been using it for months and not seconds. A name that brought with it a piece of her missing time.

. . .

ALICE'S OLD, red truck pulled to the side of the road, blue and red lights flashing behind it. Bright sun warmed the already hot cab. A cop handed back her a driver's license, the one Marci had given her. Alice's smiling face stared up at her from the ID card. The name on the ID: Donna White. Not Alice Smith.

Her heart squeezed with the loss that Kaleb's last name represented. She had to stay away from Kaleb until Marci had a way to get them out. It was the only way to end Dr. Turtle's experiment.

Play the game. Don't get caught, or you'll have to start all over.

Chapter 12

Kaleb stared up at the remains of the crumbling ceiling above him. Water moved down jagged pieces of plaster, turning them gray. He watched as the drops skated down a mangled metal beam, turning the dust of the shredded concrete into mud. Kaleb tried to move, and a sharp pain shot through his skull. Holding back a scream, he took a deep breath of pink and gray dust, causing a coughing fit.

Kaleb tried to figure out what had happened. He knew it was an explosion. It was Redding's favorite way to get rid of the evidence.

Why now?

An image flashed through his mind. Tom shot Madison. *Why would he do that? Was I wrong? Did Linc decide to work with Redding?*

No.

Linc would never put Alice at risk.

Not again.

Dark spots criss-crossed his vision, he blinked a few times to clear them, but it only worsened. *How do I keep getting myself into things like this?*

Alice, that's how. Kaleb tried to sit up, but his leg was pinned under something. He moaned. *Not Alice directly, but the people who* want her for their own sick purposes. Dad, Redding, DeeDee, and even Dr. Turtle.

He hadn't seen him yet, but he knew Turtle was part of this.

The rubble started to shift. Someone was moving near him, calling out to Kaleb. He tried to answer, but the voice moved further away.

For a second, he wondered if Alice was buried somewhere beneath this rubble. The fear that his presence got her hurt started to build in his chest, squeezing the air from his lungs. *I should have trusted my instincts and gone down to get her myself.* Heat radiated through his body, making him nauseous.

One, two, three. He took a deepish breath. *This train of thought isn't helping me.*

Alice is fine.

Marci won't let anything happen to her.

"KALEB!" Markus's panicked voice broke through the panic.

"Here." He coughed. Things were starting to take a turn for the worse. Kaleb knew if Markus didn't find him soon, he might never find him. Fighting against the impending darkness threatening to pull him under, Kaleb called out to his brother.

"Markus." His voice came out barely above a whisper this time, though it sounded louder in his head. He must find a way to get past the vibrating pain his voice caused and get Markus's attention.

Again, Kaleb tried to get his brother's attention. "Here."

"Ssh." Markus hushed the person stomping around next to him. "Kaleb?"

Kaleb nodded, causing pain to shoot through his head and his mind to go a bit wobbly. The voices above him warped into something hidden in the darkness, wrapping around him like a warm blanket. They pulled Kaleb from the present to the days after his mother disappeared. Jake and Markus took care of him just like they had when Alice died—not died, disappeared.

Tears moved down his face. *Why did everyone he loved disappear?*

Warm arms pulled at him, forcing the darkness back as cool, clean air replaced the choking dust of what he thought would become his coffin.

"Kaleb?" Markus's worried voice filled the crisp air. "Are you okay?"

He tried to say, of course I'm not, a building just fell on me, but the black of unconsciousness called. All that came out was, "Idiot."

"He's alive."

Kaleb tried to open his eyes.

Someone argued with Markus. It felt important.

"If you die inside, you die outside."

What is he talking about? His mind floated in and out of the real world. *Inside where?*

The next thing he knew, he was lying on a bed. Blinding fluorescent lights hung above, hiding the room from sight. A steady beeping filled the void. Voices, some familiar and some not, rushed around him.

Kaleb tried to move his arms, but they were strapped down. Panic crept into his throat, and his heart pounded in his ears. *This isn't right.* The tight straps dug into his arms as he struggled to escape. Someone was hovering outside his view. A white mask and dark shadows covered their face. Cold liquid moved through his arm.

Darkness.

Markus, Linc, and Tom were arguing about something.

"Why would you set off the fail-safe?" Linc asked. "It was a little extreme, don't you think?"

"If I hadn't, they would have found each other again," Tom said.

Markus asked, "Why are we trying to keep them apart?"

"Because it's the only way out, to keep things moving forward."

He knew he shouldn't, but Kaleb couldn't stay here with them. His mind floated into a dream.

"Agh, just let me sleep."

Someone tousled his hair. "Okay."

Kaleb wasn't sure how long he'd been out, but it must have been at least a few hours. He rolled over, the ache in his muscle pulling him from deep sleep. Kaleb tried to cover his eyes with a thin blanket that smelled like cedar, but with every movement, the sound of creaking wood increased the pounding in his head.

It took some time, but he gave up trying to settle into the uncomfortable bed. He covered his face with a blanket, eyes closed tight. He listened to the room, trying to get his bearings. Nearest to him were clicking fingers on a keyboard and light snoring. The familiar noises of his brother sleeping drummed inside his head.

He groaned. "Can't a guy get some peace?"

A loud bang sounded like a chair collapsed to the floor. The snoring stopped the moment the chair hit the ground. As did the typing.

Relieved, Kaleb sighed into the pillow.

The blanket was ripped from his face, and Kaleb opened his eyes to find his brother hovering above him. Markus's hot breath moved across Kaleb's face, and a sad smile crossed his lips, highlighting the dark shadows around his eyes.

"Dude," Kaleb mumbled. "Personal space, ever heard of it?"

Markus smiled at him, and the gloom Kaleb saw in his face lessened. "Sorry, baby brother. With family, there's no such thing." He pulled Kaleb into a tight hug, causing the pain in his head to make its way through the sore muscles he'd almost forgotten about.

Kaleb leaned into the hug, holding back the grimace that followed the pain. Even though he wanted to stay mad at his brother, he needed the comfort of someone else's strength. Not just anyone, but the unconditional love of his big brother.

"I thought we lost you," Markus mumbled next to Kaleb's ear.

Behind Markus, someone cleared their throat.

Letting go of Kaleb, Markus took a step back, letting Marci get closer. Kaleb saw the same darkness that haunted Markus shining through Marci's eyes. *Something's wrong.* "Did you get Alice out?"

Markus exchanged a look with her before she spoke. "Yes, but..."

Kaleb smiled. "You lost her." *That means she got my note.*

Marci moved from foot to foot. "I did. After we got her out of the building, we got on the train." She wiped her eyes. "Somehow, Kit..."

Markus pulled her to his side.

"Wait, what happened to Kit?" Kaleb asked.

Marci stared at the ground. Her breath came in short bursts.

"WonderLand," Markus answered.

He looked at Marci's and Markus's bands, both black. "Marci... I'm sorry."

"It was the Bishops. I told Alice to run." Marci sniffled.

"And Kit?"

Markus pulled Marci closer to him. "We aren't sure? But my guess is the Guard took her to one of their testing facilities in the city."

The room went silent with the weight of the situation.

Kaleb thought about the experiments he'd seen inside Red Queen while working there. Not only when he was a 'volunteer,' but those people that had been there to earn a little extra cash. He doubted the people taken from inside the wall were treated with the same respect as the college students. It wasn't much, but at least they had signed a consent form.

Awake now, Kaleb pushed aside the pain that had taken up residence in his head and scanned the room to get his bearings. He first saw a laptop in the center of the room. It sat on a flimsy black table, humming away, a folding chair in front of it. A large painting with a gold frame was on the wall above.

"Where are we?" he asked.

"Salt City Art Museum," Markus said.

"Why?"

"It's as good as a place as any," Markus shrugged.

Marci sat at the table in front of the laptop. "I've been tracking

Alice through the security cameras throughout the city, but I lost track of her."

"I might know where she is." Well, he hoped he did. Marci had mentioned she could experience some memory loss. Hopefully, she remembered their day in Salt City the same way it was etched into his soul.

It should have been their first date and the day that he finally had enough evidence to bring Red Queen and Reid Redding down. At least, that was what he thought. *I should have known better. The Reddings had too much power to let someone like me bring their empire down.*

Kaleb sat down on the folding chair in front of the computer desk. "Butte Gardens." He checked Marci's band. It was white. She'd told him not to trust anyone, including herself, especially if their band was anything other than black. But even without Marci's warning, he couldn't trust them. They'd all lied about Alice. Kaleb knew that the best way to protect Alice was to get her away from anyone involved with Red Queen, but he needed their help.

Markus and Marci exchanged a worried look.

"What?" Kaleb asked, eyes narrowing at the two of them.

Markus handed Kaleb a tablet with a city map and pulled up gray and blue lines marking the city streets. He tapped the screen, causing blobs of red and blue throughout the city. Kaleb noticed a black star above Butte Garden and a few other prominent landmarks throughout the city.

"The colors are where each faction of the Guard is active. Red Knights and Blue Bishops," Markus said.

"And the stars?"

"The infected."

Kaleb looked at the map. Not only was there a star above Butte Gardens, but it was also in Knight territory. *What have I done?*

Marci spoke, "Butte Gardens is a cache for the Knights. It's well known that you can drop off the infected there. Once a day, the Knights come through and pick up their 'volunteers.'"

"Why would anyone…"

"What's the alternative?" Markus threw a black uniform at him with a Knight chess piece stitched onto the shoulder and chest. "Gunshot to the forehead or a possible cure. What would you choose?"

Kaleb ran his fingers over the white stitching on the shoulder. Kaleb shrugged. He honestly wasn't sure.

Memories of the night that brought the Reddings into their lives started to surface. A man dressed in this uniform came for Kaleb's mother that night. He wasn't supposed to be there, but Jake was coming to visit, so Kaleb played sick.

There was a man in a dark uniform at the door.

Mom picked me up, running toward the closet in her bedroom.

The man pounded through the house, calling his mother's name.

The memory became more vivid as he remembered the closet door closing with him inside while his mom's fingers went to her lips. She told me to be as quiet as a mouse.

I watched through the slits in the closet door as the man's knife ran its silver blade over her cheek. He dragged her away. I can still hear screams drumming in my ears.

Markus's voice pulled him back to the present. "Put that on."

"Why?" Kaleb hadn't realized he'd spoken out loud. The question was more about the memory he'd just relieved. *Why had the Knights come for my mom?* He understood why he had to wear the uniform, even if he didn't want to. But it was a reminder of the man who destroyed his childhood.

"We're going to get your girl."

Chapter 13

Kaleb looked down at the black wristband, indicating he was immune to WonderLand. But, because of Marci, he suspected they meant something entirely different.

"I assume that even though you feel like shit, you're not going to let us go without you," Markus said.

Kaleb nodded, relieved his brother understood that despite the risk, he couldn't sit here and do nothing. Not while Alice was in trouble.

"Besides, this way, I can keep an eye on you. You may have survived your first encounter with WonderLand." Markus pulled on a matching uniform. "But who knows what will happen next time."

He was right, of course. Kaleb gathered up the uniform and stepped into the long hallway lined with paintings without saying a word to Markus or Marci. He walked through the gallery, past displays of clay pots and other ancient artifacts. *Why didn't I send Alice here? It was just as easy a place to get to. We'd spent most of that morning here. She really loved the impressionism paintings.*

Kaleb walked into the empty bathroom, throwing the uniform onto the counter. It slid to the floor, and the silver belt buckle bounced off the tile, echoing through the cold white room. He bent down to pick it up, and a sharp pain moved up his spine. It ping-ponged to his toes and back up again.

The room swayed with each ping, causing his view to twinkle in and out. Kaleb took a few shallow breaths. *How am I even alive? A building fell on top of me, and I'm walking around almost like nothing happened. There's no way I was that lucky. Could Turtle have done something to me while I was inside Red Queen headquarters?* Kaleb stared into the mirror and ran his fingers through his hair. *That's crazy, right? Turtle giving me superpowers? Kaleb, you've been reading too many comic books. But something is off.*

"Kaleb?" Marci called into the open space that acted as a door.

Through gritted teeth, Kaleb replied, "Out in a minute." He'd have to figure it out later.

Ignoring the pain, Kaleb gathered up the uniform and shoved his battered limbs into it. The shirt sleeves hung a few inches past his fingers, and the pants a few inches above his socks. He pulled the boots on, thankful they were tall enough to cover up the gap.

He walked out of the bathroom to find Markus, a sniper rifle across his back, and Marci, still dressed in regular clothes, having a whispered conversation. Kaleb watched the way Markus spoke to Marci. His attention focused only on her; he'd never seen Markus act the way he did with her. His brother always had girls hanging all over him, but he paid more attention to his work than a relationship. With Marci, it was different.

Markus looked up at Kaleb. "Ready to go?

Kaleb nodded. *As ready as I'll ever be.*

The three of them stepped onto the elevator, and Markus pressed the button for the garage. Marci stood in the corner, almost disappearing into the background like she did when she was Reid Redding's assistant. With her phone in hand, her fingers moved across the screen, and she paid little attention to the people around her.

It was weird. It was like she'd become a completely different person in only a few seconds. Kaleb noticed the band around her wrist was covered. He didn't want to put too much thought into what Marci had told him earlier about who to trust. He needed to get to

Alice before it was too late. Ignoring his instincts, he chose to focus on the soft cords of a piano weaving its way through the speakers above.

The hypnotic tone of the woman singing filled Kaleb's mind, leading his thoughts to a happier time. Alice sat in the passenger seat when they drove across the country to see her family. Listening to '90s pop wasn't bad.

Kaleb missed the times he got to be himself, able to forget about the past and the danger they were in, the danger he put them in. *This is my fault. If I had just left Alice alone, she wouldn't be here in this city. She never would have let Red Queen or the Reddings into her life.* He pulled himself back to the here and now; going down the rabbit hole of what was or could be wouldn't help anyone.

He needed a distraction, and since no one had mentioned it, he asked, "Does anyone know what happened to Tom and Linc? Did they make it out of the building?"

"They got out." Markus looked at Marci before speaking. "They're with Dad."

Kaleb's muscles tightened, and his stomach dropped. "Joseph's here." So, his father had made it out of Red Queen. *Is he still working for Reid Redding or someone else who pays better?*

The elevator doors opened with a ping. Marci walked past Kaleb toward a black SUV with the engine running and doors open, waiting for them.

"He came here with the rest of Reid's people a few months ago," Markus said.

Kaleb wasn't sure why his brother had kept Joseph's presence in the city from him. Sure, Kaleb didn't trust Joseph or even really like him, none of his siblings did, but if it weren't for his father, he wouldn't have gotten out of Red Queen. Though, to be fair, if Joseph hadn't pulled Kaleb into his world, Kaleb would have gotten a regular job that didn't leave the stain of death and betrayal on everything it touched. He also wouldn't have met Alice.

"Anyone else in town that I should know about?"

Marci climbed into the driver's seat as Markus got in on the passenger side. Still waiting for answers, Kaleb got into the back. As soon as he buckled in, Marci moved toward the exit, past dust-covered cars, and onto the empty city streets.

"Ryan Dixon, you know. Then there's Gryff, Reid, DeeDee, and Dr. Turtle," Markus said.

The other four weren't a surprise. Anywhere WonderLand was, Dr. Turtle and the Redding siblings weren't far behind. As for Gryff, he followed both DeeDee and Reid like a faithful guard dog.

"Is that it?"

"As far as we know," Markus replied.

Kaleb looked out the window, thinking about what Joseph being in the city meant. *What did he want with Tom and Linc?* He couldn't wrap his mind around why either of them would help his father. It didn't make sense, much like the empty snow-covered city and pink dust of WonderLand that littered the outside world.

He didn't want to think about that, not right now. "What's the plan?"

Marci held up her right arm. Her band that had been white the last time he saw it was now black. Sometime between the elevator and now, it had changed. Something in his mind clicked. That's what was bothering him in the elevator. Marci told him not to trust anyone if their band wasn't black. He looked at his brother, and his band was also black.

"I'll go in through the front doors," Marci said.

Markus clasped Marci's free hand, entwining his fingers with hers. "And we'll give cover from above."

Kaleb knew by "we" he meant himself since Kaleb was still unable to hold a gun without the fear of what he might do consuming him.

"Do you know where in the garden she'll be?" Markus asked Kaleb.

"Approximately." He hadn't said where to meet him outright, but she had enough information to figure it out.

Marci pulled over beside a hill near the garden's main entrance. She turned around in her seat, facing Kaleb, waiting for him to tell her where to go. He hated that she was the one going after Alice. It should be him. He'd been the one who sent her in there, after all.

"There's a bench to the right of the entrance. Alice should be there or at least near there."

"Should?" Marci asked.

He rubbed the back of his neck. "I didn't give her an exact location...more like clues.

Markus got out of the car, opening the door next to Kaleb. "Good thinking." He nodded toward the hill, dismissing him. Once Kaleb was out, Markus went to Marci's side of the car. She rolled down the window, and Kaleb turned his back, giving them privacy, something Markus never did for him.

Not that he and Alice had anything close to the kind of relationship Markus and Marci had. Theirs was filled with danger, but at least it was honest. Kaleb always kept Alice at arm's length when it came to his true feelings, trying to protect her from his life, but she still got dragged into the danger.

That memory refused to go away, no matter how he tried to ignore it. It pulled him into a past he'd rather forget.

ALICE STOOD OVER HIM. *Everything glowed red from the taint of WonderLand. Her words somehow made it through the torment of the boiling anger tearing through his body. "I think I might have loved you."*

KALEB PUSHED the memory away when Markus passed him. Now wasn't the time to focus on whether it had happened. He'd done that enough over the last few months, and it got him nowhere.

Markus had already started up the hill, forcing Kaleb to catch up, neither of them speaking as they walked. It was easy to fall back into the old habit of following his big brother's every move. But Kaleb still didn't forgive him for lying about Alice. Not completely.

Markus stopped. "That'll work."

They both lay down on the wet ground. Markus aimed his rifle on the bench, while Kaleb stared down at the garden waiting for Marci's signal.

"You know, at some point, you'll have to pick up a gun again."

Kaleb shrugged, "I guess."

"You can't live the life we do and not carry a weapon, Kaleb. It isn't safe."

Kaleb knew this, but he wasn't ready to admit it. "I was hoping not to live like this anymore. Once we get Alice out, I'm done."

"You've said that before."

Kaleb dropped the binoculars, turning to his brother. "Look, you don't know what it's like to lose control, not how WonderLand makes you. I can't risk it. The all-consuming rage ruined my life once and being armed only made it worse."

Markus was quiet for a while, but Kaleb saw he was working up to something, so Kaleb silently waited.

"I'm sorry I left you with dad." He rubbed the back of his neck, "And I'm sorry I lied about Alice."

Trying to push down the anger he felt toward his brother, Kaleb rubbed his temples. "Let's not go into this right now, okay?" *Maybe not ever.* If Kaleb was honest with himself, he understood why Markus had lied. But right now, he needed to feel anger for his brother. It was easier than dealing with the past.

His face went blank, almost as if he was shutting down. "Okay."

Now what? "So, you and Marci are getting pretty serious."

A far-off look filled his eyes as a smile spread across his brother's face. He pushed himself up a little from the ground, opened his jacket pocket, and pulled out a small black box tossing it to Kaleb.

Kaleb opened the box where a silver band with a teardrop-shaped, black stone surrounded by tiny diamonds twinkled in the sunlight. "Mom's ring."

Markus nodded. "Took Marci out there a few months ago. Been trying to find the right time to ask ever since."

"Wow." That was a big thing and not in the normal "meet the parents" kind of way. Markus had to trust Marci completely to introduce her to their mom. If Reid Redding found out she was still alive, she'd send the Knights to finish the job.

Kaleb handed the box back to Markus. "She'll say yes."

Marci's voice cracked through the walkie on Markus' hip. "Alice is here, and she's not alone."

Chapter 14

A giant red rock at the gardens' entrance read *Butt Gardens* in black letters. Alice held back a snicker. Sometime in recent months, the 'e' must've fallen off the sign. She didn't know if the tension made it funny or if her ten-year-old self was fighting its way to the surface. Either way, it wouldn't be a good time to have a fit of laughter.

Ian pulled into the deserted parking lot. "Are you sure your friend is meeting you here?"

"Yep." Hopefully, Kaleb was here, safe and waiting for her.

Ian and Stan exchanged a look.

"What?" she asked.

Stan nodded towards a yellow triangle painted on the glass door of the visitor center. "You may be immune, but that doesn't mean they can't hurt you."

Alice wasn't sure how, most likely one of those lost memories, but she knew the symbol on the door not only had something to do with WonderLand, it meant a lot of people had been exposed inside. "I'll be fine." *At least I know the people behind those doors have lost their minds. Unlike out here.* "It's not my first time here."

"If you're sure," Ian said.

Alice nodded before smiling at him awkwardly. "Yes, I'm sure."

That seemed to be what he needed to hear because the car door slammed shut, and they sped off. Stopping on the second step, Alice stared at the visitor center, thinking about the first time she'd come here. The sun was shining on her face, Kaleb's hand in hers. It should've been the start of something great.

"Donna," Stan called from the back seat of the car that had left moments before. Fear settled in her stomach. Alice turned to face them. There was no reason for them to be back here.

Alice walked back to the car, standing far enough that they would have to get out of the car to grab her but close enough that she could still hear them. To Alice's surprise, Stan held out a red business card, the words *Trust Nothing* printed on the front of it.

"If you ever decide you want to switch sides when you give up on the normal life thing."

Still trying to figure out what to do next, Alice took the card. "Umm, thanks."

Tucking the card into her back pocket, she stared at the building, trying to wrap her mind around what had happened.

"Good luck." He rolled up the window, and they sped off again.

Alice ran up the stairs toward the visitor center. *Well, that was—unexpected.* The large door opened with a gentle push.

Alice took a deep, calming breath before walking inside. An uneasiness settled in her stomach as the door scraped across the carpeted floor, trying to ignore the creepy, zombie-movie jazz playing overhead.

When I was here with Kaleb, there were people everywhere. Okay, it was summer, and a plague hadn't been released on an unsuspecting population. Still, this is beyond disturbing.

Alice stopped in front of the door that led outside to the gardens, giving herself a pep talk. *All I need to do is find Kaleb.* Images of what could be outside mixed with what she'd seen on the worst days of her life. Alice took another deep breath. *One, two, three, four...* She opened the heavy glass door, entering a world of sleeping flowers.

They'd spent hours here a long time ago. It was summer then, flowers everywhere, and everything was different. Alice took a few different paths before recognizing the bench Kaleb hinted at in his letter.

Alice looked around, searching for anything that might have proved Kaleb was there. *Had he forgotten? Was he safe?"*

There wasn't much to look at, though. A dead rose bush and a snow-covered bench. Maybe he left another letter for her—a way to find him.

She knelt on the cold cement looking along the curved edges of the bench, moving her fingers across the steel. There was nothing there, not even chewing gum.

Alice stood up. "Now what?"

A young girl answered. "Maybe there's something in that flowerpot over there?"

Biting back a scream, Alice spun around to face the voice. A girl, no more than eleven, stood in front of her in a flowing, white sundress. Her feet bare despite the cold temperatures. Her eyes sparkled with the effects of WonderLand.

"Oh, I'm sorry, I didn't realize anyone else was here," Alice said.

The girl's dark eyes followed Alice's every movement as she spoke. "Then why did you ask a question?" A look of confusion on her face, almost as if Alice had lost her mind.

There was something in those eyes that reminded her of someone. *Has her family left her here?* A wide grin appeared on her freckled face, and Alice knew who she looked like. Ryan.

"Guess I was talking to myself." She shrugged.

The girl looked around. "I don't see Myself. Are they a friend of yours?"

Confused and worried, Alice watched the girl. She wasn't like the people in the theater. There was a childlike quality to her, more than Alice expected from someone her age, sorta like how the guards, Madison and Harrison, at Red Queen had acted. *Did this girl get exposed to the same strain of WonderLand as them?* It explained why she wasn't shivering in her summer dress and bare feet. *WonderLand can make you run hot.*

"My name is Alice. What's yours?"

The girl looked down at her bare feet. "Most people call me TigerLily, like my mom, but that's not my real name, just what the others call me."

So there are others. Who were they?

Alice exhaled. "Is your mom here?"

TigerLily sniffled before shaking her head again. "No." She grabbed Alice's hand, leading her away from the bench. "I have friends, though."

Alice wasn't sure if she should follow the girl. Not only did she not want to leave before finding Kaleb's next clue, *if there even was one,* but she wasn't sure about this girl or her friends. What if they'd been exposed to a version of WonderLand that made them violent? The guy on the street seemed more crazy than angry, but that didn't mean everyone reacted that way.

The girl pulled her forward. *I can always run.* TigerLily led her to a small gazebo, a pastel pink and blue structure, out of place among the winter scape surrounding it. *Go back and look for Kaleb's next clue.*

A slight shiver moved through her. If Alice didn't know better, she'd think she was in a bad horror flick. Twelve girls dressed in the same white dress as TigerLily sat in a circle.

Alice guessed the oldest was around fifteen and the youngest maybe seven. They were talking and giggling until they saw Alice.

"Rose, Larkspur, look at what I found," TigerLily said.

The two oldest girls stood up, circling Alice and examining her. Their short white dresses swished around their legs with each step, WonderLand swimming in their eyes.

The tallest one stood almost at eye level, with Alice poking her side. Then turned to the other girl muttering under her breath. "She will never do."

"Not pretty enough," said the other.

"Not a flower." She poked Alice again. "A weed, maybe."

Alice rubbed at the sore spots on her chest. The girl's fingers were stronger than Alice guessed by looking at them. They were going to leave marks.

One of them came toward Alice again.

Alice shouted. "STOP."

The girls stumbled away from her, and Alice started to count. *One, two, three.* Alice was usually calm, she had to be, but for some reason, the craziness of these girls got under her skin in that annoying little brother way.

The other girls in the gazebo, who had started chatting while Rose and Larkspur examined Alice, stopped talking. Ten pairs of tiny eyes stared at her; dismay plastered across their porcelain faces.

Alice shivered again.

So *creepy*.

TigerLily's quiet voice interrupted Alice's thoughts. "See, I'm not the only person who doesn't like to be treated like livestock," she whined.

Rose and Larkspur rolled their eyes at TigerLily. Then acting as if nothing had happened, they walked back to the circle, sitting in the same places they'd left empty when Alice arrived.

Alice took a deep breath reminding herself they were suffering the effects of WonderLand. *Why else would there be kids here? Dressed like the sacrifices they were about to become.*

Alice bit her bottom lip. *Can I get them out? They're children.* She looked at the girls and then back the way she'd come. *There has to be a way to get them out.*

"TigerLily, how did you get here?" Alice asked.

Her face lit up, an infectious smile on her lips. "My uncle." She looked at the two older girls and whispered, "We're hiding."

"From who?"

A blonde girl who must have overheard them pointed at Alice's wrist. "She had a band like yours. Only hers was pink."

Alice looked at the black band on her wrist and back at the girls in the circle. She noticed that none of these girls had their own bands for the first time.

How can that be?

A memory tore her from the present.

THE CITY WAS *in lockdown and had been for three days. No one was allowed on the streets. Pink dust covered every inch of uncovered space; anyone touching it would act out nightmares beyond an average person's grasp.*

An emergency broadcast started on a nearby TV.

Do not leave your homes.

Those who leave their homes without an Optic Band will be shot.

Alice had been tested the day before and expected her band to show up anytime. When there was a knock at her door, she wasn't surprised to see the Guard on her stoop.

"Donna White, we would like to offer you a job."

THE PRESENT PUSHED Alice back into the here and now. She once again stood in front of the strangely dressed girls. Confused by what she'd remembered, she shook the memory away.

Donna White, again. Why that name? Did I end up working for the Guard? Is that why I knew this place would be okay?

TigerLily pulled on Alice's shirt sleeve. Something about the girl with dark, tight curls sticking up in all directions bothered Alice. "Why aren't you hiding from me?"

"The boy with the funny name said you were nice."

Funny name? "Was it Rabbit?"

TigerLily stopped and thought for a minute. "I don't know. Maybe. He said you'd come here. We didn't trust him at first. Only black bands can be trusted. He was funny, though, and had lots of jokes. He smiled a lot. It kinda looked like mine." She walked to an empty flowerpot and reached inside to grab something. "I almost forgot. This is for..." She gasped, and the girls in the gazebo stopped talking. Whatever they saw caused the girls to back away from Alice, terror etched on their faces.

"I'll take that," said a familiar voice.

Alice turned around. "Kit?" A joyful grin painted her smeared, pink lips. Kit's hand reached for TigerLily, who shoved something toward Alice before dropping it at her feet.

Kit's smile held an insanity Alice had never seen in her friend. WonderLand shimmered in Kit's eyes, eyes that were now focused on Alice.

How is Kit here? Alice remembered what Stan and Ian had told her about this being a drop-off point for the infected. She didn't understand why they'd drop her off here and not take her into custody or even execute her.

"Pick it up," Kit growled.

TigerLily shook her head.

Kit reached behind her, pulling a heavy-looking gun from her waistband and pointing it at TigerLily. *How had she gotten a gun?*

"What are you doing?" Alice asked.

Kit aimed the gun a few inches from TigerLily's head. "Just a little errand for the queen." She pulled the trigger, and a bullet whizzed past the girl, digging into a wooden post of the gazebo and spraying shards of wood on the girls seated inside.

How did she miss her? She's right in front of her.

Alice motioned for TigerLily to get behind her. "The queen is dead." At least, she hoped she was. The last time Alice saw Reid Redding, six months ago, she was in Red Queen headquarters, reigning over her band of crazies.

Kit narrowed her eyes, scratching her face with the gun barrel. "Are you sure?'

There was movement behind Alice. She hoped it was the girls using Kit's distraction to get away.

"Then I guess we don't need you anymore." Kit pointed the gun at Alice. "The Queen was the only reason anyone bothered with you. Without her, Marci and I would've never been, well, I guess you'd say 'friends' with you. You really are the most boring person I have ever met, Alice Smith."

Well, that hurt, even if it's a drug-induced rant.

"With you gone, Rabbit can leave this mess behind him and finally be with me."

Alice rolled her eyes. *Kaleb has no interest in Kit, not in that way. He called her draining on more than one occasion.*

Kit continued to point the gun at Alice. Her index finger on the trigger. Alice couldn't see a way out of this.

I've been exposed to WonderLand more times than anyone on the planet. Watched as the people I love succumb to its horrible side effects, and this is how I'm going to die? At the hands of a friend consumed by hatred and jealousy?

She closed her eyes. If she was going to die, she'd spend her last moments thinking of happier times. Family road trips, her brothers arguing in the back seat, and her parents sneaking a kiss when they thought no one was watching. Her friends, Tom and Linc, flirting with random girls and playing pranks on each other. And Kaleb. Even now, she could hear his voice calling out to her.

Fa-thud.

Alice opened her eyes in time to see Kit fall onto the concrete, her eyes wide open, staring straight at her. Streams of dark-red blood trickled from a perfectly circular hole in the center of her forehead. The light of life faded from her eyes.

Not sure what happened, but refusing to give the shooter time to kill her too, Alice picked up whatever TigerLily dropped and shoved it into her front pocket. Alice knew the shock of seeing her roommate and friend lying dead on the cold ground could destroy her. She needed to run. Keeping her back toward the door and watching for signs of the shooter, she made her way to the lobby.

That shot was impossibly perfect.

She didn't want to leave the girls in the white dresses behind, but she had to. Alice hoped that whoever had left them there would find them.

Drops of sweat dripped down the curve of her back in time with each step, her eyes focused on the road ahead—a silent prayer on her lips.

The black shadow of hibernating trees hung over her, protecting her from prying eyes above. Relieved, Alice inhaled the crisp winter air laced with the sweet smell of nature and gunpowder. Now that she was hidden from the tree line, Alice planned her escape. Well, sort of. She could only think of one way to get out. It was to go back the way she'd come and down the front steps.

Most of which was open space.

Not the best route, but it was my only option.

She turned toward the doors she'd gone through earlier. Her escape. Their dark- brown branches splattered with pink dust, and white snow blurred into splotches—an impressionist painting dripping with fear and confusion.

Alice ran.

Again.

Chapter 15

Kaleb's chest tightened, and his vision went fuzzy. It felt like his body was moving in all directions while his mind was stuck in one place.

Don't freeze.

He knew Alice was alive, but some part of him didn't believe it. Not until the girl in the white dress had led her into the open. Anyone could see her, and then...

The smell of gunpowder lingered in the air around him, reminding Kaleb that Kit had a gun pointed at Alice.

How did she get a gun?

She's going to shoot Alice?

Markus... Alice... Kit's dead.

I watched it and did nothing to stop it. Just like I did so many times in...

Red Queen.

Kaleb's mind floated back to the past, and he was trapped, the past mixing with the present.

The blood-soaked walls closed around him, fluorescent light flickering above, his arms tied down to a cold, steel table below. Anger swam through his veins, overwhelming his every thought. Dr. Turtle *stood over him, pumping rage through Kaleb's system with a dark grin on his face.*

RYAN'S VOICE floated in the air around him and mixed with the crackle of an old-school walkie-talkie. "What are you doing? I haven't set up the fail-safes."

ALICE.
He could hear her breathing, screaming.
Alice rescued me.
The smell of gunpowder swirled around him, fusing with rain and honeysuckle.
Not rescued.

"I CAN'T LEAVE him like this." Markus moved closer to him, his voice low. "I'm here. You're not alone." He rested a hand on Kaleb's shoulder.

"Kaleb?" The warmth of Markus's touch reminded Kaleb of the steps he'd learned in the hospital after escaping Red Queen headquarters and the effects of WonderLand.

Ryan's voice echoed around him. "Damn it! You have fifteen minutes, then I'm pulling you out."

What is going on? Am I losing my mind? Why can I hear Ryan? He shouldn't be here.

Markus's deep voice broke through Kaleb's muddled brain. "Tell me five things you see right now," he said.

Still unable to think straight, he was thankful Markus could voice the question to bring Kaleb back to the present. He blinked, trying to clear some of the static from his head. "Um... Snow."

The darkness pulled at him, consuming him. He held on to any small piece of the present he could see. *Markus shot Kit. No, don't think about it. Not right now.*

"Dead leaves."

Markus squeezed Kaleb's shoulder again, a gentle reminder that he was still there waiting for Kaleb to find his way back.

"A tree branch."

Not ready to look at his brother, he focused on the ground in front of him. *Something else to help ground me in the real world and pull me from the past.* "Your shoelaces."

Markus said in a low, patient voice, "Good, one more."

One more. I need one more thing. "Pink?"

"Good, now four things you can touch."

Kaleb reached out, picking up the wet snow, letting the cold sting his hand before speaking. "Snow." He dropped the melted snowball on the ground, wiping his wet hands on his pants. "My leg." Pushing the hair from his face, he tried to think of something else. "Hair and..." He touched his arm. "Skin."

The tension in Kaleb's body loosened a bit, and his mind started to clear. He looked up at his older brother. "Three things I can hear: birds, the train, and a stream."

A slight smile crossed Markus's lips, and they said together. "Two things I can smell."

"Dirt and..." Kaleb's jaw ticked. "Gunpowder."

Markus rushed out the last part before Kaleb could drown under anxiety's spell. "Taste, Kaleb. What do you taste?"

"Salt." Kaleb looked up at his brother, the panic that had overwhelmed him calmed to its usual dullness.

Markus looked at Kaleb, concern on his face. "What?"

"Salt City tastes like salt."

"Smartass," Markus grumbled.

A worried look crossed his brow; he turned and focused on Marci at the bottom of the hill, standing over her sister's body.

"Go," Kaleb told him.

Markus helped Kaleb to his feet. "Are you sure?"

"I'm fine."

He looked at Marci and back to Kaleb, the fear etched in lines across his face. "You're sure?"

No. "Markus, go."

His brother looked him up and down one last time before making his way to Marci. He stopped at the halfway point and looked back up at Kaleb.

Marci needs him more than I do.

Kaleb waved his brother away, needing a minute to process everything that had happened without the consuming panic that tried to devour him moments before. It had been almost a month since his last panic attack. He hadn't missed them. It was the longest he'd gone without one since the incident at Red Queen, but this one was different because someone he loved was in real danger. Not his body overreaction to a past he'd rather forget.

He watched Markus approach Marci, a rifle slung across his back. Marci lay across her twin sister's lifeless body. Her shoulders shook with sobs.

Markus shot Kit to save Alice.

Kaleb was relieved that Alice was alive, but Kit was loud, sweet, and full of life. *Will Marci ever forgive him? Markus risked his happiness to save Alice.*

Alice… She ran but to where? Kaleb made his way down the hill toward his brother and Marci, looking for any sign of the path Alice or the girls in white might have taken.

He stopped midway down the hill, watching Marci and his brother. Markus stood a few feet from Marci, scanning the area, keeping her safe, letting her grieve.

Maybe I can use Marci's computer to track Alice's movements by accessing the city's security cameras. Of course, it will take time, but…

The bouncing of a blond ponytail caught Kaleb's eye. He'd know that bounce anywhere, spent years following the woman it belonged to: DeeDee. She crept along the wall of the visitor center toward Marci and Markus. Something was off. The way she moved it was robot-like. It had taken years, but Kaleb knew she wasn't as innocent of the Redding crimes as he once thought. *I bet she's the reason Kit was here in the first place.*

Kaleb fought the urge to rush down the hill, giving up his advantage. *She has no idea I'm in the city.* Instead, he reached for the walkie that should be attached to his belt. It wasn't there. *It must have fallen off.* At that moment, Kaleb wished he'd gotten over not carrying a gun.

He had one option: get to DeeDee before she got to Marci and Markus. He quickened his pace, sliding down the rocky hillside. Snow and dirt tumbled in front of him, a red carpet announcing his approach. Markus looked up, confusion marring his features as DeeDee approached Marci from behind, a glint of evil intent shining on her lips.

"Behind you," Kaleb called out.

DeeDee wrapped her arms around Marci. A scream of surprise left Marci's lips, causing Markus to turn toward her with his hand on the gun at his waist. DeeDee pulled Marci closer, a syringe of pink liquid hovering inches from the vein in her neck.

"Tsk Tsk," DeeDee said as she looked Markus up and down, the needle pressing closer to Marci's skin. "I wouldn't do that if I were you." She glanced down at Marci. "You wouldn't want to kill an innocent, now would you."

Markus raised his hands above him.

DeeDee turned to Kaleb, who now stood next to his brother, hands at his side. Her blue eyes shimmered with malice he'd never seen.

"You survived the explosion then—You remember what this is?" she asked, nodding toward the syringe in her hand.

He nodded. *WonderLand.* He'd only ever seen it once in its liquid form but never forgot what that pink liquid did to his system.

Her grin widened into a smile. "I can see it in your eyes. You remember what it feels like."

"Yes."

"I don't want to hurt Marci. She's useful," DeeDee said. "She's brought me some of my favorite toys."

There was something off about DeeDee, and not that she was lying. Marci would never help her. It was almost as if someone was playing the part of DeeDee. Getting the basics of her right but not the essence. Kaleb tried to look at her band. It looked like it was flashing between black and white. *What does that even mean?*

Markus took a step toward them, and DeeDee tightened her grip, causing Marci to wince. "But I will."

"What do you want, DeeDee?" Kaleb asked.

She snorted. "I need her to find someone for me."

"Alice? She already tried that," Markus sighed. "That girl has a talent for disappearing."

DeeDee laughed.

Marci motioned to Kaleb. She wanted him to move closer to Markus. He took two steps in that direction while maintaining eye contact with DeeDee.

"This was never about Alice. Not for me. That was all Reid," DeeDee said.

"Then, who?" Kaleb asked.

DeeDee answered. "Huh, that's interesting. Who said I wanted a person? Maybe I just want to be left alone."

Marci's raw voice broke into the conversation. "If I can find you a place to do your experiments without interruption, will you let the others go and stop hunting them?"

"Interesting suggestion." DeeDee pressed the needle closer to Marci's throat. "The thing is, I already have one of those. Actually, more than one, but you already know that, don't you?"

Marci reached up, grabbing the hand that held the needle over her neck. Her fingers rested on the plunger. "Is that why you killed Kit?"

DeeDee looked down at Kit's lifeless form. "I'm not the one who shot her."

Kaleb glanced at his brother, Markus's lips pressed tightly

together and his body stiff. "Maybe not, but I'm betting you're the one who gave her WonderLand," Kaleb said. "You also dropped her off here to be picked up by Reid's goons, hoping she'd use that gun you gave her to end your sister's life."

DeeDee's nonanswer was all Kaleb needed to confirm his suspicions. The Redding sisters were still at war and would use anyone or anything to win.

"That's what I thought," Marci said. She slammed her elbow into DeeDee's stomach, who crumbled to the ground struggling for breath. Marci moved away from DeeDee, taking the syringe with her.

Marci stood between DeeDee and Markus, still holding the syringe to her neck. Kaleb watched as panic mixed with sadness clouded her eyes. He knew that look. It was the same one he'd seen in the mirror for months after Markus told him Alice was dead.

DeeDee got up, taking a few steps toward Marci.

Marci pushed the needle into her neck.

"Marci!" Both Kaleb and Markus took a step toward her.

She turned to face them. "Don't move. Everyone stay where you are."

A groan echoed through his mind.

Kaleb knew the tone in Marci's voice well; he'd used it himself after his mother and Alice's disappearance. It was the one someone used before doing something incredibly stupid.

Markus took a step closer, his hands outstretched. "Marci, please let me..."

"Don't, I just need..." Marci looked down at her sister's body and back up at Markus, her tear-stained face pleading with him to let her go. She swallowed. "I just need time."

She pushed the plunger down, forcing the pink liquid into her body.

Chapter 16

Marci yanked the band off her wrist, throwing it onto the litter-covered ground, and gulped down the thick, stale air around her. She closed her eyes, trying to get control of her emotions. Images of her sister's lifeless body stained the darkness behind her lids.

"No, no. It isn't true." She looked around the van that served as a mobile command center. Ryan should be in the driver's seat, ready to leave at a moment's notice. At the very least, he needed to watch over them as they slept.

Not good. How long before those goons find us?

Marci's phone dinged with an incoming message. She reached into the confines of her pockets with shaking hands.

The screen lit up with a message from Markus.

Kaleb is safe.

Come back when you are ready.

Touched by the message, Marci let herself smile. Markus had to leave Kaleb alone to send that message. It wasn't safe for Kaleb to be unmonitored by someone who knew what was happening inside Salt City. Kaleb's mind wasn't ready for the truth of what was happening.

It had taken months to find Kaleb and Alice, and every time they'd gotten close enough to get them out, Turtle found a way to turn the tables. She'd hated leaving them in Salt City to be tortured by Dr. Turtle. For now, the best she could do was track them from the outside. At least until WonderLand finished running through her avatar's system.

Marci scrolled through her phone, intending to call Ryan. Her sister's name was the first to come up, and even though she knew it was pointless, she dialed Kit anyway.

An image of Kit's lifeless body moved through her mind. Fighting back the tears, she took a deep, cleansing breath and shook the image away.

The call went straight to voicemail. Kit's cheerful voice filled Marci's ears. *No, I'm not going to focus on that, not now.*

"This is Kit. I can't come to the phone right now. I'm having a tea party with Wendy and the lost boys. Leave me a message, and I'll call you back when I get back from Neverland, or better yet, text like a normal person."

Marci hung up the phone without leaving a message that Kit would never listen to. Wiping the tears running down her cheeks, Marci pulled up Ryan's number. She'd only needed to hear Kit's voice.

It wasn't the real Kit. Not the person she'd grown up with. Markus didn't have a choice. He had killed that Kit to save Alice. It was the right thing to do, but it still hurt.

Kit wasn't really there. She was tucked away somewhere safe. Where no one can find her. She'd promised to take care of her, and Marci had to trust her.

Turtle used WonderLand to infect Salt City, and he used Kit to get Marci to give up her mission. Now that Kit was gone, it couldn't be done again, not in this round, and Marci intended to end this before Turtle found Alice and Kaleb. She texted Ryan.

Where are you?

It would be hard to go back without Kit; she'd never lived in a world without her sister. She needed to move forward and fix her mistakes.

We need to leave. NOW!

Ryan opened the van's back door with a toothy grin. Marci wanted to yell *where have you been,* but the abrupt change on his face stopped her.

He rushed over to her. "What happened? I knew Markus went in too soon. Do we need to move?"

She'd forgotten about the monitor tracking her vitals. For the first time after coming out of the simulation, Marci noticed the beeping. She pulled off the wired contraption she stole from Dr. Turtle and set it on a steel table. "Let's do it anyway, just to be safe."

Ryan leaned across the small space of the van, turning the monitor off. "Are you sure you're okay?" He reached into his pocket, pulling the car keys out before dropping them into her outstretched hand.

She nodded. *No, but we don't have time to deal with it now.*

Ryan sat in the passenger seat next to her, staring ahead, playing with a disposable cup. The smell of cheap coffee filled the van, and comfortable silence filled the air around them. This gave Marci a chance to think.

Marci focused on her conversation with the person inside DeeDee's avatar. *I don't need a place. She'd said she didn't need a place. Does that mean they weren't looking for me?* They wanted Marci out of Salt City and would do whatever they could to make that happen. Including forcing Markus to choose to kill Kit or save Alice.

"No, they aren't worried about us."

"What?"

Marci tightened her grip on the steering wheel. "Red Queen, at least what's left of it, they aren't worried about us." Her insides were too hollow to explain, but she knew Ryan would understand something terrible had happened without saying much.

"DeeDee. I think it might have been Turtle." She squinted at the road in front of her. "I think he did something to DeeDee. It was like she was her, but not."

"What do you mean?"

Marci pulled into the parking lot of a grocery store. "I'm not sure yet, but I think Turtle may have found a new way to enter Salt City."

She moved to the back of the van grabbing her laptop, before sitting in the black chair bolted to the ground. She pulled up the code for DeeDee's band. "I don't know yet. Whatever it is, DeeDee and Turtle have changed the rules." *They'd never killed someone she cared about.*

Marci could use that.

Chapter 17

Alice turned a corner, slowing down, and pulled the hood of her sweatshirt over her head. She couldn't remember ever running so far in her life, her lungs burned, and a heaviness settled in her chest. She was tired of running. There had to be a better way to survive.

Kit's dead, and I left her.

A breeze swirled around her, bringing the winter air slamming against her back. *She was my friend, and I left her bleeding out to be dissected by the same people that started this mess in the first place.*

She shivered in tune with the ding-ding of the crossing gate for the train. *Red Queen and the Guard treat human life like lab rats. Knight or Bishop doesn't matter.*

Cold and unsure what to do next, Alice walked to the nearby station. Not to ride but to get out of the wind and warm up. Once she was under one of the metal slats that covered the platform, the tingling that accompanied a memory slithered through her before tearing her from the present.

ALICE WATCHED THE NEWS. *The infected were being hunted like animals. Men dressed in camo holding hunting rifles talked about how the thrill of the chase was something everyone should experience.*

Images flashed on the screen of a burly guy with a gun aimed at a young blond woman. The camera zoomed in on the bright pink bracelet moments before she dropped to the ground. A round hole in the center of her skull.

Just like Kit.

Alice was yanked out of the past and into the snow-covered world. Fear waltzed around her heart with its partner, anger, leaving the hollowness inside behind.

Who would hunt other people like that? And why would I stay here?

Alice checked her band, and two Guards approached the station checking bands. She wasn't sure if they were Knights or Bishops, only that they were looking for someone. She considered leaving. Kaleb told Alice to avoid the Guard at all costs. But Stan and Ian helped her once they saw her black immunity band. *Maybe they'll leave me alone.*

Alice stayed in line between an older couple holding hands and a young family, not wanting to bring unwanted attention to herself. A line formed in front of her, the Guard at the end checking each wristband. Her heartbeat quickened with each step, the fear conjuring faint images of the days before the wall went up. Before the Guard came, death and blood-covered maniacs were on every corner.

She watched one of the Guard pull a dark-haired woman from the line. The girl, holding the woman's hand, cried out.

"Mommy, where are you going?"

The woman turned back to her husband, a balding man who picked the little girl up, covering the girl's face.

They're going to kill her.

That was when Alice noticed the woman's band—it was black.

She's immune.

Fear's cold fingers curled around Alice's chest. She watched as the Guard whispered something in the woman's ear, his hand pulling on the band around her wrist. Black plastic hung from his chubby fingers, revealing the actual color.

Bright pink.

Even though everything in her told her to help this family, she knew there was nothing she could do. Getting involved wouldn't save the woman; it would get Alice killed.

A shot sang into the winter sky. Followed by the sharp cries of a motherless child. The father and child disappeared onto the train behind her, leaving behind a mother and wife. Another victim of WonderLand lying in a pink-poxed snowbank.

No one around her reacted.

Alice swallowed the bile that tried to escape.

This was their new norm.

Alice stepped forward, her arm exposed, eyes trained on the ground. *It's my norm now.*

The Guard's warm hand brushed the top of her wrist, testing the band for tampering. He seemed satisfied with what he found.

"Have a nice day," he said.

Surprised by his kindness, she met his smiling blue eyes. "Uh, thank you."

Alice didn't want to be there, near a woman who lay dead two feet away and the reminder that she'd done nothing to stop it. *It's just another day behind the wall.* Alice climbed into the train car, the doors closing behind her with a swish.

None of this felt real. It was like a game. Moving from one terrible thing to another, working toward a final goal. Picking up clues along the way. Or was this her way of dealing with all the death? Either way, she hated it and herself for doing nothing about it.

Alice walked toward an empty seat in the back of the car. It was close enough to a door if she needed to get off fast, but no way for anyone to come up behind her. She sat on the blue woven fabric of the bench, the feel of it scraping against her jeans, giving her some semblance of normal.

Feeling safe-ish, Alice pulled out whatever TigerLily had tried to give her. It was a scrap of paper with her name painted in blue, distorted by crumple lines and water. Alice turned it over in her hands, trying to make out the words. *Why would Kaleb leave this for me?*

The handwriting isn't Kaleb's...is it Ryan's? How would I know what Ryan's writing looked like?

Someone tapped her on the shoulder. "Ticket."

Alice shoved the paper into her pocket before pretending to look for a ticket. She was sure she didn't have one. *Marci and DeeDee got me on the train earlier today. Maybe there's a ticket or some kind of ID in my pockets.* She emptied her jean pockets, and a crumpled twenty-dollar bill followed by two tens fell onto the steel floor, but no ticket.

What happens if I don't have a ticket? The ticket agent wasn't armed, at least as far as she could tell, but would he call the Guard to take her away?

He tapped his fingers on his watch, and a voice crackled over the intercom announcing the next stop.

The doors next to them opened with a swish. "I can't find it, but this is my stop." She pushed up her sleeves, exposing the black band on her wrist.

He sighed and motioned to the door. "Go."

Alice shoved the money into her front pockets and tried to keep her speed at a regular pace as she walked out the doors, not looking at the station name or the people who waited to get on. She crossed the street, stopping on the curb to pull out the crumpled paper from Ryan. Something about the waterlogged words popped out at her. *Rossi... Where have I seen this?* She walked aimlessly. Letting her unconscious mind guide her, she turned right down a side street.

Her stomach growled. *When was the last time I ate?* She couldn't remember. The smell of fresh bread and tomato sauce drove Alice forward, past boarded-up shops and orange construction arrows painted on speckled wood, pointing toward the delicious aroma.

The bright lights of the Hernandez Rossi Family Restaurant lit the fog-laden street. But, unlike the other shops in the alley, the red open sign flashed inside the giant, painted window near the glass door. *Was this what Ryan's note meant? Was I supposed to come here?* She pushed the door open and walked into the waiting area, letting the space heater in the corner blow warm air against her cold skin.

A curly-haired waitress behind the podium motioned to Alice's arm. "Wrist."

Alice pushed her sleeve to reveal the black band around her arm and waited for the woman's reaction. Unlike the other people she'd shown the band to, the woman seemed unimpressed.

"Come along," she barked. Alice followed her into the dining area.

Tables lined the room side by side lengthwise, reminding Alice of Thanksgiving dinner at her grandmother's house. She sat at the last chair closest to the door near a group of men and women in business suits with gold name tags on the right side of their shirts. A man in the group with salt-and-pepper hair appeared to be studying her. The streaks of silver in his dark hair caught the light when he finally turned his head away.

Alice tried to ignore him and looked over the menu, words flashing on its white pages. *Trust no one—nothing's real.* Alice blinked, not sure if what she'd read was real. The waitress plucked the menu from Alice's hands before she could look closer. She placed a bowl in front of Alice and walked away. Alice stared at the steaming red soup, confused. It was something she'd most likely have ordered, but she didn't since the menu was taken away.

"Everyone gets the same thing today," the guy with the salt-and-pepper hair said. His voice cracked like her Aunt Hazel's, who smoked a pack a day most of her life.

"Then why even have a menu?" Alice mumbled.

The guy shrugged.

When the waitress returned, she placed a cheese quesadilla next to the bowl of soup in front of Alice. Her stomach rumbled as she bit into the soft tortilla. The gooey, cheesy goodness filled her mouth.

Keeping her attention focused on her food to avoid conversation,

Alice sipped the creamy soup. Its warmth ran down her throat, heating her from the inside out, memories of her childhood swimming around her. She remembered days spent outside with her brothers and soup in odd-shaped bowls with star-shaped cheese sandwiches.

Why is it I can remember things that happened years ago but not what happened last week or even last month?

Her belly full and bowl empty, Alice looked for the waitress, but the woman with the curly hair was gone.

Not really hungry anymore but not wanting the food to go to waste, she took a bite of her now half-eaten quesadilla and decided what to do next. *I need to find Kaleb, but how?*

The gravelly voice of the guy across from her broke through her thoughts. "I know you," he said.

Alice looked up at him. Something sat on the edge of her memory, telling her she knew the old guy from somewhere, but she wasn't sure how. The gold name tag on his shirt read H.A.N.K. *Hank? The name kind of sounded familiar, though she would have remembered the odd spelling. It could be a trick of her eyes like the menu, or maybe the letters stood for something. Hidden, awareness, navigator... I can't think of anything for the K. It would be something computery, but what?*

"It's Alice, right? Alice Smith." His brow wrinkled. "You're Kaleb's friend."

Her stomach knotted. *How does he know my name? No one is supposed to know my name, not here. Alice Smith is dead.*

"You are mistaken." She stood up, took a ten from her pocket, and threw it on the table, hoping it was enough to cover her meal.

"I have to go."

As soon as she opened the glass door that led back into the alley, she regretted it, not because the cold air stung her cheeks. *Hank might know something about what happened to me in those months I can't remember.* Whoever he was, Alice didn't like the mixture of anger and fear that settled in her when she heard his voice. She looked up and down the street, trying to decide what to do next.

Her fingers touched the rough paper inside her pockets, reminding Alice of the note TigerLily had given her. *Maybe I should have stayed, looking for a sign from Ryan of where or what to do next.* She looked back at the restaurant. *Okay, so Hank makes me uncomfortable, but he might know something.*

The glass door opened behind her, and the people in the business suits walked out, including Hank. Alice watched the group as they moved past her, still trying to decide what to do.

Hank stopped. "I'm sorry if I scared you earlier, you just looked lost, and I wanted to help."

Alice nodded at him, checking in with herself. *Am I scared of him or what he might know?* She looked at the strange little man that claimed to know her. *There was something there, something important.*

She turned her attention to the group in front of them, who had kept walking after Hank stopped. *He might have information that can help me*, she reminded herself.

Alice pushed down the nagging fear, sure that what he knew about her life in the last six months was more important than her doubts. As they walked, she looked at the graffiti-covered walls and boards, noticing symbols hidden in the swirls and lines of the street art. It was as if they were somehow guiding her to her next destination.

She shook her head. *No, that's crazy.*

"Why do chicken coops only have two doors?" he asked.

What kind of question is that? She never checked his band, assuming he was fine since the waitress had demanded to see Alice when she entered. Alice looked at Hank's wrist. A white band around his arm's dark skin reassured Alice that WonderLand wasn't running through his veins. "Why?"

"Because if they had four, they'd be called chicken sedans," he said.

Alice smiled. *I was freaking out over a horrible dad joke.*

"That's better." He glanced at Alice. "I'm not sure what happened to you, but you need to do a better job of hiding. You can't go anywhere that Kaleb may have taken you. People who want you for their twisted purpose are looking for you."

"Are you one of them?"

He tsked. "Alice, if I wanted to hurt you, I would have done it long ago."

She'd assumed as much but still felt compelled to ask. They stopped walking, and Hank turned to face her, his eyebrows raised. "A funeral isn't a guarantee of death, Alice. At some point, you knew Turtle would find you."

"It was for the best," she answered out of habit, but she had no idea what it meant.

"You died months ago. Why come out of hiding now?"

She looked down the wide cement steps in front of them, steps similar to the ones at the University. They opened onto a large, pockmarked courtyard that spat out gallons of water into the air in the hot summer months. Before WonderLand, children and young couples danced and played in the water garden, laughter and screams bouncing off the brick buildings that lined the streets below.

"I'm not sure. Everyone thought I was dead, just like I planned," Alice said, unsure if it was a memory of what happened or something from Kaleb's card. "It kept them safe. It kept him safe. I had no choice."

Hank's eyes focused on Alice, looking as if he wanted to ask her something, and he changed his mind. "Everyone has secrets, Alice. At some point, you will have to face yours."

A rumble of an engine echoed through the air, and a chill moved through her body. She knew that sound.

It's Dorothy.

Kaleb's here.

Alice turned back to look at Hank, but he was gone. She looked down the street they'd come from a few minutes before and in the empty windows of the shops nearby, but Hank was nowhere to be found.

It's as if he disappeared into thin air. No, he can't do that. Can he? She shook her head. *No, that doesn't make sense.*

If she was honest with herself, very little in Salt City did. She started down the cement steps toward Kaleb's car, making her way around one of the big decorative stones that adorned the stairs every few steps.

She was halfway down when two men dressed in the black Guard uniforms stepped out of the car, a different symbol stitched into the sleeve of the black jackets.

They were arguing.

About what? Alice wasn't sure, but she was glad they were because they hadn't seen her yet, giving her enough time to duck behind a decorative rock.

When they got close enough, she could hear them. Alice peeked around the rock. Their faces were covered with dark plastic masks, but something about these two seemed familiar. It was something in the way they moved and the way they argued.

One stomped his foot while yelling, "YOU never listen."

Alice tried to get a better look at the two men that drove Kaleb's car. She didn't think one of them was him. *They have to know Kaleb. Right? I mean, they have his car.* A rock tumbled down the stairs past her, the clattering sound reverberating through the open courtyard below.

She watched in horror as it hit each step, holding her breath, hoping the men wouldn't hear it and find her hiding place. It finally stopped two steps from the bottom. Alice let out the breath she had been holding, and the man closest to her turned toward the stairs, gun drawn. "If you're going to watch our show, it's only right that you pay."

Chapter 18

How is it they didn't hear the rock, but they heard my breath?

It didn't matter if she stayed hidden; there was a good chance she'd die behind this rock. Her only choice was to surrender. Maybe once they realized she was immune, they'd let her go like the others had.

Alice raised her hands above the rock. "I'm unarmed."

"Show yourself," one of the men yelled.

She took her time standing, trying not to spook them, her knees shaking with the slow motion.

The one closest to Alice motioned for her to move closer. Alice started walking down the steps, hands above her head, pulling down her sleeve to show her black band. Their eyes followed her steps; puffs of warm breath seeped through the edges of their masks each time her foot hit the pavement.

Alice studied them, trying to place how she knew them. The black uniforms of the Guards covered everything but their eyes. She wasn't sure if she'd know who they were, even if she was close enough to see them. Eyes aren't as telling as romance novels would have you think.

Maybe they were Kaleb's or even Ryan's. A shiver ran down her spine at the thought of how she knew Ryan so well. Her afternoon on

Thavasi wasn't something she would soon forget. The way Turtle's drugs mess with your emotions is a terrible thing to experience; she wouldn't wish that on her worst enemy. No one should have to lose who they are like that.

Alice stopped, not so close that they could grab her but close enough that it seemed like she was complying. *The minute I see my out, I'm taking it.*

A thick, familiar, southern drawl came from one of the men, "Alice, is that really you?"

"Linc?" A slow smile moved across her lips, and some of the tension in her shoulders released.

The relief of seeing Linc was short-lived. *That means Tom's holding the gun.* Her throat went dry. *What had he done to get out of Red Queen?*

Linc took a step toward Alice, pulling the dark mask off, a goofy grin plastered on his face. "You're here. I found you."

Tom reached out, grabbing Linc's collar and stopping him mid-stride, inches from Alice.

"Are you sure it's her?" Tom asked.

He questions if I'm who I say I am. Alice raised her eyebrow but didn't say anything. *The last time I saw Tom, he was consumed by something from Turtle's lab.*

Linc scoffed. "Of course it's her. Look at her wrist." He motioned to Alice. "We helped Kaleb and Markus get her out of Red Queen before it was blown up. Have you already forgotten?"

Tom tightened his grip on Linc's collar pulling him closer, saying something in his ear. Linc turned to face his brother, their conversation becoming a whispered argument.

Why are they arguing? Alice lowered her arms, folding them across her chest, watching them, wondering if these were the same Sanchez brothers she'd known and loved. They seemed the same, just with more of an edge than usual.

Alice tried to see the color of Tom's band, but the uniform hid his wrist. *The way he is acting can't be WonderLand that's working its chaotic dance inside him. It must be something else.*

Alice focused on Tom and Linc's argument. She only picked up a word or two of the argument that changed from gestures to voices. Whatever had happened over the last six months must have been bad. It would explain Tom's reluctance to trust her.

"The last we heard, she was with DeeDee," Linc said. "Maybe she escaped."

She thought about speaking up and answering their questions, but Tom still had a gun pointed at her.

"Then where's Kaleb?" Tom asked. "They have to be together for this to work."

This is getting us nowhere. Alice looked around, trying to find her best way out in case things went wrong. They were in the open courtyard with no real way out. The walkway on the right wasn't too far from them, and it might give her some cover, but that would require getting around the brothers.

The car. *I'd still have to get around them, but maybe.*

Linc's raised voice interrupted her thoughts. "If it weren't for Alice, you would be dead. She didn't have to help us. She could have gotten out."

The familiar tingle that accompanied a memory started at the front of her head moving through her body moments before she was thrusted into her past.

SHE WAS *in a room with Linc and a dark-haired girl with the same green eyes as Kaleb. They were trying to find a way for her to get back into Salt City to save Kaleb and Tom. He was stuck here just like her.*

ALICE WAS PUSHED BACK to the present. Her stomach turned. Something was wrong with this memory; it didn't match up with the others.

Markus and I got Kaleb out. Right?

Did I go back in after getting Kaleb out? Was this something else? Who was the girl with green eyes?

The sound of her heart pounding echoed inside her ears. *This is wrong.* Alice took a step back, the concrete edge of the step behind her scraping against her pant leg.

"But now you're stuck here," Tom yelled. He turned toward Alice. "Why are you even here?"

With a calm voice, Linc turned to Alice. "Alice..."

"I'm just- just trying to find..." *What? What could I be trying to find?* "A store that could help me with...phone issues." *That seems like a good reason to be here. Right?*

Linc and Tom exchanged a look. "Alice, darlin,'" Linc drawled, "phones haven't worked here since the wall went up."

Tom sighed, "So what they said about your memories is true."

"How much of your memory are you still missing?" Linc asked.

Alice looked at the brothers, wondering how they knew she was missing memories and what had given her away.

Does it matter? Maybe they can help. Linc is my friend. At least, she hoped he was and could still help fill in some blanks. She hated not knowing what had happened. It scared her. *Will they help me? Kaleb's letter said to trust no one, but I'd be dead if I'd followed that advice.*

She met Linc's infection-free eyes. They were filled with concern, not malice.

They have Kaleb's car. They wouldn't have it if he didn't trust them.

She would have to take a chance they could help. Even if Tom still had a gun pointed at her.

"I'm not sure how much time exactly, maybe six months," Alice shrugged with an indifference she didn't feel. "I woke up on the train with Marci, Kit, and DeeDee." Linc tensed at the mention of the last two names but didn't stop Alice. *Does he know what happened to Kit?*

"I guess I've been in a coma or something. At least, that's what

DeeDee told me. We got separated when some guards took Kit." *And now Kit's dead; I left her to become just another faceless victim of this horrible experiment.* "Marci told me to run, so I did."

"And Kaleb, have you heard from him?" Tom asked.

Alice considered telling them about the card, but after seeing Linc's reaction to her story, she decided it was best to keep that part to herself. She looked down at the pavement. "I haven't." She looked up, shaking her head. "You?"

"No. At least not for a few hours."

She wasn't sure, but Alice thought there was some disappointment in Tom's voice. *Does he want to talk to Kaleb? Or is it something else?* Whatever it was, Tom no longer pointed the gun at her and took off his mask.

"Do you mind if we work and talk?" Linc asked.

"Work?"

He turned back to the fountain, Tom close behind. Alice thought about not following, using the opportunity to leave. She wasn't comfortable being out in the open this long because she thought they would hurt her. But the more Alice talked to people from her past, the more the memories returned, and the more she thought something wasn't right about them or this place. She needed more information, and that meant asking questions. Right now, Linc was her best hope for answers.

They'd stopped a few feet from the car, a red toolbox on the ground nearby, tools spread out in front of them. A large square of the patterned stones that made up the courtyard had been removed, leaving a person-sized hole.

Alice examined the hole's contents, a smallish tank with pipes running in multiple directions. The tank looked like it was part of the water system for the fountains, but she wasn't sure.

Linc grabbed a wrench off the ground before sticking his head in the hole. She could hear a clink and assumed he was tinkering with the pipes below. Tom leaned against the black sedan.

"What are you doing?" she asked Tom.

"What do you remember since Red Queen outbreak and the lockdown?"

Alice rolled her eyes. "Seriously, did you just answer my question with another question?"

A wolfish smile spread across his lips. He folded his arms across his chest and shrugged.

Alice bit her lip, holding back an eye roll and a smart remark. This was the Tom she knew well, the playful, lovable prankster.

Linc poked his head out of the hole. "You know these bands we all wear around our wrists?" He pulled his jacket sleeve up, revealing the black band on his wrist. "They don't detect..."

Tom cleared his throat, interrupting Linc. They exchanged a look before Tom said, "Immune, infected, and unclassified." He reached into the car's open window, grabbing an orange plastic case. "The problem is that infected could mean the person is on any of Dr. Turtle's drugs, not just WonderLand. As you know from your experience," he shrugged, "not all those drugs bring out violence."

Alice looked down at Tom's wrist. His band was pink but fading, turning white. *Is that what's going on with him? Which drug was he on?* She didn't think it was any of the ones that had been forced on her. Tom was too level-headed to be on Timore or Thavais, and she hadn't seen WonderLand shimmering in his eyes.

More of the memories from earlier sat on the edge of her conscience, taunting her.

TOM WAS SITTING *in the corner of the lobby under a fluorescent light hanging by its wires, his hands covering both ears. Blood poured from a gunshot wound and scratches that covered any exposed skin, his dark eyes staring at her, pleading with her.*

TOM'S VOICE broke through the past, "Alice? Are you okay?"

She shook her head. *NO. I can't remember months of my life. The flashes aren't helping. They don't make any sense. It's like I'm living in a bunch of different timelines.*

Alice spun the liquid-filled bracelet that Dr. Turtle gave her around her wrist. "I'm fine. Just tired, I guess." It was an important piece of the puzzle; once she remembered why, everything else would come back.

A moaning sound came from the open window of the car. Alice took a step back, looking into the car window. *Who's asleep in the back seat?*

Linc opened the box Tom had given him, revealing three vials full of colored liquid, two blue and one red. An inhaler lay cushioned in Styrofoam inside. Something about the color combination made her think of mint and regret.

Tom took the inhaler, shook it, and gave it to the man in the car, who had woken up while they talked. He sat up, his sleepy eyes looking around, not seeing.

It was Joseph.

How is Kaleb's dad here?

Kaleb's dad took two puffs from the inhaler and laid back down, falling back to sleep, a deep snore leaving his lips with every breath.

Does that mean Reid Redding is in Salt City? They should be quarantined inside Red Queen headquarters.

"How much is left?" Linc asked.

Tom put the inhaler in the box, handing Linc a vial. "If this works, it won't matter."

"What's going on?" Alice demanded, looking at Tom. "And no more answering my questions with questions."

For a moment, Linc looked at Alice like he'd forgotten she was even there.

"Just tell her," Joe moaned. "I can't..." But he didn't finish that sentence. The snoring started again.

Linc took Alice's hand, and she had to remind herself not to pull away. *He's not going to hurt me.* They walked to the center of the pockmarked square, his amber eyes meeting hers. "Alice, the Task Force was a sham. They had no intention of shutting down Red Queen."

"Okay..." Alice already knew this. Kaleb told her—when that was, she didn't know. It must have been sometime between being trapped in Red Queen and now.

"It was about money and keeping anyone who tried to stop them under their control. The Task Force wasn't trying to find a cure or even get Dr. Turtle's drugs out of the corrupted company. They are part of Red Queen and somehow, you and Kaleb figured it all out."

Tom interrupted his brother. "I don't know how you found out, but I think that's why your and Kaleb's memories keep disappearing. Every time you two get too close to finding something, we have to start this game again."

"Game? What game are you talking about?" Alice tried to pull her hand from Linc's. "This is not a game. I'm not missing a short time, Linc. I'm missing six months. And Kaleb..."

Tom stopped her rant. "It's something Dr. Turtle's been working on. They wiped more time away from you this round. No one knows why, but it's why you had to disappear."

A white mist started to come through the holes in the ground that sprayed water into the air during the summer months. Alice's heart raced. *It's a trap.* She tried to pull away again. Linc's grip tightened.

"Why what? Why are you doing this to me, or why would they drug me? Why did I have to disappear?"

Linc shook his head. "It doesn't matter. Not anymore. What matters now is that you must find a way out. To do that, you have to see what is going on." He motioned to the building mist around them. "This will help with that."

Alice bit down on her cheek, fighting back a scream. *How does this make sense?*

The cool, white mist rolled up her pant leg, moving across her knee.

She took a deep breath holding onto the air in her lungs. Her chest tightened.

What am I supposed to do now?

A tingle spread through her hand, and she had difficulty focusing.

Tom touched her shoulder. "Alice, you need to breathe."

She shook her head. Dark spots danced across her vision. *Why did I let my guard down? Kaleb said to trust no one.*

The mist was on her stomach now.

"Alice, open your eyes," Linc said.

The mist moved to her chest, and the thud of her heart moved through her ears. Finally, she could no longer hold her breath. Alice coughed in as she gulped down the mist-filled air.

"I don't..." Alice coughed. A cold sweat moved down her back. *Why did I follow Hank?* Tom stood in front of her, his dark eyes staring down at her.

"The mist can't hurt you, Alice," Linc's voice called from somewhere else. "It's a cover, so the people watching us can't see what's happening. You need to open your eyes. Tell me what you see."

She wanted to believe him; she needed to. *But?* The mist was at her neck. Tom placed his head in the thick white smoke taking a deep breath. "See," he said.

She shook her head. Her mind was saying no, but her body wasn't listening.

Alice took a deep breath letting the white mist move through her lungs. Each inhale brings a mint flavor different from WonderLand's grass and dirt taste.

Linc released her arm. He and Tom stood near her as the world enclosed her in white fog. A steady beeping echoed around her, worming its way past the quiet of the broken city. The click of frantic typing mixed with angry voices pulled her forward, past the sleep fog of her brain.

"She's waking up," a raspy unfamiliar voice said from somewhere above.

Alice tried to move, but achy limbs pushed at her encouraging her to go back to sleep and forget.

Something pinched the skin on her arm, followed by a cold liquid moving through her.

Dr. Turtle's voice echoed off the walls. "Not for long."

Chapter 19

Alice was yanked backward. She tried to scream as the collar of her sweatshirt dug into her neck. Only a hoarse cry moved past her lips.

Something or someone fell hard near her, crashing into the ground and releasing the tension around her neck.

Alice crawled away toward the clearing mist. Arms and legs pulled and pushed against her now bruised skin. She pushed herself up on scraped hands, struggling to stand up, trying to get away.

Her heart pounded in her ears. The footfall of boots echoed off the walls as they hit the pavement behind her. Wet snow seeped into her jeans, weighing her down. Her chest burned with each breath.

I need to find somewhere to hide.

Alice ducked into a nearby alley. Her options were limited to a silver metal door without a handle or a big green dumpster. Neither was great. There *might be something I can hide under inside.* It would be gross, but she knew her best chance would be to climb inside the dumpster.

She pushed the black lid back, the smell of rotting food stinging her nose, making her rethink the plan. The thud of boots nearby compelled her into action. Alice moved to one side of the dumpster. She placed her foot into the square opening meant for garbage truck arms, placed her hands on the thick metal ledge, and pulled herself up.

Looking into the stinky box of discarded junk, she knew it wouldn't work. *There has to be somewhere else.* Using the height advantage granted by the dumpster, Alice tried to find somewhere, anywhere really, that she could hide.

That's when she saw it. An orange arrow hidden in the graffiti on the wall across from her.

She'd seen it before.

The same arrow directed her to the restaurant earlier that day.

Now, it pointed up to a black, fire escape ladder.

Someone nearby shouted, "She can't be far."

The hair on her arms stood up straight. She had to be quick. Standing on top of the small square arm of the dumpster, Alice pulled on the black plastic lid, closing the can and locking the horrible smell inside.

The cover popped under her weight as she crawled onto it. The sound of cracking plastic was louder than she'd expected, causing her stomach to flutter with panic.

She wasn't sure if she'd be able to reach the ladder rungs. *Maybe if I stand on my tiptoes.* On unsteady feet, Alice stood with her arms outstretched, using them to balance herself on the lid before reaching for the ladder. It took a few seconds before she was able to drop her arms and stand without the fear of falling.

Now I just need to grab the ladder.

She lifted her heels off the lid, stretching her arms high above her head, her fingers brushing against the cold metal of the ladder.

Almost got it.

The plastic groaned beneath her feet, and Alice threw her arms out to recenter herself.

I wish I hadn't quit ballet.

Standing on her tiptoes once again, Alice reached up. This time she could get one finger around the bottom rung before her ankles gave way.

So close.

She bent over and rubbed the pain from her ankle, checking for any serious injury. Thankfully, it was only twisted.

Movement caught her eye. A man stood at the end of the alley, his back to her. Alice recognized the black uniform of the Guard. Unlike her previous encounters with the Guard, she wouldn't be able to lie her way to freedom this time—they were looking for her. She had seconds before he turned around and discovered her.

Alice knew she'd have to jump. It was the only way she could reach the ladder. Hoping it didn't make too much noise before she could get away, she looked down at the ground below. Alice hesitated.

If I fall...no, I won't fall. I can't.

Alice stood, lifting her heels off the dumpster lid, stretching her arms to their limits, reaching without looking, preparing to jump.

A warm hand encircled her wrist from above, pulling. *They found me. No, no, no, this can't be happening.* Alice looked up, expecting to see the dark uniform of the Guard.

Marci's dark shimmering eyes met hers. Alice's relief was short-lived as warm blood dripped from Marci's eyes onto Alice's hand, leaving a warm, sticky trail of red. Fear settled in her stomach.

It's fine.

Just WonderLand.

Marci is strong. She can fight this.

She will fight it.

Marci yanked her upward, pulling Alice onto the hard landing of the fire escape with a dull thud, causing the air in her lungs to leave with a whoosh. Marci pulled at Alice, trying to get her through the open window. Heavy steps echoed off the walls of the dark alley below as Alice crawled toward the window. The crisscrossing metal of the landing dug into her skin. The sound of the dumpster lid being yanked open moved through the alley while Alice tumbled through the open window.

A gunshot echoed off the thick concrete walls below, confirming her suspicions that the garbage can was not a good place to hide, and if she were caught by the Guard again, she wouldn't live.

Marci walked into the dark room behind them toward the only other light source besides the window.

"Wait," Alice called out.

Sighing, Marci turned to face Alice. Her dark hair covered her face, making it impossible for Alice to tell if she was indeed affected by WonderLand or if she'd imagined it.

Still a bit wobbly from having the wind knocked out of her, Alice's questions came out as a breath. "Marci, are you…WonderLand?"

Marci didn't answer. Only stepped into the light provided by the open window. Her hands pushed her long dark hair from her blood-streaked face, confirming Alice's fears.

Marci's dark eyes looked through Alice.

"How?"

Marci shook her head, as if trying to clear her mind. A grin spread across her face, and with a giggle, she said, "That's the effect of living backward. It always makes one a little giddy."

Marci was at the stage of what Alice liked to call nonsense. If she could get through this, everything would be fine. Alice moved closer to Marci. Shaking her head, Marci turned away and walked further into the dark apartment.

Do I follow her? Alice looked back at the open window. She could hear the Guard stomping about in the alley below, still looking for her. *I mean, I don't think she's violent, and I really shouldn't leave her alone.*

Alice moved further into the dark room, her eyes adjusting to the darkness with each step. The main room was empty, with nothing on the walls. Instead of a door to lock the outside world away, there was just a metal frame covered with a thin yellow sheet separating the living room from the hall.

She walked in the direction she thought Marci had gone, into what would have been the master bedroom. Like the door to the hall, this room also had a thin sheet instead of a door.

Alice pushed past it, surprised to see that this room wasn't empty. The room was lit by a haphazard assortment of candles that smelled so bad Alice had to hold back a gag. A large stack of what looked like packs of toilet paper sat in the center of the room, covered in blankets as if someone had been using them as a makeshift bed.

"Marci," she called into the room. "Are you in here?"

One of the blankets moved, and a woman with long blond hair that glimmered in the candlelight glared in Alice's direction. Her eyes didn't have the shimmer of WonderLand, but something was off about her. *It's like she's looking through me. Not at me.*

"Who are you?" the blond woman asked.

"Alice." The woman picked up a blue tube, shaped like a toothpaste container, and spread it across her skin. "Have you seen my friend?" With each swipe, the women's glare disappeared, replaced with a goofy, almost lovesick smile. "I think she c-came in here," Alice stuttered.

"That way," she giggled while hiding her face and pointing behind her at what was most likely the master bathroom.

"Uh, thanks."

Alice walked past her. She looked at the tube that now lay discarded on the floor near the makeshift bed. Alice shivered. She knew what was in that tube without seeing the rest of the word printed in big blue letters. That blue goo made her forget her anger with Ryan, trading it for puppy love for an entire afternoon. Alice shuddered. *Who would use that willingly?*

Marci sat on the bathroom floor near the long neck of a pedestal sink. A piece of thick brown rope lay across her lap. She looked up at Alice. "I can't get it."

"Can't get what?" Alice asked.

"The rope," she huffed. "I have to tie my arms down."

Alice sat down on the smooth tile next to Marci, who'd started wrapping the rope around her wrist. "Why do you need to tie your arms?" Alice asked.

"WonderLand." Marci pushed the neck of her shirt down, revealing a dark bruise around a small pinprick scab. "It was the only way."

"Did someone inject you with WonderLand?"

"No, I did it."

"Why?"

"Kit. They had to think it worked."

"What are you talking about?"

Marci shook her head. "No, the other me, she's only part me. She knows what's going on. You have to wait here for me to come back." Marci shoved the rope into Alice's hands. "You have to do it. You have to tie my hands."

The other her? "I..." Alice looked at the rope and back at Marci. She didn't know what to do. Marci's eyes weren't clear of WonderLand, and her bracelet wasn't black or white but a weird tie-dye mixture of pink and black. "I don't think tying you up is going to help."

"Please." In what looked like a moment of clarity, Marci clasped Alice's hands. "I need to keep you safe from the other me. I can't stay here."

"Okay." Alice wrapped the rope around her right wrist. "But I'm only tying one wrist. You've been in the city since the outbreak and haven't had an episode yet. If you have one now, I doubt it will be violent."

Satisfied, Marci slumped down next to Alice, her back against the nearby wall as Alice secured her wrist to the thickest part of the sink. Once the rope was tied, Alice clasped Marci's free hand in hers and leaned against the wall next to her friend.

"Alice," Marci croaked. "I can't..."

Sure that Marci would tell her to leave, Alice interrupted her. "Ssh."

Marci laid her head on Alice's knee, her eyes blinking at the candlelight that crept in from the master bedroom. Alice pushed the hair from Marci's face. The blood streaming down her cheeks had stopped, leaving behind dry patches of speckled skin.

Alice rested her head against the wall behind them, slowly listening to Marci's breath and reviewing what she knew about the missing six months. First, there was the funeral for her, and she'd disappeared in Salt City. She might have faked her death and changed her name to Donna White. Second, Dr. Turtle's drugs were here in Salt City. Third, Linc and Tom released something into the air, and she saw what looked like Dr. Turtle's lab after inhaling it. *Was it a hallucination? Or something else?*

Kit's dead. Marci gave herself WonderLand, and Kaleb was somewhere in the city looking for her.

Alice rubbed her temples to fight off a headache and something else: the tingle of a memory. Something from her life before Salt City —when she was still Alice.

She fell into the past with a thump.

The smell of antiseptic overwhelmed her. Alice looked at the pills in her hand. After everything they had gone through...she couldn't finish that thought. She looked at Kaleb.

He lay under a thin, yellow blanket in a hospital bed. The beeping of the heart monitors and their breathing were the only sounds in the room.

She reached for Kaleb, intertwining her fingers with his, a last goodbye before the drug took over, wiping her memories of what it was like being controlled by WonderLand.

There wasn't much time.

Someone's shoes squeaked behind her. A beefy hand covered her mouth, muffling her scream as she fought to get away. Thick arms wrapped around her stomach, tossing her over a square shoulder.

It's a trap.

. . .

ALICE WOKE with a start knowing she was no longer in the past, and for a moment she wasn't sure where she was. Alice looked around the dark room, a candle burning in the center of the room, and the morning sun peeked through a paper-covered window behind her. Her body ached. She tried to stretch her legs only to find Marci was still asleep in her lap.

"Here we go again..." She rubbed her head. *A half memory that leaves me more confused than when they started.*

Marci sat up and looked at Alice with bright, clear eyes. "Did you say something?"

"I was just...never mind. How are you?" *It looks like the drug might finally be out of her system.*

She tugged at her tied wrist. "Better." She moved to sit in front of the sink's base. Alice helped her undo the knot.

Marci stared down at the floor. "I was there. I saw it."

"Saw what?"

"Kit."

Bile burned her throat. "Is that why you injected yourself with WonderLand? Because of what happened..." Alice tried to swallow.

Marci nodded.

"I'm..." Alice stopped mid-sentence, the tingling that brought memories of her lost time dragged Alice into the past.

MARCI PLOPPED *down in a chair across from Alice. "Seriously, D, how can you drink hot coffee? It's a hundred degrees outside?"*

"If you're asking that, then you don't understand the purpose of coffee," she snapped.

Marci put her phone on the table. "Wow, that was a bit...well, I'm not sure, not like you."

Alice sighed. "Sorry. It's just—we're getting nowhere. I've been here for three months, and still no Dr. Turtle. Are you sure this is the best way to draw him out?"

"We are." Marci spun her phone around on the table. "I could ask…"

Alice interrupted her. "Absolutely not." She knew what Marci wanted. "We can't do that to him." She wouldn't be the reason Kaleb threw himself back into this life. Not yet. It was too risky. If they were found together, the investigation would have to start over, and their memories would be wiped again. "He thinks I'm dead, and it needs to stay that way. At least until we have a way out for all of us."

ONCE AGAIN ALICE's reality shifted to the present, the memory faded, leaving Alice with more questions than answers. "How many times has my memory been wiped?"

Marci studied the now black band around her wrist. "Six that we know of, but it could be more."

A weight settled on her chest, and Alice's mind drifted, looking for a hold on reality. But unfortunately, there were too many images flashing through her mind, re-living the heartbreak of being ripped from her life moments after finding Kaleb, over and over again. She tried to rub away the pain that settled in her chest.

"And Kaleb?"

Marci met her eyes. A sadness Alice had never seen swam in them. "Only five. Before yesterday, he thought you'd died inside Red Queen headquarters. Now he's scouring Salt City looking for you."

Alice sighed. "He can't find me. Not until we find a way to get everyone out of Salt City."

Marci studied her. "How much do you remember?"

"Not enough. But I can't go through the heartbreak of losing Kaleb again."

Marci stared down the empty hall spinning the black band around her wrist. "I might have found a way out for both of you."

"Just us?"

Marci shrugged. "For now."

Chapter 20

Alice ran her hands through her hair. "What do you mean for now?"

Marci didn't answer. Instead, she got a far-off look in her eyes and started talking to someone not in the room, making Alice question if WonderLand was indeed out of her system. "What time is it? Okay, give me just a second."

Then as if nothing out of the ordinary happened, Marci focused on Alice. "Look, I want to tell you everything, but we've done that before, and well, let's just say it didn't end well. For now, you're going to have to trust me."

Using the wall to support herself, Marci stood up. "I've got to put a few things in motion on my side." Her eyes looked unfocused for a moment before she started talking again. "Meet me at the Sheep and Oar in two hours." She walked toward the fire escape, Alice following close behind. "Fingers crossed, you will remember enough that we can finally end this."

Something had been bothering Alice since their conversation started. Not the fact that WonderLand wasn't affecting her as Alice expected it to, but something else. "I need to know who I can trust. Who is 'we'?"

Marci looked at her through the open window. "Markus, Ryan, me, and Linc, sort of. He doesn't know everything but enough to be effective." Marci looked behind her, then back at Alice. "This is important. If you run into one of them and they aren't wearing a black band, they don't have your best interest at heart. Understand?"

Alice nodded. "What about Kaleb?"

"He's just as much in the dark as you are, maybe more."

Marci started down the metal ladder. "Oh, and Alice," she called up. "If you're ever lost, follow the arrows. They'll get you where you need to go."

She jumped onto the garbage can lid. "Good luck."

As if she had never been there at all, Marci disappeared.

It didn't make sense, but Alice had seen it with her own eyes. One second, she was there, and the next, she was gone.

Alice waited in the abandoned apartment. She hated feeling like a pawn in a giant chess game.

She tried to focus on something else. Like why she hadn't freaked out. Marci disappearing should have bothered her more, but her mind kept returning to the memory wipes. *Six times. Marci said my memory had been reset six times.* Alice started to pace. *That she knows of.*

How is that even possible?

Is that why everything seems so jumbled?

She stopped pacing and peeked out of a hole in a board covering a broken window. *What am I supposed to do now?*

She pushed the board aside. "Whatever it is, I'm done waiting."

A tightness of panic built up inside her, gripping her lungs. Memories that didn't make sense jumped from one time to another, pushing her to places she wasn't ready to go.

She needed to find a way out.

Now.

Just like every time she tried to leave, something stopped her. As usual, the woman from last night with the *Thavasi* came out of her room, followed by the sound of Guard boots echoing off the walls outside. Hopefully, this time the exit won't disappear. How that had happened didn't make sense, but it happened.

Alice waited until the two hours passed before she searched the abandoned building for a good exit.

There was a door to the street. It wasn't a door exactly, but a piece of plywood with a square hole in the middle. Alice wouldn't have to go down the fire escape and fall to her death.

She looked out the makeshift door, ensuring no one was waiting for her to come out. When she was sure it was safe, Alice moved the board aside and stepped into the cool air. The street was empty.

Alice started to walk toward the Sheep and Oar. She knew she was somewhere in the middle of the city and had a vague idea of where the shop should be. Memories of her life as Donna and the start of WonderLand's release into Salt City burned inside her mind, swirling around her with every step.

Alice crossed the street without looking, stopping in front of a red brick wall speckled with pink. *Maybe if I'd brought Kaleb in like Marci suggested, we would have found Dr. Turtle, and none of this would have happened.* But she knew that wasn't true. *They would have found us, whoever they are, and wiped mine and Kaleb's memories, again.* Marci said it had happened to Alice six times but only five to Kaleb.

I must have gotten close to something. That's why I can't remember anything from the last six months. Why only five times for Kaleb? What was it?

In the last two hours, Alice had pieced a few things together.

Marci isn't always Marci. If her band is black, she's okay.

There is a way out of this, whatever this is, but first, I need to find Dr. Turtle. He is the key.

Kaleb and I agreed to no more secrets, but something changed, and I let him think I was dead because of it.

Alice looked down the street lined with black lamps and sleeping plum trees. She stared at the glass doors of the Sheep and Oar, realizing it was the place from her memory. The one where Marci had made fun of her coffee choice.

A heaviness settled in her limbs, telling her to run. It was hard to ignore. *You're fine.* The smell of old books mixed with coffee and pumpkin swirled in the air around her, bringing a comfort she'd forgotten existed. *It's just a coffee shop.* Her gaze swept over the back of the room. *No bogeymen.* Books lined the walls; comfy chairs were tucked away, hidden between more bookshelves.

Alice entered the shop, and a bell rang above her, announcing her entrance. The people in the store turned to look, and Alice knew without prompting to show her wristband. She lifted her arm, ensuring the black band around her arm was visible.

The Guard and the few other customers not in uniform stood in line waiting to get their morning fix.

Alice looked at the line, tempted to spend her last few dollars on something sweet and bready but decided against it. She didn't want to chance one of the people in line recognizing her. Who knew if they were still looking for her after the incident yesterday? Instead, Alice walked around the store looking for the best place to sit: somewhere she could see Marci come in and still avoid the Guard's gaze.

Why would Marci want to meet here? The place is crawling with Guards.

Alice picked up a book as a way to hide in plain sight without looking suspicious. The cover should have been a clue to the wonders it held inside.

Even though she started in the middle, she was hooked. She should have known better. Books had always been a way to forget her problems and escape the real world.

...Still caught in the moment, Vera nodded before making her way through the maze of unpacked boxes to sit on the second-hand couch. Wendy sat on a box across from her, munching on a breakfast of fortune cookies.

Vera sighed. "I did something stupid."

Wendy didn't move, waiting for Vera to speak, giving her time to organize her thoughts.

"I tried to kiss Grimm," Vera said before covering her face with her hands.

Wendy didn't say anything, but Vera could feel the grin that danced on Wendy's lips. Shaking her head, Vera looked at Wendy, her eyes shining with warmth. "Was it stupid...or brilliant!?"

A loud crash pulled Alice from the fictitious world she'd immersed herself in. Alice looked up at the clock on the wall above the exit. Marci was late. *Maybe she came in, couldn't find me, and returned to the apartment? No, Marci would have found me.*

Worried, Alice stood up, intending to return to the abandoned apartment. It was the last place she'd seen Marci, so it made sense to start there. *I hope Wonderland isn't still affecting Marci. I hope she wasn't picked up by the Guard.* Alice scanned the coffee shop, looking for the best way out without running into people.

That was when she noticed that the store was empty.

Not empty. Abandoned.

Steaming cups of coffee and half-eaten pastries littered the empty tables. The same creepy, horror-movie jazz from the Butte Gardens played overhead. A cell phone that shouldn't have worked vibrated across one table, falling to the floor.

Don't overreact. Maybe there was some kind of emergency.

Alice looked at the glass door. The sign had been turned over, letting the outside world know that the shop was closed. A chill that had nothing to do with the winter weather moved through her. The store wasn't supposed to close for three more hours.

It could be new hours due to the outbreak, but they would have asked me to leave if they were closed. Right?

A young girl with a green apron and a name tag came out of one of the back rooms. Her arms were full of books, and bright red, noise-canceling headphones covered her ears. Alice thought about stopping her to ask what had happened to everyone. Something was off about the girl. It was as if she was there but not.

Alice wasn't sure what would happen if someone found her here, not with the abandoned way the coffee shop looked. She waited until the girl's back was turned to make her way to the door. Hoping the bell above the door wouldn't be heard, Alice pushed on the door and opened it. The smell of cold, crisp air sped through the opening.

DeeDee's voice filled the shop behind Alice. "It's not my fault Alice isn't with us, and I had nothing to do with what happened to Reid."

Alice stopped. *What does she mean?*

A familiar male voice she couldn't place yelled at DeeDee, "Dinah, she's dead."

Who's dead?

Reid?

Alice turned around and walked back into the store. She hid behind a tall bookshelf hoping to get more information. *When had Reid died? How had she died? The last time I saw Reid, she was alive and well. Okay, maybe not well, but not dead.*

"Your Task Force is responsible for it. They destroyed Red Queen headquarters, killing everyone inside, including our sister," the familiar male voice growled.

"I had nothing to do with that, and you know it. Besides, who let Dr. Turtle get away?"

The Task Force has Turtle?

A memory trickled up, tearing her from the present.

DR. TURTLE *and Gryff escaped from Red Queen using the exit made for her and Kaleb. Turtle agreed to help get Kaleb out of Red Queen after he got Alice out. Still, Dr. Turtle disappeared after he gave her the cure in the hospital.*

Only it wasn't a cure.

What was it? Sedative?

. . .

BACK IN THE present Alice realized she knew that voice. It was Gryff, the bulky head of security for Red Queen and Reid Redding.

"You're blaming me for that?" Gryff screamed. "It was that boy, you know, the one you said you had under control?"

So he hadn't gone to Argentina like Marci thought. How do I know Marci thought this? Maybe she told me before the memory loss.

He went on. "What is that ridiculous name you call him? Rabbit?"

"It wasn't Rabbit!" DeeDee screamed.

Alice agreed. *It wasn't Kaleb.* He was in the hospital fighting for his life when Turtle escaped.

"Poor baby sister always trusting the wrong people."

Huh, so Gryff is DeeDee and Reid's brother.

The sharp sound of a hand meeting skin rang through the air moments before the hard thunk of a large body, Gryff's most likely, hit the bookshelf that Alice hid behind. Books rained down on the ground around her. *DeeDee isn't usually violent like this.* She bent down, hoping to get a peek at DeeDee or even her bracelet while still being hidden.

Gryff's heavy breath vibrated through the shelf near Alice, causing her to rethink her decision to return to the bookstore. The soft footsteps of sneakers on the carpet moved closer to where Alice guessed Gryff was. Alice imagined DeeDee leaning over her brother, who lay on the floor where he'd fallen.

DeeDee's voice came out in a hiss. "Know your place. You don't get to tell me who to trust."

Gryff huffed out a pain-filled grunt of someone who had been kicked.

"Why can't you be a good little goon and do as you are told? You don't have the brains to pull this off, and we all know it."

A shiver moved down Alice's spine at the venom in DeeDee's voice. It reminded her of Reid months ago, inside Red Queen headquarters, sitting on that horrible throne, drops of blood and a bleeding heart carved into its dark wood. The words, "Off with her head!" moving through the crowd of the WonderLand-crazed staff, looking for a way to release the violence that burned inside their infected minds.

Alice thought about running, but she knew that would only bring attention to her presence. So, she stood in place, waiting for her chance to move. She crawled back to the spot where she had watched the cashier.

The girl was still sorting books. *Why hasn't she moved? Sure, she has noise-canceling headphones, but she could still see.*

Relieved that she hadn't been spotted, Alice scanned the window at the front end of the store, making sure the coast was clear before exiting. From her spot, the street outside looked abandoned like it had been when she went in.

On her hands and knees, Alice crawled across the floor, hiding behind bookshelves whenever possible and trying to avoid the girl in the front of the store, who was still sorting books. All Alice needed to do was stand up and push the door open. Ignoring the aching in her knees, she took a deep breath. Standing up slowly, she walked out the open door. The sound of a gunshot echoed through the empty store behind her.

Chapter 21

Marci looked down at her watch. She should have met Alice an hour ago. Ryan slammed on the brakes causing her chair to slide across the van's carpeted floor.

Red Queen had found them. *What changed?*

She grabbed for the table mounted to the side of the van, pulling herself forward. *Turtle said he didn't need me.* Marci opened her laptop, looking for the code programmed into Alice's band. There was no way Marci would be able to meet Alice now.

They'd have to find somewhere safe to hide.

If they found me, it would only be a matter of time before they found Alice and Kaleb and wiped their memories.

Again.

They wouldn't have another chance to get Alice and Kaleb out.

Marci pulled up the program she'd written to send Markus a message using his band. They were out of time.

Red Queen found us.
Find Alice.

Marci searched the screen in front of her looking for Alice. She was on the move but still near the coffee shop where they should have met.

Last seen near Sheep and Oar.

Will meet you as soon as it's safe.

They had to get Kaleb and Alice together and out of Salt City. Now.

Chapter 22

Not sure what to do next, Alice walked around the corner of the store, acting as if nothing had happened inside. *It's not like gunfire is a new thing in Salt City.* She came to a crossroads, not sure which way to turn. There was something familiar about it, but the memory was still gone.

Alice growled.

She looked down both roads trying to find something familiar, but nothing came. *I don't want to go back.* Alice turned in circles, trying to decide her next move. A yellow arrow painted on the sidewalk caught Alice's eye.

Marci had told Alice if ever she was lost to follow those arrows.

"Right it is."

Alice walked down the deserted road, feeling lost both physically and mentally. She rubbed her hands together, wishing she had more than a hoodie to keep her warm. Maybe some gloves or even an actual coat. She walked past an office building, a large green plant blocking most of the large window.

This can't be my life. When did lies become my new norm? Running, hiding...hunted.

Snippets of memory from the last six months flashed through Alice's mind. *Did I do this to myself? No, why would I erase my memory? The letter from Kaleb said I had died.*

Alice followed another arrow and turned the corner.

Two of the Guards stepped out of a building in front of her. With their backs to her, they stopped to pull on the black masks of their uniforms before turning in her direction. She looked around for somewhere she could go to avoid them. A grime-covered car pulled out of a nearby parking structure, causing the Guards to look up. She made eye contact with one of them, and he started toward her.

She ignored the arrows that seemed to glow, leading Alice straight into the arms of the Guard. Instead, she walked into the garage, hoping they wouldn't follow her. Her mind spun with too many questions to keep any lies she'd tell them straight.

The garage was full of cars. Cars Alice could hide behind if they hadn't been covered in a pink-colored film. She wasn't sure if or how strong the dose of WonderLand trapped in its pink confines was or how it would affect her, but now was not the time to find out.

Alice moved through the garage, avoiding the cars and trying to keep her shoes from squeaking on the painted concrete.

She walked up the incline to the next level, car after car covered in a thicker film the higher she got. Heavy footsteps echoed behind her. Her heart pounded faster with each step as the sound got closer. *This is crazy. Maybe they aren't even looking for me. Maybe it's not even the Guard, just someone who likes black.* Alice slowed, letting the owner of the steps get closer.

Not everyone in the Guard had tried to kill me. Some were even helpful. Alice looked down at her arm. The black band stood out next to the multi-colored bracelet Dr. Turtle had given her. *After all, I'm immune.* Alice stopped. *How can I be immune?*

Something knocked at the back of her memory.

The virus is a distraction.

She concentrated on reaching for that part of her missing past. But it wouldn't budge, mocking her.

"I think it was Alice," a male voice said from a few cars down.

Another male voice huffed, "You said that about the last three brunettes we saw."

Alice ducked behind the closest car and waited. *They're looking for me.* Black boots stopped at the end of the vehicle she hid behind. She listened to their conversation.

"No, that bird brain that follows your every move thought he saw Alice," one of them said.

That voice, she knew. It sounded like Kaleb, but she couldn't be sure, not with it being muffled by the mask. Trying to make as little noise as possible, she moved closer.

"You know he hates when you call him that," he said.

"That's why I do it. How are the two of you even working together? Aren't you the one who told me not to trust him?"

Alice peeked around the car's bumper; both men had their backs to her and had moved up the row. She stared at them, willing herself to recognize them. Still, the only thing she noticed was the insignia on their uniforms. One was a Knight, and the other a Bishop. From what Alice had been told, the two groups didn't work together.

The other man huffed, "Marci said she was around here."

Marci? My Marci?

A woman's scream rang out from somewhere above, and the men took off in a run. Not worried about the scream—they were expected in Salt City these days—Alice waited for them to disappear before moving from her hiding spot. She looked at the exit to the street. *Do I follow them or leave?*

Alice sighed.

What if one of them was Kaleb? And Marci had told them where to find me? What should I do?

The elevator dinged behind her. Alice turned around to find Dr. Turtle standing in the middle of the open elevator. His dark eyes followed her every movement. Challenging her.

Alice's hands tightened into fists, her fingernails breaking the skin of her palms. He was responsible for this, and he'd ruined their lives. She stomped toward the elevator. Now he was here. It was too perfect, and Alice knew it. It didn't make sense. How did he know where she was at this exact moment?

She took a step toward him, intending to ask him that very question, when the thick metal doors closed, hiding the doctor and his ugly green scrubs from her view.

Alice watched the red numbers above the door count up each floor, fighting back the memory that tingled at the back of her mind. Since waking up on the train for the first time, she didn't want them. Not now.

She counted with the elevator, letting it calm her nerves like it had when WonderLand consumed her life. The numbers stopped on the eighty-seventh floor.

Alice pressed the up button and waited for the elevator to return. She entered the little metal box when the silver door opened with a ping. Unable to fight the pull of her past, she let images yank her back to the past.

IT HAD BEEN *two weeks since she'd left Kaleb in the hospital, and her memories had returned. Every one of them. The life and identity that Marci had made for her crumbled with each passing day. Alice wanted her old life back. Her friends Linc, Tom, and even Ryan.*

Kaleb.

She needed to find him to tell him everything.

Someone knocked on her front door. Alice stared at the red and white polka dot couch that sat in the apartment's living room she now lived in, debating whether to open it. Her phone chirped with a message from Marci.

You'll want to hear what she has to say.

Confused, Alice went to the door, expecting to see Marci. She wasn't there; instead, it was an older man with salt-and-pepper hair and a woman with silver hair. Their over-analyzing stares made her insides squirm.

"Can I help you?" Alice asked.

The woman's voice came out barely above a whisper. "Alice Smith."

Alice squinted at them. "I'm sorry you have the wrong person."

Marci had said she could trust them, but Alice knew better. Everyone had their own reasons for doing things. Alice wasn't giving away anything until she understood why this woman was here.

The man stepped to the side, motioning to the car behind him. Marci leaned against a black sedan glaring at her pink phone, her fingers frantically typing.

So that's what Marci's message meant.

Alice couldn't understand why Marci didn't come in with them.

She nodded at the couple, stepping aside to let them in. The woman came in first, sitting in the big, teal chair in the corner near the window, making herself at home. The guy waited for Alice to come into the room before asking if he could move one of the kitchen chairs into the living room.

Once they were all seated, Alice asked. "So, you know my name, but I don't know yours."

The man looked to his partner, who slid a card across the coffee table. Alice picked up the card. "We've investigated misconduct at Red Queen since Reid Redding became the CEO."

Blossom Bobbins
The Midnight Group

"Bobbins?" Alice asked.

Alice looked the woman and her partner over. Nothing about the guy screamed, "I can't be trusted." Bobbins, on the other hand, with her long silver hair pulled up into an elaborate bun and dark business suit, was a different story. She wore bright blue glitter eyeshadow that looked like a child had applied, not a fifty-plus-year-old woman. But who was Alice to judge? She didn't even wear makeup.

The woman groaned. "Blossom makes me sound like someone's fairy godmother. It's Bobbins."

"And you're here," Alice looked between them. "Why?"

"Alice, we know you are starting to remember your old life. You can't go back," Bobbins stated.

Alice wanted to yell but knew it wouldn't get her the information she wanted. "Who are you to tell me what I can and can't do?" she asked.

Alice could feel Hank studying her, judging her. She held his gaze, not letting him see that he made her uncomfortable. Releasing Alice's gaze, he leaned back in his chair.

"Look," Bobbins started, "we weren't sure you'd get your memories back. After a month or two, most people exposed to Dr. Turtle's experiments are beyond help. You have been on them longer than anyone, with little to no side effects."

"What do you mean 'I've been on them longer than anyone?'" Alice asked.

Bobbins pulled a tan folder from her bag and handed it to Alice. "This was hidden in Dr. Turtle's labs inside Red Queen headquarters."

Annoyed, Alice took the folder and flipped through the pages and notes, not really looking at what was written, but scanning. There was an entire section devoted to the questions he'd asked her at the start of every visit.

"They're Dr. Turtle's notes on me and the progression of WonderLand. So what? It's not a secret that Turtle experimented on me."

Alice stopped near the end of the notes, Kaleb's name catching her eye. She read the text that followed his name:

"Kaleb White, like Alice, shows incredible control of his emotions. Even after exposing him to the newest strain of WonderLand, like Alice, he has survived the first application with little effect. The next step..."

Alice flipped the page. That was it. Where were the rest of his notes? That couldn't be it.

"Why did you give this to me?" She looked between the two people in front of her, remembering when the Task Force gave her a file like this before she went into Red Queen to get Kaleb. "What do you want?"

Bobbins' voice came out more graveled than before. "We need you to stay Donna White for a bit longer.

"Let me guess. You want to use me as bait."

Both spoke at once—Bobbins with a resounding yes and Hank with a hesitant no.

Bobbins moved to the edge of her seat. "I'm sure you've seen Marci around. She's been watching you."

Alice nodded. She'd noticed Marci a day or two after moving into the apartment in Salt City. Something about her felt familiar, too familiar. She started doubting the life that was built for her. The day Alice introduced herself to Marci, the memories started to come back.

"Now that you remember who you were, we hope you can help us," Bobbins said.

Alice crossed her arms. "Why should I?"

Bobbins got up and started pacing. "The lab at Red Queen wasn't the only one. There are more spread across the country, and we need your help finding them."

"So that you can do what with them?"

"Find them and shut them down," Bobbins said matter of factly.

Bobbin's words held a certainty that Alice wanted to believe. Alice spun the bracelet Dr. Turtle gave her around her wrist, trying to decide if she should trust them.

Bobbins stopped pacing, placing her hands on the back of the couch. "We could have Kaleb here by the end of the day. Of course, he couldn't be visible, but if he was here watching you, maybe that would draw Dr. Turtle out."

Alice wanted to see Kaleb and know he was okay. He was the first thing she'd remembered. The first person she'd asked Marci about, but Kaleb was trying to live a normal life without her. She couldn't be the one to bring him back into this world. "No. Leave Kaleb out of it. Let him keep believing I died inside Red Queen headquarters."

It's for the best, she told herself. Besides, she didn't need Kaleb to rescue her.

Hank nodded.

They spent the next few hours making a plan. Who Alice would check in with. What to do if Dr. Turtle contacted her and a bunch of little things that needed to happen to make this mission successful. Alice walked them to the door. Her initial discomfort with them was nearly gone.

"One last thing, WonderLand is a distraction, not the issue," Hank whispered, stopping on the doorstep and moving close to her. "Look for the things that don't fit."

Chapter 23

Back in the present Alice collapsed against the elevator wall, using the rail to support her. She watched the red numbers count toward the eighty-seventh floor and Dr. Turtle.

She couldn't believe it.

For years she'd feared the worst, that she would eventually lose her mind and kill everyone around her. *That entire time Dr. Turtle experimented on me, WonderLand was his excuse.*

Things were starting to make sense. Even if she couldn't remember everything. Why everyone thought she was dead, her complete trust in Marci, and why she was compelled to follow Dr. Turtle. *Everything wrong in my life since I was sixteen was because of WonderLand and Dr. Turtle.* The door opened with a ping, the metal slats revealed a large, open room. *He's probably why things are so fuzzy—one of his stupid drugs.*

Alice stepped out of the elevator as the smell of burnt coffee and something she couldn't quite place stung her nose. She started to navigate her way through the room, stopping a few steps from the elevator door. Bright light streamed through the broken blinds. It had been a long time since she'd seen the sun so bright. Alice suspected that most days, the pink dust cloud hanging over the city blocked the full blaze of the sun.

A movement in the corner of the room caught her eye.

Dr. Turtle sat on one of the windowsills, his sleek form silhouetted by the sun's natural light.

Alice walked through the large room that once served as an observation deck. Two large, circular, blueish-white couches sat in the middle of the room, now stained with a pink hue. A metal folding chair splattered with blood lay discarded among flyers that littered the expensive-looking wood floor.

Bathing in the anger that always boiled below the surface, Alice let her emotions take over. The heat of rage filled the emptiness that loss had left behind. Memories swirled around her: the theater, her mother's funeral, and the glowing red in a black-and-white world when she almost lost control. *This man was responsible for all of it.*

"Alice, dear, it's rude to stare." He pointed to a nearby chair, exposing the black band on his wrist. "Please come sit."

She tensed, and the sound of his voice pushed her forward. She wanted him gone. It would be so easy. One hard push through the open window behind him, and he would plummet to the ground below. Splat. All her troubles would be gone. Then she could find Kaleb and get out of this hellscape. Alice thought about the file from her memory, the one Bobbins had brought. Dr. Turtle wasn't only after her. He wanted Kaleb too.

"Why?" she asked.

A smile crept across his face sending a shiver down Alice's spine. "Tsk tsk," he murmured as he crossed his legs. "You're asking the wrong question."

Alice held back the scoff that bubbled in her throat and crossed her arms, waiting for Dr. Turtle to explain the right question.

He leaned back against the windowpane. "All those years spent in control of your every emotion, not succumbing to the effects of WonderLand, and your first real question has no meaning. It only serves to satisfy an emotional need for resolution."

She wanted to smack him. "If you hadn't spent the last four years drugging me, then maybe I wouldn't need to. What was it you said?"

Alice did air quotes to emphasize her next few words, "satisfy my emotional need for resolution."

Dr. Turtle cleared broken glass on the window's ledge near where he sat. The dark-blue, silky material of the jumpsuit he now wore, in place of the ugly scrubs she'd seen him in earlier, seemed out of place among the broken pieces of this world. The suit cracked, echoing through the empty room with each movement. Once the glass was cleared away, he pointed to the spot next to him. "Sit."

Alice stepped forward, craning her neck to peer out the window. The trees and cars that lined the streets below looked like toys from this height. It was beautiful, and under different circumstances, she would have loved to watch the world below, but she didn't trust Dr. Turtle. Shaking her head, she said, "I'm good here."

He smiled at her, his eyes meeting hers for the first time. "Afraid of heights?"

Alice shook her head. "Falling."

Not so much falling, but you pushing me through the window.

Turtle shrugged and then looked back out over the city. "I've been waiting a long time."

"Since?"

He turned to her, studying her. "The world is different than you remember."

That's an understatement.

"How long has it been since your last solid memory? Six months? A day? How about the headaches? They don't seem to be getting better, do they? Do you really want to live like this?" He shrugged, "I could help you, but you'd have to—"

Alice cut him off. "Let me guess, trust you? Yeah, that's never going to happen. You've been experimenting on me without my consent might I add, for," Alice held up four fingers, "four years."

"Before WonderLand, you had no control over your emotions," Dr. Turtle smiled. "I did you a favor. Not having to deal with those nasty feelings of loss."

Did he really just say he did me a favor? Alice scoffed. "I don't have control. I've been too afraid to feel anything, and I've been consumed by anger. That's not control."

"Ah, yes, but there is power in anger. Right?"

Alice stared at him. She couldn't believe it. He'd used her as an unwitting guinea pig, killed a bunch of people, and felt nothing. And she was supposed to be grateful? She remembered something from their time trapped in the little office at Red Queen. When he'd played Kaleb's video, she noticed him watching her. *What was he hoping for?*

Dr. Turtle started muttering to himself as if he were conversing with someone not in the room. "It couldn't be more than a day or two. Kaleb's only been in Salt City for what, a few hours? They wouldn't have brought him in otherwise."

Alice raised an eyebrow. "What are you going on about?"

Dr. Turtle smiled at Alice with a practiced grin that was most likely meant to comfort but gave off a creepy vibe instead. "Oh, I just thought you wouldn't be here without Kaleb. Where is he?"

I wish I knew. "You know Kaleb is never too far behind."

"You remember him then?"

She thought of the best way to answer this question, feeling like he was trying to bait her into a reaction. Alice pushed the sleeves of her hoodie up, intentionally revealing the bracelet he'd given her on her wrist. "Mostly."

Dr. Turtle scooted closer, his backside barely touching the edge of the windowsill. His eyes focused on her arm. "I could help you remember even more."

Alice took a step back. With time, all her memories would return. She knew he'd never let her go if he got his hands on her again. Something tickled at the back of her mind telling her this was not how it should be. *Turtle can always find you in Salt City. Why doesn't he know where Kaleb is? He's been tracking us from the start of this little game of his.*

Has Marci found a way to hide us? Is that why Bobbins and Hank needed me?

Alice shook her head. A tidal wave of memories knocked around her brain. Lives that she didn't remember living threatened to pull her under. Turtle was trying to distract her. Why? What was he hiding? She needed to get away from him. Get somewhere safe before the memories come.

She looked back at the elevator door, noticing the heavy-looking, white door to the side with a black square sign showing a picture of stairs. *I can make it to those stairs before he even stands up.* She took a step toward the white door. *But if I run, he'll still find me, and how many more people will get hurt in the process?* She needed to distract him.

"You trapped us here," Alice said.

Dr. Turtle's eyes twinkled with amusement. "Like I always said, smart."

"Why?"

The heavy doors that led to the stairs opened with a crash behind Alice. She held back the squeak that threatened to leave her lips, glancing behind her while still keeping an eye on Dr. Turtle. The two Guard members that had followed her into the parking garage stormed into the room. This time they weren't alone. Alice's heartbeat kicked up. Now she really was trapped.

Dr. Turtle stood up, shuffling back toward the broken window. "To find you." He kicked a crumpled pile of fabric like the stuff he wore toward Alice. "Put that on," he barked.

Alice didn't move.

A red dot appeared on Dr. Turtles' chest. "Don't move," one of the Guards yelled. "Alexander Turtle, you are coming with us."

A smile twitched across his lips, and three more dots appeared on his chest. Dr. Turtle reached for Alice. "Come along, dear."

Alice shook her head. No way was she going to be his shield. If he died...

"They'll never find you," he said in a low growl that only Alice could hear.

Cold fear moved through her, freezing her from the inside.

Alice tried to take a step away from him.

A brick wall of a man stopped her advance. His strong arms wrapped around Alice from behind, pulling her against his warm body.

She tried to scream, but his hand covered her mouth. He opened his mouth next to Alice's ear. Warm breath brushed against her ear, but before he could say anything, she bit down into his hand's warm, salty flesh. Alice slammed her head against his chin at the same time and stomped on his foot.

The man released her with a scream. A new set of arms moved to grab her. His viper-like grip caused Alice to fall to her knees. She watched as black boots moved closer to the window and Dr. Turtle. The leader yelled commands with each advancing step. *If they catch him, will they kill him or put him to work?*

Alice looked up, she'd heard her name coming from the direction of the Guard. Not the fake one but her real name. One of the Guards near her had used it.

A flash of blue distracted her from finding out. She watched as Dr. Turtle stood on the very edge of the window. He spread his arms out wide, his back turned to the Guard. *Why haven't they shot him yet?* The sleeves of the silky blue jumpsuit attached like wings. The sound of glass scraping bounced off the walls as Dr. Turtle turned and faced the room, his back to the broken-out window.

He turned to Alice, a smile spread across his thin lips. "Until next time."

Turtle jumped.

Chapter 24

Alice pulled away from her captor, rushing to the window. She knew it was stupid but needed to see Turtle's broken body. It was the only way Alice would believe he was dead. The only way she could have a normal life.

She looked down at the empty street, expecting to see Dr. Turtle's broken body on the ground below. Her eyes frantically searched for the mangled corpse of the man who had tortured her for all those years. Nothing. There was no one on the ground below.

Turning back to her captor, Alice sighed. When a flash of blue caught her eyes, she saw Dr. Turtle not only alive but gliding through the air. A glee-filled laugh echoed around them.

Of course, he must have known the Guard was coming. That's why Turtle changed clothes?

The guy behind Alice moved closer. "Damn it."

Alice understood the feeling. Not only had she let Dr. Turtle get away, but she'd thrown away her chance to escape. Her only option was to try and talk her way out.

She studied the guy next to her, his face still covered by a black mask, trying to get a feel for what kind of person he was.

He wore the black uniform of the Guard, a white knight stitched on both the shoulders and chest. But...there was something familiar about him.

He didn't stand straight like the others; he slouched as if he held the world on his shoulders. This could be because his uniform didn't fit right, but she doubted it. The pants were short and tight around the legs, while the jacket billowed around his thin frame.

He was missing the confidence that she expected from the Guard. His stance said the world had beat the hope for change from him. The slump of his shoulders told Alice that he no longer believed the lies the Guard told themselves to justify the terrible things they did to the infected bearable. This man didn't seem to buy into this world they were trapped in.

Added to all that, there was the fact that this Guard wasn't carrying a gun. Alice had never seen any Guard member without at least a gun on their hip. This one had something, but it wasn't a gun, maybe a taser. Which totally didn't fit with the Knights' MO.

Maybe he's a lab tech out on a raid.

He turned to face Alice, studying her the way she did him. Usually, this would have bothered her. But this felt different. She met the man's eyes, the blue-green color shining through the plastic mask.

"Kaleb?"

His bare hands reached up, pulling the mask from his face. A tentative smile crossed his lips. "Hey, Ace."

Her heart fluttered. Oh, how she'd missed that nickname. Alice took a step closer to him. "Kaleb?"

He nodded.

She held back the nervous giggle that tried to escape her lips. *He's really here.* Alice reached out and grabbed the edge of Kaleb's too-big jacket, pulling him toward her. Wrapping her arms around his waist, she released the smile twitching at the corners of her mouth.

"Is it really you?"

His warm arms moved around her, pulling her close. "It's me. I'm really here."

Alice rested her head on his chest, letting his warmth blanket her, listening to his heartbeat match hers. Alice asked the question that had plagued her since the parking garage. "How did you find me?"

"I got your letter."

That wasn't what she meant. She knew Kaleb was in the city. Marci had told her that though she hadn't mentioned a letter.

"My letter?" *Did I write him a letter?* She tried to think back to the last time she remembered seeing him.

"The one from the hospital. You were dying. That's why I took the 'cure'— that wasn't really a cure—it was to save you. The letter was goodbye forever. But that wasn't what happened."

Rubbing her temple, she stepped out of his embrace. "Something happened. What?"

Kaleb opened his mouth to reply, but Alice stopped him. She needed to think. There was more, something tugging at the edge of her memory. "I was lying on the floor. Markus, he was fighting with someone. I couldn't keep my eyes open, couldn't move. Then I woke up here. Well, not here, but here, in Salt City. That doesn't make any sense. Does it? I don't know anymore."

He stepped toward her. "Ace, are you okay?"

She shook her head. Seeing him awakened something. Memories started flashing, burning through her faster than she could speak: Mirrors with the wrong reflection, a virus that wasn't an illness but a person, Linc looking for Tom, Ryan helping her while he searched for his sister. And Marci always there. Even why she needed Kaleb to think she was dead this time around.

This is a game.

And whoever was running it always found a way to separate her and Kaleb. Erasing their memories when they got too close to the truth. *But what truth?* She'd come too close the last time around. Then Kaleb did something to alert them, and they had to start again.

Fear crept out of its dark hiding place inside Alice, threatening to take control. The cold sweat of it twirling around the anger she spent her life trying to control, reminding Alice of all the times Kaleb had tried to 'save her. *The big bad protector that nearly got us both killed again.*

She took a deep breath.

Not now. One, two, three...

When Marci found her this time around, Alice told her to leave Kaleb out of it. It wasn't only to keep him safe but out of the way until they needed him.

Marci was to give him just enough information so that his mind wouldn't unravel when this was finished. The truth of what was going on in Salt City would destroy him, and even though she only had a piece of it, she knew without a doubt that he'd blame himself for what happened to those of us trapped here.

They'd been so close last time. If Kaleb had worked with her to find the final pieces of this puzzle, maybe they'd be out of Red Queen's grasp, but no...he had to keep his secrets. To protect her. Now it was her turn to do the same for him. Even if it hurt her to do it.

Alice wiped at the tears she hadn't realized she'd shed. "Kaleb, what are you doing here?"

"I came to find you."

Her throat tightened with the thought of what she'd have to say next. "Why?"

Kaleb looked around the room, the confusion clear on his face. "Ace, I..." he stopped.

She glared at him. "What, Kaleb? What were you going to say? 'I'm sorry you're here in Salt City?' 'That I left you alone?' Oh, I know. How about you leave me another cryptic note?"

Alice turned her back to him, watching the men that had come up with him leave the room. Everyone except for a now-maskless Markus.

"I was trying to protect you, Ace."

She snorted, "Protect me? Those notes got me drugged—twice. That I know of."

"Maybe if you had done what I told you..." He ran his fingers through his hair. "Neither of us would be in this mess."

Alice turned on him, angry tears running down her face. "If I had done what you told me." *Breathe Alice. You're fine.* "You're kidding me, right? I'm not one of your 'yes men,' Kaleb." She pointed at him. "That requires trust, and we don't have that."

"Obviously," Kaleb mumbled. "Whose fault is that?"

Now she really was mad. Alice had kept one secret from him until six months ago—that she was infected with WonderLand.

"Whose fault is that?" She repeated back angrily, pushing him for good measure. "You've got to be kidding me."

"Are you saying it's mine? You let me think you had died...just like my mother did." Kaleb gritted his teeth. "Would I even know you were still alive if you didn't need me to save you?"

Alice had forgotten about his mother faking her death to protect her sons. Hiding away up north somewhere. It was why he didn't let people get close, and for a moment, her anger receded, imagining what it must have been like and how she'd feel if it was her mother.

"Save me." She sighed. "How are you saving me, Kaleb?"

He stared at her open mouth. "Dr. Turtle—"

She cut him off. "What, you think I didn't have that under control? I know what he wants." She shrugged. "Not that you cared to ask. Let's be honest here. The only thing that matters is your secrets don't come out, and everyone does everything the way you think they should. You can't control the world, Kaleb. You just live in it."

"You think I don't know that? My life has been nothing but one tragedy after another. All because of Red Queen and Turtle."

"You think Red Queen only destroyed your life? Let's talk about mothers. You were there the day my mom died." She let the white-hot anger that burned inside lace her next sentence. "You were the one who chained us in that theater."

Kaleb's face went white. "Ace, I..."

She cut him off. "Didn't think I remembered? Well, I do." Alice started to pace. "If that wasn't bad enough, you befriended me. I confided in you, trusted you. Told you things I'd never told anyone." She turned her back on him. *Why am I doing this? This is going too far. I need him to return to where Marci hid him away until I find a way out of this game. I'm losing control.* Every frustration and betrayal she'd had with him came bubbling to the surface, and she didn't know how to stop it. "Are you going to say anything? Wait, I know. 'I'll explain later.' Kaleb code for 'Forget what you saw.'"

He sighed. "That's not fair, Ace."

"Fair. You want to talk to me about fair? Really, Kaleb?" She glared at him. "We wouldn't be in this mess if you'd just shared things with me. I'm not a damsel in distress. Stop treating me like one."

Kaleb rolled his eyes. "Obviously."

"What do you mean by that?"

He crossed his arms. "I sacrificed everything for you. I was out, and I don't mean six months ago when you 'disappeared.' Four years ago. That day at the theater, the day your mom died, was my last day at Red Queen. At least, it was supposed to be. That was until that day in the coffee shop, the day we officially met. DeeDee was there staking you out."

"And you thought I'd go with her. Ha. That's rich," Alice scoffed. "The only reason I even let DeeDee into my orbit is because of you. I wanted nothing to do with DeeDee, Reid, or even Turtle. Did you know they were calling me once a day to come in for this test or that? No. Or that they offered to pay for college or anything else I wanted for the rest of my life?"

She shook her head. "Of course not. But you were investigating them, telling me not to trust them. Well, everyone but DeeDee." Alice laced her voice with as much sarcasm as she could. "How did that work out for you?"

He ran his fingers through his hair. "It doesn't matter."

"Of course not. Why would it?"

Kaleb asked, "What do you want from me? I came back for you."

"I didn't ask you to," she yelled.

"But you did, in your letter. 'Never stop fighting for what you believe is right. Don't let what happens to me stop you from finishing what you started all those years ago. Don't let what happened to me happen to anyone else. Stop Reid Redding.'" He pointed at her, "Those are your words."

Did I write a letter? Wait, did he memorize it?

"I thought you needed me," Kaleb shrugged. "I guess I was wrong. Should have known better. Sooner or later, everyone disappears." He turned away from her and walked out the door to the stairs without looking back.

Alice glared at his retreating back. Her emotions jumped around her brain, leaving her more confused than ever. She started to count. "One, two, three..." Her chest rose with each number, calming and clearing her mind. *That's not what was supposed to happen.*

"I just wanted him to go back to his normal life, work at Jake's coffee shop, and forget all about Red Queen," she said out loud to no one in particular.

She slumped against the wall wiping at the tears streaming down her cheeks. "He deserved that much." Her body relaxed. The anger that had overwhelmed her, boiling over and burning the friend closest to her, dimmed to a simmer.

Markus appeared next to Alice, thrusting a tissue at her.

"I didn't know you had that in you," he smiled.

She kicked at something on the floor. "Was it too much?"

"Not sure." He shrugged. "You're right about at least one thing."

"Yeah?"

He pushed off the wall. "You both deserve that normal life you're looking for."

Chapter 25

Kaleb stopped halfway down the first set of stairs. He needed a minute to think, to pull himself together. His heart pounded in his ears. Alice, his Alice, was here. Right in front of him. It wasn't a dream.

Alice is alive, and she's pissed. He clenched his fist. *Hell, I'm pissed.*

Someone cleared their throat behind him. Kaleb reached for the stun gun—his only weapon. He turned to find Markus rubbing the back of his neck, looking for words. "Rabbit, sorry, I know that... Well, that sucked."

"It's fine. Besides, it needed to be said."

His brother opened his mouth, but Kaleb cut him off.

"Markus, I'm fine."

"You're not. But Marci called. Both factions of the Guard are on their way here. She's tracking their movements. We have maybe fifteen minutes to get to HQ."

"The art museum?" Kaleb wasn't ready to go back there. Not with Alice in her current mood. The place had been happy for them, and he wanted to keep it that way.

"Of course." Markus turned toward the stairs expecting Kaleb to follow him into the stairwell. "Oh, and one more thing. Alice will need to be cuffed to keep the real Guard from stopping us." He started to rub the back of his neck again. He only did that when he was nervous. "So yeah, you'll need to do that."

"What? Why me?"

"I've got to go find those men you two scared off. Be downstairs in five." In classic Markus fashion, he disappeared, leaving Kaleb to deal with a mess.

At least this time, it's my mess. Kaleb pushed the stairway door open to find Alice standing in the middle of the room, arms wrapped around her chest, looking completely lost.

She turned to face him rolling her shoulders back, and stood up straighter, meeting his gaze. *She's going to hate this.* A nervous smile on her lips, the one she used when she was faking confidence. It was her "ready for war" face; Kaleb loved that smile and the false sense of confidence.

He took a step toward her. The smile fell away. The light the smile brought, even a fake one, faded away, replaced by a glare.

"Where's Markus?" she snapped.

How am I going to do this?

"He'll meet us downstairs," he growled. *The coward ran at the first sign of conflict.* "Marci called. The Guard are on their way to this location."

Relief flashed in Alice's eyes. "Marci's okay?"

Did she know about Marci and WonderLand? Or is she asking because of Kit?

"Not really, but you know Marci, she'll act like all is good until it's not." He looked down at the blood-stained floor, trying to find the best way to ask Alice to surrender her freedom. "Um, Alice, I need your wrists."

Without a word, like it was second nature, Alice shoved up the sleeves of her sweatshirt, revealing her black band. Her reaction scared him.

How has she lived in this city for so long?
What had she seen?

How has it changed her?

He wrapped his fingers around one of her open hands. "I'm sorry to do this, but I'm going to have to restrain you."

Alice jerked her hand away from him, holding her arm close to her chest. "Why?" She breathed.

The fear in her eyes made his heart squeeze in his chest. Kaleb reached out for her, wanting her to trust him like she had before. She didn't move, didn't even look at him. "Look, you are obviously not a part of the Guard." He pinched the bridge of his nose, fighting the tension building behind his eyes. He didn't want to do this either. "It's the only way. You need to be a prisoner."

She shook her head. "Never going to happen."

"It's the safest way to get you across town." *We don't have time for this. If DeeDee or Reid get their hands on Alice, then this, whatever she's been working towards, will be for nothing.* "Is this going to be how it is from now on? Fighting me on every little thing."

Alice huffed.

I guess so.

He was tempted to leave her there but knew he could never do that. Even after everything she'd said, he'd do anything he could to protect her. So, he played the only card he had. "If you want to see Marci, this is the only way to get there."

Alice looked at the door that led to the stairwell and then back at him. "Fine." She held out her hand. "But I'll put them on myself."

Relieved, Kaleb held out the zip ties from his belt. He watched her clip each one into place, noticing the two bracelets on her wrist. One that let the world know if WonderLand was running through her veins, and another that had bulbs of multi-colored liquids.

I know that bracelet.

Kaleb waited until they reached the elevator to ask Alice about it. "How... When... Turtle?"

Alice raised an eyebrow, "Spit it out, Kaleb."

"The bracelet on your wrist."

She looked at the black band. "What about it? It's black. I'm sure you've seen one before. I bet yours is the same color."

"Not that one."

He reached out to touch her arm.

She pulled away.

His stomach dropped a bit with the movement.

How are we ever going to get past this?

He rubbed the back of his neck. "Ace, I—"

"Dr. Turtle forced it on me when we were trapped inside Red Queen headquarters." She huffed. "You were standing there when it happened."

"Honestly, I don't remember much about what happened at Red Queen that day." He did dream about it, though. Red-hot anger clouding the simplest of tasks. Death and a lot of blood. And the screaming. They still rang in his ears even after waking.

With a slight hitch in her voice, as if she'd been holding back tears, Alice said, "That's probably a good thing."

Is it a good thing? He wasn't sure. Changing the subject back to the present, he asked, "Do you know why Turtle gave you the bracelet?"

Alice shrugged, "Why does he do anything?"

A game.

"Did he say anything to you about it?"

She looked at her shoes.

So, yes. Kaleb watched the numbers change on the display above the elevator doors. *She doesn't trust me. There is no way Turtle didn't say something, but Alice isn't going to tell me anything. Not right now.* He didn't know what else to say to her. After months of wishing he could talk to Alice, he couldn't find the words.

He stared straight ahead, studying their reflection on the elevator doors. He saw his ill-fitting uniform in contrast to Alice's jeans and sweatshirt. Alice stared down at her wrist, strands of hair covering her face.

With a heavy sigh, she said. "I think the bracelet might be a sample of Turtle's drugs."

What?

"I was so close." She started to ramble. "If I'd just gone with him. My mission, the reason I'm here. Why did I let you think I was dead? This would be over." Alice shook her head. "I could have shut down Turtle's experiments."

"Alice, slow down. What are you talking about?"

"I was bait. Marci, and some woman named Bobbins and a guy named Hank, they asked me." She met his eyes. "I just needed Turtle to trust me long enough for me to get the location of the other labs and maybe get a sample of the drugs. Though I didn't know until now." She nodded to the bracelet. "I already have the drugs."

"Hank? Salt-and-pepper hair, tall?" Kaleb asked.

Alice gave him a look like he was crazy. "Yes, he said he knew you."

"We've met," he grumbled.

He couldn't believe that not only was Alice going after the same things Kaleb had been trying to get all those years, but the people helping her had been watching him for months. *If we can get the info, we can both be done with this stupid game and have a normal-ish life.*

"Do you know if Marci was able to get into the thumb drive I gave her?" Kaleb asked.

Some unknown emotion moved across her face—maybe annoyance? "Of course."

Relief washed over him. He hadn't thought about the drive since he gave it to Marci six months ago after finding Alice in the creepy rotunda near his house. The one thing he had found on the drive before giving it to Marci was the location of at least one of Turtle's labs. The code was simple enough to figure out. *So why did Alice look for them? Marci is a lot better at the computer stuff than I am. Did I miss something, or was it the drug samples she needed?*

It didn't matter now. They could end the meaningless

experiments and murders between the two of them. Alice's mission was almost over, and she had no idea.

"Alice?"

The elevator dinged, and the doors slid open, cutting Kaleb off. Markus and his team waited for them on the other side. Before Kaleb could share the news, Alice walked past him. Not waiting for him, she moved into the center of the waiting team and pulled the hood of her sweatshirt over her head.

Chapter 26

Alice chewed on her lower lip. The walk was not as eventful as Kaleb would have made it out to be. The worst part was feeling like a prisoner. The streets were empty, like always, and the cuffs were unnecessary. It did give her time to reflect on the argument she'd had with Kaleb, though.

How did I let this get so out of hand? There was real anger and hurt about things they'd never dealt with.

They stopped in front of the blacked-out glass doors of the museum. The last time Alice visited this museum was one of the best days of her life. She was full of hope and love. *At least all that anger is out in the open now.* Alice looked at Kaleb, his brow furrowed in thought as he focused on the door in front of them.

"What's going to happen to us now?" she mumbled.

He shrugged, taking a step forward, and she followed.

The door slid open, revealing the museum's lobby, and they moved in as a group. *We go on as if nothing happened, I guess.* Everyone split in different directions, leaving Alice alone with Kaleb.

He moved in front of her, motioning to her wrist with a small knife. Realizing what he was asking, Alice raised her hands so he could remove the restraints. *Not that I needed them.* They hadn't seen a single Guard on their way here. He slid the knife into the space between her wrists, pulling upward and causing the plastic strip to fall away from her hands.

Unsure what to do next, she walked around Kaleb and further into the building. Alice was surprised to see the normalness of the lobby in front of them. Strings of lights hung high above them, twinkling off the bronze etchings set into the wall.

Everything is so messed up.

Kaleb moved next to her, holding his hand out to her. She stared at it for a moment, trying to decide if she should take it. *I said horrible things, even if they were true.* She only picked a fight with him to push him away, to protect him. *How can he forgive me?*

It must have taken her too long to decide because Kaleb slipped his hands into his pockets and walked wordlessly to the escalator, leaving her in the lobby. Alice watched him go, his shoulders slumped in defeat. *What have I done?*

Unsure what to do next, Alice followed. *Maybe Marci could help.* Alice needed to talk things out. Find her footing in the ever-changing world. *She should be here somewhere.*

No one acknowledged Kaleb or Alice as they got on and off three escalators. Not that there had been a lot of people in the museum to begin with. The few people they saw along the way wore mismatched Guard uniforms like Kaleb's or jeans with a touristy t-shirt.

Once they got to the top floor, Kaleb turned left, passed a room full of clay pots in glass displays, and disappeared into one of the smaller rooms. For a split second, Alice thought about not following. Where she would go, she didn't know...*anything would be better than this.*

Would it, though? Or am I just embarrassed by my loss of temper? Grr...

Alice knew she had to find a way to talk to Kaleb and make things right. She followed him into one of the small exhibit rooms.

Alice didn't know what she expected, but it wasn't this. A bed made of blankets took up the floor in one corner, and a map of the city marked with black and white dots hung on the opposite wall. There was a makeshift desk made from some old boxes with an open laptop below the map and cans of orange soda littering the floor.

Kaleb sat alone on a short wooden bench bolted to the floor, staring at the picture hanging on the wall in front of him. *I should have taken his hand.* Alice walked across the room to stand next to him, the emotions of the last twenty-four hours swirling around her. Kaleb reached out his hand again. She took it, his long fingers entwining with hers, pulling Alice down to sit next to him.

Something crossed his face, and he loosened his grip, pulling away from her. Alice held on tight, pulling their joined hands closer. She didn't know what to say, but she wanted him close to her while she tried to explain why she'd not only pushed him away but let the anger that had been boiling inside lose.

Alice didn't meet his eyes, letting his warmth seep into her, holding onto this moment before the peace of it slipped away. She focused on the painting in front of them.

They sat silently, staring at the gold-encrusted frame that housed a painting of a small, black-and-white cottage. A white sand beach spread in front, and red poppies swayed in the distance behind the cottage. It was one of Alice's favorite paintings. She even had a small copy of it in her wallet.

"Ace—" Kaleb turned to her, breaking the silent truce between them.

Alice interrupted him. "Kaleb." She knew that tone. It was his 'this-is-too dangerous-for-you' tone, and Alice didn't want to hear it. Not this time. "Can we agree, no more lies or half-truths? No more protecting each other at the cost of the other. We deserve better than that."

He looked down at the tiled floor but didn't say anything. Alice was losing him and didn't know what to do.

Alice kept talking, letting the words come without thought. "Don't get me wrong, I'm happy to see you and glad you're alive," *more than glad,* "but here's the thing, I can walk out the door right now." She stood up to leave. "I've been on my own for a long time now and doing just fine."

She walked toward the door, stopping in the doorway. "Everyone I have come in contact with since my mother's death has lied to me."

Please don't let me walk away.

"I had hoped after everything we had been through—"

"Alice." It was the first time he called her by name since they met, and it did something funny to her stomach. "Don't go."

She stopped, watching people move through the corridors in front of her, waiting for him to say more. When he didn't, she rested her head on the metal door frame, gathering her strength. It was going to take everything she had to walk away now.

Kaleb's warm hand settled on her shoulder, pulling the tension from her. Alice turned to face him, waiting.

He shook his head, sadness creeping into his eyes. "You're right. I don't want to keep things from you."

Kaleb took a step back and looked at Alice, the fake confidence he held like a shield falling, leaving behind the boy she met in the coffee shop.

Something like hope fluttered inside. Hope? She let a half-smile move across her lips as he began to pace.

"Where do I start?" he muttered. "Before we knew who DeeDee really was, Linc, Tom, and I joined her Task Force. We started working undercover in Red Queen." He rubbed the back of his neck. "And in your life."

Alice leaned against the wall. "So, when you told me you were afraid to leave Red Queen because of your father, was that a lie?"

"Not exactly."

She raised an eyebrow waiting for him to explain.

"My father can be a tyrant." Kaleb tensed. "I was afraid of his reaction when he found out my plan." He ran his fingers through his hair. "I couldn't get us away from Red Queen without some kind of leverage. The green card plan was there if I was discovered before I got what we needed to be safe."

"Okay?" Alice asked.

Kaleb went on. "Linc and I started to notice little things about DeeDee. Info on her sister's daily dealings, employee lists, and things like that. Then one day, DeeDee asked for a sample of one of the drugs from Red Queen's lab. Linc caught her experimenting with it on, well, it doesn't matter who, just that she was doing it."

He looked at Alice, and she saw guilt swing in his eyes. She wanted to stop him from going on, to comfort him. Tell him none of this was his fault. They'd been caught up in something their parents had started. The words wouldn't come. She needed to understand why, and she suspected he needed to tell her.

Alice settled for clasping his hands with hers.

"A couple of days after the lake incident, DeeDee went to Linc and asked him to bring her WonderLand. That's when I showed Linc the footage from the theater experiments."

Remembering something from the day he'd given Alice the bright green index card telling her to run, she asked, "Was that the video on your laptop? The one I watched when Ryan gave me Timore?"

Kaleb nodded. "Yeah, Marci sent it to me. You remember that?"

"I remember everything from that day. It's the stuff after that's a bit fuzzy." She shook her head, "It's starting to come back, though. Things I need to tell you, but you finish first."

He smiled at her, and a few more things started to click in place. Things that caused the tingle of memories to come knocking. Alice rubbed them away. Right now, she needed to focus on Kaleb.

He must have noticed something was wrong. Alice nodded, encouraging him to continue. "Keep going."

"DeeDee didn't know I'd shown Linc the footage from the theater, and that he knew what WonderLand really did," Kaleb shrugged. "Linc quit that day. It's why he wasn't inside Red Queen when WonderLand was released. After finding you curled up in that creepy statue thing you love, he volunteered to rejoin the Task Force to find out what DeeDee was up to."

"What happened?"

"I was wrong." He took a step toward her. "It wasn't just DeeDee, the entire Task Force was all a lie. A way to keep me busy, from stopping the Redding's real goal." Kaleb clasped Alice's hands tighter. "They only wanted one thing; it was always you."

"But I don't understand. Why me?"

"I'm not sure, but I think it's because you survived at the theater. That day changed everything; it wove doubt into the organization." Kaleb placed his hand on her face, and Alice leaned into it. "Now, we have everything we need to stop them with the drive."

"Come on, bro." Markus cleared his throat as he walked past them. "Seriously, get a room."

Kaleb sighed, "I'm in a room."

"Then, get a door."

Kaleb stepped away from Alice, shaking his head, leaving her more confused than she'd been. *What does he mean they had everything they needed to stop them?*

"So, you decided to forgive him. Bad move," Markus scoffed, plopping on the makeshift bed.

It was more like he forgave me.

Alice tried to glare at Markus, but the smile he gave her made it hard to be mad. "For now," she told him.

Kaleb rolled his eyes. "Shut up, Markus."

Markus pulled an apple from one of his pockets, his black wristband a dark contrast to the apple's bright green skin. "The White Queen is on the move."

Was Markus's band white earlier? She couldn't remember. "The White Queen?"

Marci walked into the room, dressed all in black, with dark circles under her eyes, but alive. A bit of the tension Alice had been holding onto left her body. She checked the band on Marci's wrist to be sure she was clear. It was...black?

"DeeDee. It's the code name they gave her: The White Queen," Marci said.

Marci took a tentative step toward Alice, her hands at her sides. "Sorry about leaving you and then not meeting up with you."

"Not meeting you was my fault," Markus offered.

Marci smiled at him with a pained look in her eyes. "He found me wandering the streets and brought me back here." She turned back to Alice. "I guess the virus isn't completely out of my system yet."

Alice looked at Marci's wrist again. Sure enough, the band flickered pink for a few seconds before turning black again. Marci gave Alice a pained smile and squeezed her hand. "I'll be okay. I'm fighting with everything I have to stay." She made her way to the laptop on the makeshift desk in the corner.

Kaleb whispered to Alice, "Don't tell them yet."

Alice twisted the multi-colored bracelet Dr. Turtle had given her around her wrist. She knew without a doubt that Kaleb trusted Marci. *Why else did Marci give me the birthday card? Has something happened between him and Markus? Maybe he's just giving Marci time to recover, or did he see the band flicker?* Alice followed Kaleb to stand behind Marci, whose nimble fingers clicked on the laptop keys.

Lines of code flew across the screen. She pulled up a map of what should have been the city, but it was a black spot with no roads or landmarks. Code moved across the screen again. A maze of what Alice assumed were streets appeared along with a single red dot moving upward.

"There," Marci moved from the computer. "Now, we can follow her."

"Can you find Tom and Linc?" Alice asked.

"You've seen them?" Kaleb wondered.

Alice was confused. "Yeah, right before I found Marci. They were with your dad."

"They had something to combat the effects of the dust that still litters the ground," Marci said. "Did it work?"

Alice looked at Marci's hope-filled face and didn't want to tell her the truth. "I don't know. We got separated. They did something to a fountain that released some kind of gas into the air." Alice rubbed her head. She couldn't quite remember what had happened. She thought she heard something about waking up. "Then I was running from the Guard, and Marci helped me escape."

Kaleb placed a hand on his brother's shoulder. "You knew they made it out of the building. Why didn't you tell me?"

"Not now," Markus said.

Gryff's deep male voice boomed behind them, "Your brother's right."

The four of them turned. Gryff, the big man she had met at Red Queen headquarters and the other voice in the bookstore, stood in the doorway with a gun pointed at Alice. Kaleb moved to stand in front of her.

Gryff tsked and motioned with the gun for Kaleb to move away from Alice. "Sorry, Rabbit, but I have business with the girl, and you will not be interfering this time."

So, DeeDee didn't kill him.

Chapter 27

Alice squared her shoulders. She wouldn't let this man intimidate her, even if he was armed. "What do you want?"

"Like you don't know," Gryff scoffed. "A way out of this stupid game. I know the doctor gave it to you when we escaped Red Queen the last time."

What is he talking about?

The only thing Alice remembered Turtle giving her was that stupid bracelet. *There is no way a bracelet is a key to all this.*

Alice stared Gryff down. In a clear, flat tone, she said, " Turtle didn't give me anything."

Marci leaned close to her ear, whispering, "Are you sure?"

Yes... Maybe. She was still missing time, and if what Marci told Alice was true, her memory has been wiped at least six times. He might have given her something else.

Gryff scratched his face with the gun's barrel, revealing the black band around his wrist.

"That's unfortunate," he said. "I guess there's only one way to end this."

He pointed the gun at Alice; its smooth, black cylinder promised her demise. A warm hand pressed into the small of her back. Alice's throat tightened. She needed to say something and convince Gryff that killing them wouldn't change things. He'd still be stuck in Salt City. But the words wouldn't come out.

Alice's mind was being torn into pieces. One told her to stay and the other to run.

"We have a problem," a voice from somewhere else said.

No kidding.

A somber expression moved across Gryff's face. "I'll have to do what my sisters were never able to do."

"What should I do?" the same voice asked.

Alice closed her eyes. She knew what was coming and didn't want to see it. Kaleb's hand slipped into hers as he whispered something she didn't hear in her ear.

An alarm sounded in the distance.

I really thought we'd get out this time.

Strong hands pushed Alice to the floor. Her knees slammed onto the cold concrete and knocked the breath from her lungs. The crack of a gun sounded above her. Alice struggled to breathe. A deep pain filled each breath with the sweet charcoal smell of burnt gunpowder.

Alice opened her eyes, and blue lights flashed in the dark room. The loud buzzing of a fire alarm filled the room. With each flash of the lights, she tried to find Kaleb or Marci. Alice wasn't sure what had happened or where anyone was, but she was grateful it did.

Someone touched her arm, sending a chill through her rattled mind.

"Ace?" Kaleb was kneeling on the floor next to her.

He motioned to the outline of a door with a green exit sign above it.

Alice nodded her understanding. They needed to get out.

She crawled across the cold floor toward the door despite the heaviness in her limbs and her unsteady breath. She concentrated on the exit, blocking out everything around her.

The exit was close enough that Alice pushed up on her hands, readying herself to run. She slipped on something covering the floor, her fingers covered in a slick, warm substance.

She knew without looking–even before the copper smell reached her nose–that she'd crawled through blood. This wasn't the first time she'd crawled through the sticky substance. *There was so much blood that day in the theater. It was everywhere.*

Alice tried to shove that day away, trapping it in the box with everything else she didn't have time to deal with. But the thoughts kept creeping back. *The walls were covered in it. So was I.*

Her breath came faster, the panic pulling her under. *One, two, three.* She needed to get control. Someone or something on the ground pulled her back to the present. *Kaleb.* Alice scanned the room between flashes of the indigo light above, expecting to find Kaleb nearby. She was alone, and the dark edges of the puddle of blood crept closer.

Terrified at who she might find but needing to know that it wasn't one of her friends, Alice's eyes followed the edges of the puddle, looking for the source. The sound of her heart pounded in her ears with each inch. A scream brewed below the surface of her lips when she found the source of the blood.

She focused on the tattered, blood-soaked flesh of a bullet wound for longer than necessary, not ready to know who it was. Fear slithered its way into her limbs, making a home near her frantic, beating heart. Alice moved closer to the body. Letting her eyes adjust with each blink of the blue security lights.

She hoped it was Gryff and not... The lights flashed on, catching blood-streaked blonde hair.

Alice's stomach dropped.

It can't be Kaleb.

I saw him.

He was behind me.

She moved closer, her hands sliding across the blood.

Was there one shot or two?

Again, the room lit up. Shadows fell over the hulking, lifeless body.

It was Gryff. Alice released the breath she'd been holding.

Then where's Kaleb? And Marci? Even Markus?

She scanned the room, but she couldn't see them anywhere. *What happened to them?* A cold sweat ran down her back. *Is one of them hurt?*

Something like a whimper came from the far corner of the room. The light flashed a blue halo over a cowering figure in a mismatched uniform, his knees held to his chest. Haunted eyes tracked her every move.

"Kaleb?" Alice crawled across the floor toward him.

His heavy breathing became more erratic with each movement that brought her closer. She'd never seen him like this. It was almost as if he was having some kind of panic attack, like the ones she'd had when WonderLand ran through her system. Alice moved closer; she waited for the lights to flash again so she could see his armband.

It was black.

She placed her hands on his. They were ice cold. "Kaleb?"

He whimpered but didn't move.

She didn't know what to do. *Markus, he'll know.* The lights flashed, and Alice scanned the room, looking for Markus. He wasn't there. Neither was Marci. Had they left without her and Kaleb?

There was only one thing she could think of doing for Kaleb. The same thing her mother had done for her in the movie theater parking lot on the day she died. Alice clasped Kaleb's fisted hands in hers, avoiding the cool steel of the weapon he still clenched, and stared into his eyes, forcing him to look at her.

"Kaleb, breathe."

He didn't move. So Alice started to count. "One, two, three, four..." When she reached twenty, his hands squeezed hers, and he began to move. She stood, helping Kaleb to his feet while still holding one of his hands, and even though his eyes were vacant, he followed her.

Alice tugged him behind her, out of the room and down the stairs. She ignored the sound of dozens of boots rushing through the halls below them. She let the concrete walls dull the alarms buzzing around them and concentrated on getting them out.

Chapter 28

Marci slammed back to the world with a jolt, the black band on her wrist vibrating with its distaste. Red Queen had found a way past her safeguards and forced them out again. She looked at the chair beside her; Markus's heavy breathing filled the van. His panic-stricken eyes met hers.

"We have to go back."

She shook her head. How could she tell him there was no way back? "I don't—"

The computer screen lit up with an incoming call from Bobbins. Markus moved to the other side of the van and pressed the accept button.

"Mom, I lost him." Markus crumbled onto the floor, tears running down his face.

Bobbins pushed her blond curls that she shared with her youngest son, Kaleb away from her face, a stark contrast from the image she chose to us inside Salt City. "And we will get him back. Right, Marci?"

"Right." And just like that, she'd agreed to do the impossible. It was hard to refuse Isabella Button, AKA Blossom Bobbins, anything. Marci pulled up the program she had written all those months ago to find Kaleb and Alice looking for anything that might get them back in.

Her fingers moved over the keys as she listened to Markus and his mom talk. Sometime over the last few months, she'd let herself fall in love with him. She hated seeing him so broken. Marci rubbed at the pain in her chest. Not that she'd tell him. At least not until Kaleb and Alice are safe and out of Salt City.

"I told him to shoot Gryff. It's my fault if he gets lost inside his mind again."

Marci didn't hear what Bobbins said, but it sounded like it was meant to comfort her son.

"He might forgive me, but will he forgive himself?"

Marci stopped typing even though she knew the answer. *No.* She sighed. Gryff was dead, and Kaleb had done it. If you die in Salt City, you die in real life.

The computer beeped with an alert. H.A.N.K had found a way in. There was only one way to prevent detection: they'd have to play their parts. Any help they gave them had to be small.

Markus was going to hate this.

Chapter 29

The cold, crisp air stung Kaleb's cheeks. *How did I get outside?* Alice. She was dragging him behind her. He ran the fingers of his free hand through his hair. *The last thing I remember...*

His brother's words echoed in his mind. *"You know what to do."*

No... I don't want to go back. But Kaleb was sucked back into the moments before he shot Gryff.

Years of training took over when Markus placed the cold steel of the revolver into Kaleb's hand. The blue warning lights flashed above as he pulled the trigger without a thought, watching Gryff fall to the ground between flashes of light.

I killed Gryff.

It was like an old-time movie on the big screen, too slow, too dramatic to be real. But it happened. The fear of what Kaleb would become, the reason he hadn't touched a gun since leaving Red Queen, had come true. *I'm a murderer and can't blame it on WonderLand this time.*

Kaleb's knees hit the cold ground. *How did I get here?* He stared down at his hands, the revolver clenched in his right fist. Pain rolled through his stomach as the little bit of food he'd eaten since coming here threatened to come up.

Alice turned to look at him, her hand brushed against him, and he wasn't sure if it was real. *Am I still in the past?*

Her eyes were so sad. Kaleb couldn't let her see him like this. She needed to get far away from him. He tried to yell at her to go but could only mouth the words.

He sighed, relieved that Alice started to move away from him.

She'll be safer without me.

It's better if I stay here with the other monsters.

The memory of Gryff's dead eyes stared through him, damning him each time the blue flashing light chased the darkness away and made his stomach spin even more. *Still in the past.* Kaleb couldn't look at the proof of his descent into madness that he knew would come, so he covered his eyes, pressing the soft flesh of his palms against the sockets.

Nightmares of the past flared behind the pulsing of the pressure of his hands. *There's no escape.* He whimpered. Wrapping his arms around his knees, Kaleb began to rock, his sight plagued with black spots, blue light, and Alice. Markus's voice whispered in his ear again, and those horrible moments played all over.

No, no, no.

Alice's soft voice was in his ear. "Ssh, it's okay. You're safe." He tried to grab onto that sound.

Kaleb's eyes started to focus on the world around him. He was standing in the center of what looked like a large master bathroom.

"There you are," Alice smiled at him. "Let's get you cleaned up."

He nodded but didn't say anything. Instead, he went through the grounding steps.

Alice led him to a sink.

Five things I can see: The mirror, a bathtub, broken tile, chipped paint, and Alice.

In front of him, Alice rubbed her hands under the running water of a sink. Dark red changed to pink and swirled around the drain. He met her eyes in the clouded mirror that hung above the sink. She gave him a sad smile before turning to Kaleb and clasping both hands in hers, leading him to the sink and placing his hands under the warm water.

Four things I can touch: hair, jacket, skin, and tears.
Three things I can hear: water, humming, Alice.

She placed soap into his hands and scrubbed them together, rubbing the dark red from his skin. The same red that had been on hers. Turning the water off, Alice clasped his hands in hers, drying them with the damp sleeves of her shirt.

Two things I can smell: mold and lavender.
One thing I can taste: Salt.

Alice led him into the next room. It was a larger room that might have once been a bedroom. The room was lit by candles spread around the floor, giving it an unearthly glow.

"Where are we?" he asked.

Alice shrugged. "This is where I found Marci when she was riding out the worst part of WonderLand." She leaned against a sun-bleached wall. "It was the only place I could think to go," she sighed.

He looked around the room—it had been framed, and drywall rested against boards, holding down plastic and old blankets that had been nailed into the exposed wood. A case of toilet paper lay in the middle of the room, surrounded by the majority of the candles and empty silver tubes. He didn't need to read the words printed on them to know they were Turtle's drugs.

Alice's cold fingers clasped his hand, pulling him onto the floor beside her. The movement made the floor creak beneath them. He straightened his legs and leaned against the wall behind them.

Once they were both settled, Alice reached for his hand, entwining them together. "Okay?"

Not wanting to break the quiet truths between them, Kaleb stared into the flickering flames of a nearby candle. "Yeah." He traced the faded scars that marked Alice's knuckles, remnants of the worst day of her life. The day that changed both of their lives forever.

A cold sweat moved down his back as memories of that day threatened to pull him under, back to the hidden, dark corners of his mind. He couldn't breathe under the tidal wave of all he'd done and what he'd almost done. Alice shifted next to him.

Kaleb focused on Alice's still form. Her head rested on the wall behind them, and her eyes closed. He studied her, looking for the girl he'd fallen in love with. She'd been so angry when they'd found her on the top floor of that building moments before Turtle jumped. An emotion he'd never seen her express, but he knew now that was because of WonderLand.

How she kept the effects of WonderLand under control for so long was a marvel. After only a few hours, Kaleb held onto the edge of sanity by the tips of his fingers. After the incident at Red Queen, he had to be sedated those first few days in the hospital. When he finally came around, Alice was gone.

Dead.

He looked at the woman he thought was gone forever. *Is she the same person?* She looked the same, lighter even. Kaleb knew that she'd suffered from memory loss, but how much?

She'd faked her death, and he needed to know why. "Alice?"

Alice looked at him with tired eyes.

He let go of her hand, rubbing the back of his neck, trying to find the best way to ask without starting an argument—deep down, he knew there was a good chance there wasn't one. "Why did you let me think you were dead?"

Something crossed her face, maybe anger. Kaleb wasn't sure. For a moment, he thought she might try to change the subject or tell him it wasn't important.

Alice took a deep breath, squaring her shoulders as if preparing herself for a battle. "I didn't, at least not at first."

So, she was afraid this was going to cause an argument too.

"What do you mean not at first?"

Alice groaned. "That 'cure' that Dr. Turtle gave me in the hospital after we escaped Red Queen had some side effects. The biggest one is memory loss. By the time my memories returned, everyone thought I was dead. My name was different, and I was living in Salt City. Marci and her boss asked me to help find Turtle. I couldn't be the one to bring you back into this life. Not after you worked so hard to have a normal one."

He guessed that made sense but... "How did you know what my life was like?"

For a moment, Alice looked as if she'd gone somewhere else. "I didn't want to believe them when they told me you'd moved on. But Marci took me to your brother's coffee shop, and there you were, sitting at the cash register, a textbook in front of you, flirting with a woman at the counter." She shrugged. "The best thing I could do for you was to stay dead. It was the only way to be sure you were safe." Alice shook her head and focused on him again.

She'd been to the coffee shop? "When...when did you come to see me?"

He'd seen Marci outside the shop a few times watching him, but she was always alone. At least, he thought she was.

Alice scrunched up her face. "I'm not sure." She rubbed her temples. "Sorry, my mind is still a bit fragmented."

Frustrated, Kaleb sank back against the wall. *Is this our life? Who can be trusted? Lies and secrets around every corner, with the added bonus of being unwilling guinea pigs.*

"It was never your job to keep me safe," he sighed.

Alice raised an eyebrow. "I could say the same to you. Everything you sacrificed to protect me from Reid Redding, Red Queen, and even myself."

She's right. Kaleb ran his fingers through his hair again. "I—"

Alice cut him off. "Before this turns into another argument that neither of us will win, can we just agree from here on out—no more secrets? Even if we think it's going to hurt the other person? Neither of us is a damsel needing saving."

Kaleb smirked at her vague reference to their lives being fairy tales. "I don't know. It seems to me that we're trapped in a tower guarded by a dragon. Are you sure you're not a princess that needs to be saved?"

Alice rolled her eyes at him before resting against the wall behind them with a yawn. "Sorry, not this time. The dragon and I are on a quest to destroy the evil queen and restore the land." She laid her head on his shoulder, and in a sleepy voice, she said, "No more secrets. Partners."

He rested his head on hers. "No more secrets."

Chapter 30

Alice struggled against an imaginary adversary. Their tight arms forced her down. Pinning her. She knew it was a dream. The one with talking animals and a lunatic queen trying to kill her. Warm arms surrounded her.

"You're safe," a familiar voice mumbled in her ear.

For a moment, within the world between sleep and awake, Alice thought she'd been drugged again. She could even see the IV bag hanging above her, the black words of the drug washed out by bright white light. Someone in green scrubs leaned over her, a needle in their gloved hand.

Alice tried to open her eyes, the lids heavy, and her head foggy. Her breath caught in her throat, her mind racing; something was wrong.

"Ssh, everything is fine." Kaleb pushed the hair from her face. "You're okay."

Everything that had happened the day before rushed past her. The anger and betrayal and—love. Kaleb agreed there would be no more secrets between them. *If I can't remember everything, is it still a secret? Do I tell him about the memory wipes? What if it sends him spiraling and I lose him again?*

She'd never seen Kaleb act the way he did last night. He'd

disappeared to somewhere inside his mind, and Alice was scared. *What if he doesn't come back next time?*

Kaleb stood up. "We should get going."

"What? Where?"

He helped her to her feet. "The fairgrounds."

"Why?"

Kaleb ran his finger through his hair. "I don't know, something Marci said yesterday before..." He swallowed, and a far-off look crossed his face, followed by a deep breath.

Alice squeezed his hand, hoping it would keep him in the present. "You don't happen to know how to get there, do you?"

He didn't say anything for a few seconds. Alice would have thought she lost him again if it wasn't for his thumb rubbing across her wrist.

"It's where Markus found Marci after the WonderLand." He took a deep breath before going on. "After Marci disappeared. Markus said it would be a good place to meet if we ever got separated."

Alice tried to keep her voice light. "I guess we're going to the fairgrounds."

A knock echoed through the empty room, causing them both to jump.

Alice looked toward the noise.

Ryan stood in the doorframe; the dirty sheet that served as a door pushed aside.

"Sorry, but this is the only way." He pointed a gun toward her. "I need you to come with me."

Kaleb took a step toward him. "What the hell, Ryan."

"I'm sorry, Rabbit. If there was any other way, you know I'd do it."

Alice heard Marci's voice in her head. *We all have to play our parts.*

Did that explain Ryan's sudden appearance or even the gun in his hand? *Maybe?* Alice knew without remembering that he'd done this a few times since she'd been in Salt City.

A memory tingled through Alice shoving her into the past.

She was at the Sheep and Oar. Ryan sat across from her, a cooling coffee cup in his hand. "That's why I took the job with Red Queen. I'm not sure how, but the Reddings had something to do with my sister's disappearance."

Alice reached out to him. "I'm sorry. But I'm still not sure what I can do to help."

"Don't give up on drawing Turtle out." He met Alice's gaze. "You're the last lead I have. If you go back now, Turtle may never come out of hiding. Without him, there is no way to make the Reddings pay for their crimes."

Alice hated to ask it, but she needed to know. "Are you sure she's still alive?"

He pulled up a photo on his phone. A woman not much older than him, her face kissed by the same freckles, sat on the steps of a rundown, old building. A child played in front of her. "I got this last week. Marci traced it. She's here. Somewhere."

Alice came back from the past with a start and a realization. *The girl playing in front of Ryan's sister was TigerLily, the girl I met at Butte Gardens.*

Alice placed a hand on Kaleb's chest, stopping his advance. Ryan wasn't the same guy who had licked her and drugged her so long ago. He was her–partner of sorts. He showed up whenever she needed help.

She studied Ryan. He had lost weight since she had last seen him, and the black band on his wrist wasn't as tight as it should have been. He'd also aged. Gray strands specked his hair. There was something else she couldn't quite place—something in his eyes, a sadness.

"What changed?" Alice asked.

Ryan didn't look at Alice when he answered. "They found my sister."

"Who?" Kaleb asked at the same time Alice asked. "When?"

Panic seeped into Ryan's voice. "I thought it was the Reddings. It wasn't, and DeeDee—it doesn't matter. I have to get my sister back. This is the only way."

Alice took a step forward, feeling the heat of Kaleb's glare on her back. Alice said in a low, calm voice, "Ryan, I don't know where your sister is, but I saw your niece. She was waiting for you."

Ryan's voice shook, "When? Where?"

"Alice," Kaleb growled. "We have to go."

Alice followed Kaleb's gaze. A group of guards—Knights—moved toward the building. They needed to get out of here before they made it upstairs. "You sent them here," she said to Ryan.

"No, but he did." Ryan sighed. "Turtle found a way to track me. I'm sorry."

His voice went flat. "We all have to play our parts now."

"What about Marci? She was helping you, is she—"

He nodded. "Her too."

Alice wasn't sure what that meant for her and Kaleb. It's just that it was bad. *Now what?*

The Knights moved closer, their boots echoing off the brick walls outside. If they took them—Alice shook the thought away. She didn't like using the girl as leverage, but she needed to get her and Kaleb out of there.

TigerLily said something to me, something that Ryan told her. What was it? Some craziness about tarts, maybe, yes. Alice hoped it would be enough for Ryan to let them go before the Guard arrived. "Tarts and flowers, a spot of tea in the sun."

She saw the look of confusion on Kaleb's face. It was the best she could think of to get the message to Ryan. The Guard was too close not to overhear her say, "Your niece is at Butte Gardens with a bunch of other girls. That is, if the Guard hasn't picked them up already."

Ryan smiled a toothy grin, putting the gun in his belt and tossing Alice a set of familiar keys. "Past time to go." He handed her a black helmet with a blue A painted on it.

Alice started toward the makeshift door, but Kaleb stopped with a hand on her shoulder. "What are you doing?" he asked.

"Leaving."

Kaleb rolled his eyes at her. "Are you sure we can trust him?"

Alice looked to Ryan, who was pretending not to watch them, then back to Kaleb. "Aren't you the one that told me he wasn't a bad guy?"

"He pointed a gun at you."

"And now he's not."

Kaleb took a few deep breaths, frustration marking his brow. "Alice."

"Look, you said it yourself, we have to go. So, we can take a chance Ryan is a good guy and get out before the Guard gets here. Or get caught." She pulled from Kaleb's grasp. "I'm choosing to trust Ryan."

Chapter 31

Alice let the buzz of the motorcycle wash over her as she moved through the city. Her mind raced through the things she couldn't put together, like how she knew that Turtle had Ryan's sister.

She pulled into an empty space, parking the bike next to the brick wall of an abandoned convenience store. Alice was surprised she'd found this place.

Thankfully, the Guard followed Ryan instead of us.

Kaleb hadn't been much help beyond an occasional grunt.

Hopefully he got away.

Alice thought about the promise she'd made to Kaleb about not keeping secrets. She knew she should tell him about the half-memories and the things she suspected, but how? He was barely holding on as it was. *How am I supposed to tell him that Salt City isn't real? That this was one of Turtle's games when I'm not sure it's true.* She rubbed her temples. *It could be a side effect of one of the many drugs Turtle and his cronies gave me.*

She scanned the gated area in front of her, looking for signs of life. Alice played the conversation she'd had with Kaleb over in her mind. Trying to find a way to not break her promise.

No more secrets.

A stillness hung in the air around the tent city that covered the open space behind the gate. The smell of campfires and bread hung in the crisp air. Alice thought about asking Kaleb if he was sure this was where Marci said to meet. It looked like one of the places where families dropped off people under the influence of WonderLand. Unlike the gardens, the people here had made a home.

"Gaaahhh."

Kaleb had Markus pinned against the wall, his fist hovering above his brother's head. Kaleb's posture was rigid, and the look in his eyes scared Alice. She'd never seen him this disconnected from the world, not without warning.

Markus moved his hands above him, giving up his slight advantage over Kaleb. Alice stepped toward them, but Markus motioned for her to stay.

"Kaleb, it's Markus," he said with a steady voice. "You're safe."

Alice watched Kaleb for any change. Beyond the rising of his chest, as he took a deep breath, nothing changed. She wasn't sure what to do and was ready to start counting. *It worked last night.* Before Alice could say anything, Markus's calming voice moved through the cold air.

"Kaleb, five things you can see."

Alice watched Kaleb's breath slow as he started to name things in and around the alley.

"Brick... Snow... Fence... Tents... Campfire.

"Good. Now four things you can touch."

Again, Kaleb named things in the alley. *This must be what he does instead of counting to get back to the real world.* Kaleb's muscles loosened, and his breathing returned to normal.

Markus smiled. "Now, something you can taste."

"It's supposed to be three things I can hear," Kaleb muttered. "Idiot."

To Alice's relief, Kaleb let Markus go. Alice made a mental note to ask Markus about the grounding he'd just done with Kaleb. It worked better than the counting she'd used most of her life. *I'll have to keep a few things to myself until I understand how to help Kaleb through this and determine what triggers his extreme reaction.*

"You know, if I wanted you dead, little bro, I would have done it already," Markus said.

Alice could see the eye roll coming before Kaleb did it. *This is the Kaleb I remember. The sarcastic, take-nothing-too-seriously guy.*

"What's going on?" Kaleb asked. "I thought we were supposed to meet you inside."

Markus looked everywhere but at them. "The old man's back. He's looking for you, says he needs to talk to Alice."

Kaleb gritted his teeth. "NO!"

Wide-eyed, Alice took a step back from Kaleb. Sure, Joe and Kaleb had their issues, but without Joe's help, she would never have gotten him out of Red Queen in the first place. Ignoring Kaleb's statement, Alice turned to Markus and asked. "Why?"

Markus shrugged. "You'll have to ask him." He didn't wait for a response; he walked away toward the chain-link fence surrounding the fairgrounds and tent city.

Alice looked at Kaleb, every muscle in his body tense, and asked, "What's going on with you and Joe?"

"He ordered your execution." Kaleb started to pace. "That's why I went into Red Queen in the first place. We were all set to leave. The car was packed, and you were asleep in the passenger seat."

Alice interrupted. "The convenience store." *That was so long ago.* "I remember waking up in your car surrounded by the smell of pine." *I followed DeeDee into the store and got drugged again, but Kaleb didn't need to know that right now.* "I thought you left me there."

Kaleb shook his head. "Joe called. He said he'd send Reid's goon squad after you if I didn't come in. I couldn't..."

Alice clasped one of his hands in hers to stop his pacing, waiting for him to meet her eyes. She remembered being angry that he'd left her for the second time in less than twenty-four hours. Then Linc and DeeDee asked her to go into Red Queen headquarters to get the cure, using the fact that Kaleb was trapped inside to get her to do their bidding.

So many secrets came out that day, and new ones were made. They were still coming to light now. Alice took a deep breath, clearing her mind. Alice finally understood why he'd left her in the car alone. He couldn't let what had happened to his mother happen to her. Then she'd gone and disappeared, letting him think she'd died.

"You're not alone," she reminded him. "Not anymore."

He relaxed a little, but the lost look in his eyes was still there.

"What do you think we should do?" she asked.

Kaleb shrugged. "I don't know."

"Let's go over the facts," she went on. "We know Marci was found here, and Markus thought it was a good place to meet. I'm assuming Marci is most likely here since—"

Kaleb interrupted her. "Markus won't let her out of his sight, not after the incident with WonderLand earlier."

"It's also safe to assume that Markus wouldn't do anything to put her in harm's way, and since we both trust Marci, then..."

Kaleb sighed. "We should see what Joseph wants."

Alice nodded and squeezed Kaleb's hand before walking across the street to meet Markus, who waited for them at the gate. Markus walked through the park without saying anything to either of them. He showed the black band on his wrist to anyone who came near. Children ran away at their approach, and scared faces of all ages peeked at them through hidden openings in their temporary homes. A fire burned in a large metal garbage can in the center of the camp. They walked silently, Kaleb brooding next to her, and Markus focused on the path ahead.

A large building that looked like a barn came into view. Markus stopped and knocked in some kind of code on the closed door. It creaked open, and Markus beckoned them forward, stopping Alice before she could enter.

She met his eyes, a flash of emotion she couldn't read passed between them as if he wanted to tell her something important. "I'm sorry. We have to play our parts. I have no choice."

He led them into a large room. Heavy beams lined the ceiling. Once Alice was in the room, Markus slammed the door behind them, breaking the silence and causing Alice and Kaleb to jump.

Alice was trapped. The walls were moving toward her. *No, that's not right.* She took a deep breath, trying to calm herself. *Someone has to have their wits about them.* There was what looked like a long hallway nearby. *Maybe there's a door down at the end.*

"What the hell is going on?" Kaleb shouted at his brother.

A long, wooden table had been placed in the center of the room. Reid and DeeDee sat across from each other: DeeDee in a white business suit trimmed with blue and Reid dressed in red. They both were disheveled and covered in bruises. Reid looked up and smiled a crooked smile, blood oozing from her split lip.

"Reid?" Alice said. *She's supposed to be dead.*

Reid lifted her hand to wave, her arm rising only inches from the chair's arm. A thick chain attached to a metal bracelet hung from her wrist.

Nope, not happening. She was going nowhere near either of them. Not when she was so close to getting out of this messed-up world they'd created.

Alice turned around to walk out the door they came through.

Kaleb turned to his brother. "What's going on?" he demanded.

The door creaked open, and Joe's deep voice echoed through the nearly empty room. "Hear me out."

Chapter 32

The muscles in Kaleb's jaw tightened. There was no way he would do anything his father wanted. Especially if those two women were involved.

"No," he growled.

Alice squeezed his hand in silent agreement.

"We are leaving," Kaleb said. He moved toward the door that his father had come from. He'd spent a lifetime dealing with the Reddings and their games. He wouldn't be caught up in their schemes ever again.

DeeDee's light, airy voice floated through the room, causing Kaleb to stop. "Rabbit, dear."

He hated when she called him that.

"Don't be like that," DeeDee continued, her voice a singsong whine. "We just want to have a friendly chat with your girlfriend."

Don't do it, just keep walking.

Alice looked up at him, rolling her eyes and shaking her head. "Not happening." She tugged him toward the door, clearly not taking DeeDee's bait.

Reid glared at her sister. "Hush." She turned to look at Alice. The sugary sweet smile plastered on her broken lips sent shivers down

Kaleb's spine. "You must excuse her. She means well but can't help saying foolish things as a general rule."

It was Kaleb's turn to roll his eyes. *Do they think I'm dumb? They both know exactly what they're doing at all times. This is nothing more than a game to them. Alice and I are pieces moving toward some kind of horrible end.* He wasn't playing anymore.

Reid motioned with her handcuffed hand to Kaleb's father, who had moved to stand next to his sons. "Joseph, explain."

Kaleb tightened his grip on Alice's hand, crushing her fingers with his, tugging her toward the door. He didn't wait for his father's explanation. Kaleb pushed the door hard enough to crash into the wall.

"They're going to destroy the city," Joe called after them.

"What?" Alice stopped in the doorway, turning to face Joe.

Kaleb groaned next to her. "Don't do it. Don't turn around." He mumbled to her. "He's lying."

He's always lying.

"Are you sure?" she whispered.

For the first time since this madness started, Kaleb really looked at his father. His clothes were a few sizes too big, and patches of skin hung loosely around his face. Dark circles marked the skin under his eyes, and his hair was now gray.

What happened over the last six months?

Joseph stared at the ground, his feet shuffling back and forth nervously. The confidence that his father carried around like a shield had disappeared. Kaleb wasn't sure if this was part of the game or if his father was telling the truth. He ran his fingers through his hair, considering their options.

Can we take the chance?

Kaleb huffed. "Destroying the city does sound like something they'd do."

The balloon of hope inside his chest deflated. *I should have known better.* He squeezed Alice's hand. *They'll never let us go.*

Marci entered from a door Kaleb hadn't noticed before. "The

Reddings planted a bomb somewhere in the city." She announced as the door swung shut behind her and disappeared as if it was never there. "At least that's what they want us to think."

Of course, Marci is here. He watched her walk across the room toward them. She was distracted by something.

Kaleb tried to meet his brother's eyes. Markus wasn't going anywhere without Marci. Even now, he watched her every move. *Is he worried about her?*

Alice turned to face her friend, letting go of Kaleb's hand to hug Marci. Kaleb watched the two of them, wondering what had happened over the last few months. He didn't remember them being so close. Alice bit her lip before leaning in, whispering something to Marci that sounded like, "Can you get us out?"

Kaleb knew Alice meant more than out of this room. *Can she really get us out of this whole mess?* Kaleb wanted to share a normal life he'd started to build with Alice. One where he could take her on a date and not worry about who it might benefit or upset. A place where they could figure out their life together without interference from their past. *If she even wants to be with me.*

Marci mouthed the word *maybe*. She stepped out of Alice's embrace, nearly knocking Markus over in the process. She said in an almost normal voice, "I'm glad you're okay."

Remembering what Marci had said about the Redding sisters, Kaleb asked, "What do you mean, at least that's what they want us to think?"

Marci leaned into Markus. Her arms entwined with his, the black band on her wrist a contrast to his now white band. "It just doesn't make sense. I mean, it's been six months since the Salt City experiment started. Why now? There has to be more."

"One of those two did something." Markus motioned with his head toward the table. "If we can't find a way to clear out the city in the next forty-eight hours, Salt City will be no more."

Marci glared at Joseph, who hadn't said anything since Marci walked into the room. She motioned to Joseph. "He tried to get the information from them. Obviously, it didn't work. He's been nothing but a problem since Linc and Tom woke him up."

Kaleb looked at the Reddings trying not to let anger cloud his thoughts. They watched the conversation around them, not saying a word. Eyes vacant of any emotions, hands flat on the table in front of them. "That explains the bruises but not why they aren't talking. Let me guess, torture didn't work."

Alice glared at Joe and said, "And now they won't talk to anyone but me."

"Of course, they want Alice," Kaleb growled. "The two of them are obsessed. They both think she has something the other wants. A pawn in their sick game of chess." He scoffed. "Everyone in this room has given in to their demands. Does anyone here even know why they want Alice?"

Everyone avoided meeting his gaze. "That's what I thought."

"Does anyone even care what I want?" Alice asked.

Kaleb turned to Alice, a pinkish blush on his face. He should have asked her sooner. Rubbing the back of his neck, Kaleb met Alice's gaze.

"What do you want to do?"

Chapter 33

Alice looked around the room at the three men; all had the same color eyes and delicate features. Each of them reflected a different emotion back to her. Fear, hope, and uncertainty filled the air around them. Unsure what to do next Alice turned to Marci for advice. She shifted from one foot to the other worried wrinkling her brow. *What if there is a bomb?* Alice would have to figure this out on her own.

She thought about the people she knew in the city: Ryan and TigerLily.

Has he found her?

Alice looked down at her hand still in Kaleb's grip, thinking about Dr. Turtle using them as lab rats. *There are so many who aren't affected by WonderLand. People who are stuck in Salt City too.*

Even if we get out of this, how can I live with myself if the city is destroyed and I can stop it?

"I'll talk to them on one condition," Alice said cautiously. They needed a way to get the information to Bobbins and Hank. They were the only people Alice trusted at this point to find Dr. Turtle and stop this madness.

"We're out." She motioned to Kaleb and herself. "Out of Salt City. Out of whatever organization you currently work for or will be working for. New identities, a new place to live, and no way for any of you to find us."

"An average and normal life." She looked up at Kaleb.

Surprise and warmth marked Kaleb's face. "Are you sure?"

"Absolutely." Alice smiled at him.

She thought of the nights they'd spent together streaming their favorite shows on the tiny computer in her dorm room. Of the green card plan. Their dreams of having a normal life once his mission was over. A mission that would never end. Not until they made a choice to walk away.

It wasn't going to be easy, but she wanted it. More than anything.

"Agreed," Joe stated as he approached Alice. "Let's get started then."

Joe grabbed Alice's arm, and Kaleb growled at him. "Don't touch her."

The two men glared at each other, each holding one of Alice's arms. A silent tug of war, and she was the rope. Alice pulled her arms from their grasp, unwilling to be a prize, and moved further into the room.

She opened her mouth to yell something about not being a dog's chew toy or something with a bit of wit and bite, but Markus's voice boomed through the barn's rafters. "Stop. This isn't helping anyone."

Alice watched DeeDee and Reid, who hadn't said a word since Joe announced the city would be destroyed. She couldn't remember a time when the sisters had sat back and watched the world around them.

She met Kaleb's gaze, and for a minute, she thought about taking his hand and running, getting out of the city, and letting it burn. It wasn't the right thing to do, but if it meant she didn't have to be here with the Reddings, it might be worth it. Only she couldn't do it. She couldn't let someone else become a victim of their sick game.

Kaleb pulled her into his arms, surrounding Alice with his warmth, calming the tidal wave of emotion that threatened to overtake her. She relaxed against him, silently counting, trying to make her breath match his.

Cold metal touched her back, stopping at the waistband of her jeans. Kaleb whispered in her ear, "Just in case." She knew it was the gun he had been carrying since the night before at the museum. The same one that had killed Gryff.

Kaleb's breath hitched as his fingers traced her back. "I can't lose you again."

Alice leaned closer to him, words from a dream hanging between them. *They found each other again.* Alice moved from Kaleb's grasp and sat in the empty chair at the head of the table. The weight of a possible bomb pulled her down. If these women didn't tell her what she needed to know, a lot of people might die.

The cold plastic of the chair seeped through Alice's clothes, settling in her veins. Alice stared at the grains of the table, trying not to feel trapped. Memories of a fan and Dr. Turtle flashed through her mind.

Markus kneeled in front of Alice, acting as if he was going to strap her to the chair with handcuffs like the other two.

"What are you doing?"

"Part of the deal," he called out.

Markus winked at her as he placed both ends of the cuffs around the chair leg. Even though she wasn't attached to the chair, her heart moved in time with the clicking metal as it attached to the chair legs.

Markus's warm hand moved to her ankle, and bile churned in her stomach. She hated being stuck without escape, even if it was a facade. It reminded her of the day her life had turned into one crazy trauma after another.

Alice closed her eyes, taking a deep breath, numbers moving through her mind. Cold steel touched the inside of her ankle, and Alice suppressed a scream, letting the wave of fear move past her with the numbers.

Markus tapped her ankle. Alice looked down; the cold steel wasn't the handcuff but a slender pocketknife. Both sides of the cuffs wrapped around the chair leg. Markus moved to her wrist, and, like her ankle, he didn't attach them to the chair. He whispered in Alice's ear. "Don't forget you're supposed to be bound to the chair."

Markus stood up and clasped Marci's hand. Alice thought she saw a flash of pain move across Marci's face, but it disappeared as quickly as it appeared.

"Remember, we'll be right outside that door if you need us," Marci rubbed her temple, then turned to Reid and DeeDee. "That goes for you two as well. Any hint of trouble, and this 'interview' is over."

Reid smirked at Marci but kept her mouth shut.

Kaleb placed his hand on Alice's cheek. "You got this."

She smiled up at him. The confidence he placed in that one statement settled her nerves. *I can totally do this.* "Whatever this is."

Kaleb kissed her forehead and walked out the door. Markus and Marci trailed behind Kaleb, pulling Joseph behind them.

As soon as the door shut, Reid spoke. "Glad you could make it to our little party."

Chapter 34

A sharp pain moved through Marci's head, and she could no longer pretend it wasn't affecting her. She yanked off the wristband that connected her to the program and threw it on the van floor. Red Queen had found her intrusion in their system again. Her legs wobbled underneath her as she made her way to the computer, calling out to Ryan.

He didn't answer.

He was still inside the system.

Marci sighed. She should have never let Ryan go in. After watching Kit die, she didn't have the strength to tell him no. Marci understood why he needed to go in. She would tear the world apart to find her sister. She had done it once already.

Where was Markus? He's supposed to be watching over us.

Marci's fingers moved across the keyboard, looking for the code representing Kaleb, Alice, and DeeDee.

The doors to the van rear opened, and Marci reached for the weapon attached to the desk below.

She exhaled the breath she hadn't realized she'd been holding. Somewhere in the back of her mind, Marci worried that Markus had been taken by Turtle's goons, even if Turtle said he didn't need her anymore. Marci knew Turtle would do whatever he could to find her; she's the only one who could stop him from doing his experiments.

"What happened? Markus rushed toward her. "Why aren't you with Kaleb and Alice?"

"They found a way to force me out." *Again.*

She turned back to the computer, fingers moving across the screen. Markus sat beside the chair, placing a comforting hand on her leg.

"I still haven't found a way to get Alice and Kaleb out of the system, but..." She typed a quick message to Ryan, telling him to get his sister somewhere safe and then get out. "I might have found a way to keep them hidden until we can get them back."

But first, I need to get Alice away from Reid and DeeDee.

Chapter 35

For a moment, Alice thought about not saying anything. *They are the ones who want to talk, not me.* But she knew from past experience if she didn't speak, neither would DeeDee.

"Let's get something straight right now," Alice said. "I don't trust either of you. I'm only here because of the small chance that you're telling the truth, and there is a way to stop the destruction of Salt City."

DeeDee tapped her once-manicured fingers on the table, the nail on her index finger gone. "I understand why you don't trust my sister. She has been using you for years, even tried to kill you once. Me, on the other hand, I've done nothing but try to protect you."

Alice snorted. "You're the one who sent Ryan into Red Queen to kill me."

"You remember that, huh?" She shrugged. "Guess the drugs are starting to wear off."

Before Alice could come back at her with a snappy retort, the familiar tingle of memory thrusted Alice into the past.

ALICE STOOD *on the sidewalk outside her apartment a black sedan pulled up behind her truck. A girl she didn't recognize stepped out of the car. "Alice, I know you don't remember me, but I can help you get your memories back if you like."*

Alice took a step closer; she did remember her. DeeDee was Reid Redding's sister and Kaleb's friend.

She shouldn't be here. "How did you find me?"

Besides Marci, Bobbins, and Hank, everyone thought Alice had died six months ago. Not even Kaleb knew she was alive and playing spy—not yet, anyway. Not until Marci found a way to get them out.

DeeDee walked toward Alice, a crazed smile moving across her perfectly painted lips, WonderLand swimming in her ever-shifting gaze. "I was hoping we could do this the easy way." She snapped her fingers.

Someone wrapped their arms around Alice, trapping her. She struggled with the unknown captor as DeeDee moved closer with a syringe in her dainty fingers.

ALICE SLAMMED BACK into the present, the pressure of the needle still on her skin. The sisters watched her but didn't say anything. She studied them, looking for the tell-tale signs that WonderLand was affecting them while going over what she'd just remembered. *DeeDee was the one who erased my memories that time. Why?* Alice tapped her fingers on the arm of the chair she was supposed to be attached to. *To get Kaleb here.* It was the only explanation that made sense.

She shook her head. This was crazy. These two had the power to stop the terror that ran through the city's streets and the rest of the world. Instead, they wanted to have a little tea party and rehash the past, bringing her and the people she cared about along for the ride.

Anger washed over Alice as she thought of the deaths that could be prevented if these two could just get along or kill each other.

"What is wrong with you?" Alice muttered through gritted teeth.

"You're alive, aren't you?" DeeDee popped her gum. "It's not like I killed you or anyone else. I couldn't hurt someone like that."

Reid scoffed but didn't say anything.

"But you could drug them," Alice growled. "That's why I couldn't remember what happened since I woke up on the train. How did you even find me?"

Reid slammed her fist on the table and yelled at DeeDee, "Enough. I want to talk about DeeDee trying to kill our brother."

Ignoring her sister's outburst, DeeDee shrugged before answering Alice's question. "You aren't the only one who has been keeping an eye on Rabbit." She turned to Reid. "Gryff was fine when I last saw him."

The band on DeeDee's wrist flickered from black to pink. A crazed smile that Alice had seen in the vision appeared on her lipstick-smeared lips. "What about you, Alice? Can you say the same?"

The memory of Gryff's sticky blood on her hands, shining under the flash of blue light, sent spikes of cold through Alice. She could feel the color draining from her face and wondered how DeeDee knew she'd watched the life leave Gryff's eyes. "How do you know he's dead?"

DeeDee scoffed, not answering Alice. Turning to stare at her sister with a scowl. "And you haven't killed anyone?"

"I haven't," Reid insisted. "Besides, those other people don't count."

All those people in the theater, my mom, don't count.

"Because you were infected or affected?" DeeDee turned to Alice, "I can never get those two straight."

"Yes," Reid stated.

"Even Elizabeth?"

Mom? Alice longed to know more, but this wasn't the time. This conversation had taken a turn that wouldn't help the people stuck in Salt City.

"Enough." Alice turned to Reid. "You and I both know you didn't kill those people inside Red Queen headquarters because of WonderLand. You did it because you wanted to, maybe even enjoyed it. As for the others—"

DeeDee snorted, "Told you she was smart."

"Yes, she is," Reid said, smiling at her sister. "Too bad Elizabeth kept her away from us for so long. Maybe then—"

"Don't." Alice ground her teeth. She didn't want to hear what they had to say. Not when it came to her mom. "You don't get to talk about my mother."

DeeDee's shoulders fell. Her eyes went vacant for a moment before pulling a black notebook that matched the now black wristband from her jacket. At that moment, Alice realized DeeDee's hands weren't bound to the chair. The handcuffs hanging off the chair were free of their hostage. A paperclip, or something like it, was sticking out of the lock.

Alice was relieved DeeDee had freed herself, that she hadn't been betrayed by people she'd placed her trust in. But worried what the Reddings being free could mean for her safety. Alice took a few calming breaths and counted to ten. *I can't let them get in my head. There's more going on here, and I need to keep my wits.* Alice tried to pick up the thread of conversation she'd lost between Reid and DeeDee.

"Of course, our people wouldn't..." DeeDee motioned to Alice. "Well, you know."

"Kill people?" Alice said sarcastically, trying to keep the conversation going and see if Reid's hands and feet were fastened to the chair. Or if, like DeeDee, she had found a way out of her restraints.

"There you go saying foolish things again," Reid hissed. "Ruining someone's life is just as bad; it's worse than killing them. At least when I was done with them, the pain was gone. None of this grounding nonsense Alice is doing all the time. Counting? Ha! Who does that? Does it even work? Oh, and your precious Rabbit." Reid turned to her sister, letting hate fill her words. "What you did to him is, well, genius. That boy is so messed up. For what? He loves Alice and hates, well, not you, but what you represent."

Alice swallowed the disgust that rose up with Reid's statement. *What did they do to Kaleb?*

No, now is not the time for that.

She concentrated on the cuffs around Reid's wrist. They looked so loose that Alice thought Reid could slip right out of them. She thought about calling out to Kaleb or Marci, but she still didn't have the bomb's location.

"Oh, yes, well..." DeeDee shoved the notebook into her jacket pocket.

Alice had lost track of the sisters' conversation again. Not that it mattered. They seemed to have forgotten she was there and were having a nonsensical conversation about cats talking over each other.

It would be easier to understand someone on WonderLand than these two. Alice fell back into her chair with a sigh. She needed to change her approach.

Reid and DeeDee stopped talking and turned to Alice.

"That's right, the Turtle, he contacted you," Reid stated.

DeeDee raised up a glass that appeared in front of her. "A toast," she said, "to Queen Alice, long may she reign."

Alice shook her head, telling herself that the glass had always been there. *Are they pumping some kind of mind-altering chemical in here?* Her mind was playing tricks on her. She focused on the words DeeDee had said. *Queen Alice?*

This was an unusual statement, even for these two women. Alice studied them. Sweat pooled across their foreheads and their bodies shivered despite the room's heat. Alice couldn't believe she hadn't noticed sooner.

She'd been wrong.

The bands hadn't detected it. *Is this what Marci meant about not trusting them?* Reid and DeeDee's eyes had the shimmery look of someone on WonderLand.

How did Joe and Markus not realize? They were never going to help me. How can they?

Alice turned in her chair, forgetting to pretend to be strapped in, looking for a way out. *But DeeDee's hand, it's black.* She opened her mouth to scream but could only squeak. *Why can't I talk?*

A smile crossed Reid's blood-smeared lips, the same smile she had worn while pointing a gun at the guy cleaning blood off the walls in Red Queen. "You're finally getting it," Reid said.

"It was intentional," DeeDee said. "He injected us with WonderLand."

Reid sat back in her chair, her fingers tapping the arm. "Dear, dear Alice, he wants you dead."

"Who? Joe?"

"You're smart. Too smart," DeeDee barked. "But no, he has no idea what's happening here."

Reid examined her nails. "He just woke up, poor dear. Too bad he won't survive to see the end of today."

"Then who?" Alice stood and backed away from the table. "Who drugged you?" The weight of cold steel pressed against her back, reminding her that Kaleb had given her a weapon.

Reid stood, taking a step toward Alice, that crooked grin sending shivers down her spine. Alice wrapped her hand around the grip of the gun.

"You're mad," Alice stammered. "Why would anyone besides you want me dead?" She let the weapon's weight in her hand remind her of its potential.

She pointed it at Reid and then at DeeDee, who sat in her chair writing again in her black notebook. Both of them had done horrible things, but Alice wasn't a killer and didn't want to be. "Reid, sit down."

Reid shook her head, pulling a revolver, the same one she'd had inside Red Queen during the outbreak, from her waistband.

How did Joe or Markus miss it?

Reid's finger moved to the trigger, pointing the gun from DeeDee and back to Alice. She began singing, "Who will it be? Ting tang bang."

A gunshot echoed through the room.

Alice blinked.

DeeDee sat slack in her chair. Blood trickled down her face from a bullet hole in the center of her forehead. *No—how could she, that shot, it's impossible!*

Reid turned the weapon on Alice, but still faced DeeDee, her hands shaking with laughter.

"Stuck in a book and not the real world, told you it would get you killed." Reid turned to face Alice. "Guess I forgot to mention I would be the one to kill her."

"But why would you? She's your sister."

Reid took a step toward Alice, her gun at her side. "Is she? Are you sure?" She shrugged. "To be fair, she always bothered me, acting like she was better than everyone else."

Reid looked back at DeeDee's lifeless body. "But when it came down to it, she was just like the rest of you. Weak. Besides, she's not the first sibling I've killed.

Reid gestured to DeeDee with the gun. "Elizabeth wasn't supposed to die. Just learn her place."

"Elizabeth—My mom?"

Reid laughed, "Oh, don't tell me you didn't know. Elizabeth, like DeeDee, was too good for her own family. Running off and marrying that trash you call a father. Alice, you're a Redding." She motioned around her. "Red Queen is yours. It always was."

A pounding sounded at the door behind Alice, but she couldn't focus on it. *No, it isn't true. Reid lies.* She could hear Kaleb's strained voice calling her name. She wanted to go to him. To hide from this world.

"Oh, poor thing, did you think you were special?" Reid laughed. "No, we just wanted you to give us what was rightfully ours."

Alice kept her gaze focused on Reid, bloodlust shining in her eyes. The same look on many faces in the theater the day her mother died. The one that haunted her: a look of complete loss of control. This time Alice refused to succumb to her fear.

"I had hoped to turn you to my side. Mold you into someone I could be proud of." Reid raised a steady hand at Alice. "But now you're a liability."

Alice thought about the gun in her own hand. Could she pull the trigger before Reid? Could she take someone's life, even with her own life hanging in the balance?

Kaleb screamed her name again. Closer this time, but Alice couldn't tell where it was coming from.

"You're weak," Reid mocked.

I have to.

It's the only way to stop her.

Alice swiped at the tears on her face, closed her eyes, and fired, hoping for the best.

"How cowardly. You can't even look me in the eyes as you kill me," Reid heckled.

Alice opened her eyes, wanting to prove the woman wrong who had caused all the trouble in her life.

Reid was too close, her well-manicured hand wrapped around Alice's throat knocking the weapon from Alice's hands. Her expensive perfume stung Alice's eyes, its sour taste tainting what little air she could get.

Reid stepped forward, slamming Alice against the hardwood of a door and knocking the breath from her lungs.

Alice tore at Reid's hands.

Her finger dug into the soft flesh of her neck, trying to get away. Spots fluttered in her vision as her back slid down the wall.

Reid followed her to the floor, her weight putting more pressure on Alice's throat.

Frantic and losing air, Alice kicked her assailant off. For a moment, the pressure eased, and a rush of fresh air filled Alice's lungs. She coughed as the burn from lack of oxygen started to disappear. Alice tried to crawl away, but she didn't get far.

Alice's mind searched for an escape. Never had she wished more than in that moment for the strength that WonderLand gave her.

Reid's warm flesh wrapped around Alice, pushing her into the cold concrete floor. Her long fingers coiled around her neck, applying more pressure, crushing Alice's air source.

She reached for the knife Markus had slipped into her shoe, her fingers brushing across it before it clattered to the floor. Alice stretched her arm out, reaching for the knife, her fingertips grazing the hard plastic cover.

Damn.

The burning in her chest intensified, and her need for air was getting desperate. Reid cackled above her, and Alice felt the familiar pull of anger rush through her. There was no way Alice would to let this woman win.

She walked her fingers across the concrete floor, fighting against the black spots swimming in her vision. Alice knew she didn't have long. The plastic cover of the knife met the tip of her index finger. Alice's eyes rolled back.

Hold on. Alice internally shook herself. *Not like this.*

Her fingers wrapped around the cover, pulling it closer, struggling to release the blade from its confines. Reid sunk further into Alice, putting more pressure on her throat.

The knife opened.

With a strangled scream, Alice plunged the knife into what she thought was Reid's arm. Warm liquid dripped down Alice's arm, and the pressure around her throat disappeared. She gulped down the metallic-tasting air, coughing with each breath.

Reid stared at Alice with wide eyes, her hands clasping her throat. Blood oozed through her fingers and dripped down her chest onto the red suit, making the red a dark crimson. She collapsed on her side, facing Alice, a smile on her twisted face.

Life faded from her eyes.

Reid whispered, "I win."

Chapter 36

Alice watched the blood pool around Reid's lifeless body, her once vibrant green eyes staring at her. Reid's last words played over in Alice's head. *I win.* Alice looked around the room at what she'd done. Had Reid won? Alice still didn't know if or what would destroy the city. She got the impression the reason for this little meeting was to get the three of them in the same room. Not stop a bomb.

Glass shattered somewhere in the distance.

Kaleb called her name.

Alice didn't answer. She was lost in her thoughts, trying to connect the dots but overwhelmed with her past images.

The theater.

Her mother with clumps of hair in her hands.

Red Queen Inc.

With tears streaming down his face, Harrison shot Madison and then himself.

The unknown man Alice hadn't saved from the Guard.

Gryff, DeeDee... Reid.

All dead.

Warm hands touched her cheeks, forcing Alice to look up.

"Ace? Ace. Open your eyes."

Her voice cracked, "I...I killed her."

Kaleb didn't look away. His green eyes focused on her face. "You did what you had to."

"I didn't mean to." Alice looked down at her blood-soaked hands, the knife still clenched in her fingers. A hot tear moved down her face. "I didn't have a choice."

Kaleb's calloused hands brushed across hers, loosening Alice's grip on the knife and placing it on the floor. "I know." He wrapped his arms around her. "It's okay."

She relaxed against him, letting the warmth and love seep into her. "You're safe now." His hands moved up and down her back. "You're safe," he repeated, sounding like he wasn't only trying to reassure her but himself.

Kaleb tightened his arms around Alice for a moment before letting go. He stepped away from her, using his body to shield Alice from the death she had caused. Reid's words, the words of a madwoman, ran through her head again. *I win.* Alice sniffled.

"Alice?"

She shook her head. Alice wasn't ready to talk. "Just get me out of here."

Kaleb helped her to her feet. "The door is locked; we'll have to go out the way I came."

"Fine."

They made their way through the large room, past fallen chairs and a large wooden table. Kaleb tried to shield her from the carnage. A single white shoe, now stained red with DeeDee's blood, lay in their path.

"Why is the door locked?"

Kaleb grabbed Alice's hand and pulled her forward. "I don't know." He stopped and stroked her cheek until she met his gaze. "I need you to be brave for just a moment more. It's the only way I know to get out of here."

He smiled at her and clasped her hand, looking into the dark corridor behind him.

Alice nodded. *None of this makes any sense.* She looked past him to the tightly enclosed, dark space he had to lead her through, and her stomach dropped. Tight spaces were not her friend, but there was no way they were going back into that room.

"Okay?"

She took a deep breath. *I can do this.* "Okay."

Glass crunched under her feet, and cold air danced through the hall. The walls around her started to move in. She couldn't see an exit. Her lungs and throat burned from her near-death encounter and the panic that threatened to take hold.

"We're almost there," he squeezed her hand.

Above a mint-colored door, a shattered window let what looked like moonlight through its broken confines, lighting their way out.

Marci and Markus stood outside the door with a gun at their sides. Marci called out to them. "The Guard is here."

They pushed through the door. The night air cooled Alice's heated skin, a balm on her bruised throat. Booted footsteps echoed through the nearly empty street as they made their way into the camp's densely populated area.

Kaleb led her to stand at a large barrel, orange flames dancing and reaching from its depths. A group of men, women, and a few young children warmed themselves. None of them looked up but moved closer, hiding them from the Guard patrolling the area.

Alice watched through the gaps between the people surrounding them. The Guard, who seemed to be running things, pointed to the building they'd come from and the people standing around the barrel. All but one person surrounded the building, their flashlights bouncing across it.

The Guard who stayed behind came toward them, but his hands were held up in surrender. "Alice, it's me. Linc."

Alice moved forward, but Kaleb gripped her arm. He shook his head and mouthed the word, *Stay.*

Why? she mouthed back.

"Trust me," he whispered in her ear.

Linc stepped closer to the group. The people around Kaleb,

Alice, and Markus moved in, tightening their protective wall. The heat of the burning barrel licked at her blood-soaked clothes, stealing what little breath Alice had.

She looked up at the star-covered sky. *What should I do?*

Alice didn't think Linc was a threat, but Kaleb did. Maybe it had something to do with why the door was locked. She looked over at Kaleb, jaw clenched and his hand in a tight fist.

She wanted to trust that Kaleb knew what was going on here but knew he didn't always do what was in their best interest when it came to Alice's safety. Linc had risked everything to get them to this point. Alice pushed her way through the crowd. He could have hurt her back at the fountains if he'd wanted to.

Kaleb swore but followed Alice.

"Linc," Alice called.

He looked back at the building before saying with a voice full of relief. "Alice!" He took a step forward, ready to pull her into a hug. "I was afraid they wouldn't get to you in time."

Kaleb moved closer to Alice, shoving Linc. "No thanks to you."

"Really, Rabbit?" Linc glared at Kaleb. "This is how it's going to be now?"

"She almost died."

Alice tried to interrupt them, but both men ignored her.

"I had nothing to do with that. I contacted Marci the moment I learned about Turtle's plan to use Reid to kill Alice." Linc raised his voice, "I risked everything, and now I'm stuck here."

Alice looked between the two, her body tense, nostrils flaring, and something snapped. She was done with all of it. The running, hiding, people trying to kill her, and the overprotective Alice-needs-someone-to-save-her junk. Kaleb dropped her hand to get into Linc's face, shoving him.

Alice opened her mouth to yell at them to stop. Nothing came out. Not because of her injured throat but because she didn't care. This was all pointless. Alice wasn't sure if there was a bomb in the city.

She didn't care.

Linc made it sound like the whole thing was a way to get Alice alone. Again. She believed it. Reid wanted her dead. Alice suspected she wanted anyone dead who got too close to the truth. Turtle was running everything.

He no longer wanted to 'help' her. He wanted her dead. *Maybe I should be.* There was no getting away from them. How many more long-lost relatives would find her? Try to kill, and for what? Red Queen? Alice would be happy to watch it burn.

She walked away from Kaleb and Linc into the dark street. Away from the Guard. Away from Markus and Marci. Where she was going, she didn't know, and she didn't care. All of this was her fault. *This would never have happened if I had died that day in the theater like everyone else.*

A set of soft steps echoed behind her, following at a safe distance. Alice hoped it was Kaleb but knew he was too caught up with Linc's issues to even notice she'd left. *It has to be Marci. She's the only one who would have noticed my exit.* Sure she was right, Alice walked fast. She let her anger and despair disappear with each step, knowing Marci had her back if trouble decided to follow them.

Alice stopped and stared at the fresh, white snow glittering in the moonlight. Marci walked past her and bent down in front of her, balling up the fluffy white flakes and handing it to Alice. She rubbed it across her blood-stained hands. "What the hell happened back there?" Alice asked.

Marci sighed. "I don't know. But you should know, there was never a bomb in the city. I have no idea why they told you that." Marci leaned against the wall, looking exhausted. "I'm sorry. This world is wrong. We don't belong here. You, Kaleb, and Linc are all trapped here, and I can't find a way out."

Markus interrupted them, "Did you get it? Did DeeDee or Reid give you a location?"

Alice glared at him as she scrubbed her hands. "Did you know they weren't chained to the chairs either? Is that why you gave me the knife?" She threw the snow on the ground. "And did you know they both took WonderLand? They weren't there to talk. They wanted to kill me, and you served me up on a silver platter."

She knew it wasn't fair to blame Markus for the cuffs; it had been obvious that both women had picked them.

"Alice—" Marci started.

She interrupted her. "Once again, I got sent off to die. At least last time, I had some warning. They told me that WonderLand had been released inside Red Queen." Alice turned her back to Markus. "And I didn't have to kill anyone."

Marci's hand rested on her shoulder. "Alice, I'm…"

She shrugged her arm away and, with a sniff, asked, "What happened with Kaleb and Linc?"

Kaleb moved into the moonlight, a black eye forming on his face. "Linc didn't want to blow his cover with the Guard, even if it meant your death."

Linc moved from behind Kaleb and handed Alice a black jacket. "That's not fair. I told you how to get in, and I even found out where you needed to go to get out of the city." His words had more S sounds than needed due to his split lip.

He met Marci's gaze. "Besides, my cover is definitely blown now."

Alice saw something pass between the two of them that seemed important, but she didn't have the energy to figure it out.

Kaleb shook his head. "It's not a great way out, Linc. First, we need a car that won't stand out. Second, how would we even get there if we are lucky enough to get said car? The Guard is looking for us." Kaleb grumbled.

"I have a car," Alice announced. And just like that, a memory clicked into place among the rest.

Chapter 37

Alice strolled out of a red brick apartment, a book bag hung from one shoulder and her blue-and-white class schedule in her hand. She threw her bag into the back of an old, red truck and leaned against the tailgate.

What was the point of going to class? She thought. The city was fenced off. Quarantined. Alice pushed up her hoodie's sleeves to look at the black wristband that told the world she was something she wasn't.

It was just like it had been after she'd disappeared from Kaleb's hospital room. Instead of the memories being forced on her like the others she'd had since waking, this one slid into place like a puzzle completing a picture she'd been searching for. How she got to the city, why she took the so-called cure, how she met Markus. It all made sense now. Alice rubbed her head. They were all there but jumbled, almost as if she'd lived the same day over and over. Only nothing changed. It always reset, and the timeline started over as soon as she or Kaleb acknowledged it.

One thing was always constant. Marci. *This doesn't make sense.* "When did my life become a Bill Murray movie?"

"What do you remember?" Marci asked.

Alice rubbed her temples. "It's all kind of a tangled mess, but I feel like we have been here before. Like we keep living the same life but a little different. Does that even make any sense?"

Marci, Markus, and Linc all exchanged a look.

"What's going on?" Kaleb demanded.

Markus took a step closer to his brother. "I promise we will explain everything, but first, we need to get you and Alice out of Salt City." He placed his hands on Kaleb's shoulders. "It's not safe to talk about it here in the open."

Kaleb nodded, but Alice could tell he wasn't happy by his stance. To be honest, neither was she. She was tired of this stupid, spy-game stuff.

"Alice, you said you have a car?" Marci asked.

Alice shook the frustration away, focusing on something that might help them. "A truck, actually." She sighed. "I live about three stops from here."

"Did you just say you live?" Kaleb asked.

Alice nodded, pulling on the jacket Linc had given her tighter around her. "Yes. I'm still unsure of all the details of my life here." *This time.* "But I remember the last place I parked my truck."

Marci's shoulders sagged. She looked as if she'd lost something important. "But not everything?" she asked.

Alice debated telling her she remembered many things, maybe even most things that had happened since coming to Salt City. But a lot of it didn't make sense, and it hurt her head to focus on it. The only clear thing was that Marci was always there when things went wrong, helping Alice and Kaleb to the very end.

Linc looked behind him and back at the group. "Alice, this is great and all," a flash of light moved across the darkness, "but you need to go."

He was right. They couldn't get caught by the Guard. Not after what Alice had done. There was no way she could talk her way out of that. Their leaders were dead, and they'd be looking for justice, at least the ones loyal to the Reddings.

If she and Kaleb could get out and talk to the right people about WonderLand, then maybe, just maybe, they could stop all of this. The experiments on unwilling participants, a lockdown of a city that wasn't really sick, and every horrible thing the Reddings and Dr. Turtle had done.

Alice started toward the train, knowing it might not be the safest way to get to her apartment, but it would be the quickest. The Guard had found her on the train once before and seemed to patrol it often.

By now, the news of what had happened to both DeeDee and Reid would have traveled. They would be on high alert, and there was no way to know who remained loyal to the Reddings.

"I need your hoodie," Linc said.

"Why?"

Linc kicked at a rock. "If I can give it to my commander, maybe I can send them in a different direction, giving you time to get out."

"But—"

Linc met her eyes. "I can't leave. Not without my brother."

She had forgotten about Tom and wanted to ask what had happened to him, but she knew there wasn't time.

"Okay."

The black jacket Linc had given Alice fell to the ground with a thud. She pulled the hoodie over her head, careful not to touch any bloody spots, and noticed that her favorite white T-shirt, with a black kitten in front of a mirror looking at a panther, was stained pink.

Alice shivered, not because the winter air bit her bare arms but at the memory of what she'd done. Kaleb wrapped the jacket around her shoulders, pulling her close as she handed Linc the red sweatshirt.

"Thank you." He smiled at her. "Maybe it will be enough to earn back my commander's good graces."

Alice took a step toward him, pulling Linc into a hug, and slipped the red business card Stan gave her at Butte Gardens into his back pocket.

She whispered into his ear, "He helped me once."

Linc pulled away, turning his back on them, jogging away without saying goodbye.

I hope this isn't the last time I see him.

Chapter 38

Alice relaxed against one of the chairs. The train car was empty and warm. Kaleb's knees touched hers as he sat across from her. Markus sat next to her, and Marci next to Kaleb. None of them spoke, each caught up in their own thoughts. Markus's and Marci's hands hung in the center of the row, barely touching, Marci's white band a bright contrast to Markus's black.

Alice shifted in the seat, noticing the heaviness of the jacket's front inside pocket for the first time. She examined the jacket and noticed the white knight stitched on the arm and chest. She wasn't sure who it had belonged to before Linc gave it to her. *Anything could be in the pocket.* She suspected it was a weapon of some sort and hoped it wasn't a gun.

A coldness settled into her.

Or a knife.

Her hand skimmed the top of the object. The smooth edges of bonded paper soothed her nerves—a book. Curious, Alice pulled the book from its confines and recognized it at once. It was the black notebook DeeDee took notes in. She almost dropped it. The pages were no longer white, and there was a burn mark on the corner.

"Ace."

Alice looked up and met Kaleb's eyes. Eyes looked at her with pity, like she was a wounded bunny. "Don't," she said.

"What?" Kaleb asked.

"Look at me like that. I'm not broken." Alice opened the notebook. "I'm not."

"No more than me." His warm hand clasped hers. "At least now we can be broken together."

She smiled up at him, letting the warmth of his words give her a weird kind of comfort. She didn't like being called broken, but the idea of being together filled her with hope for the future.

Markus leaned across the row, whispering something to Kaleb, a cheesy grin plastered on his face. Alice suspected it had something to do with what Kaleb had said to her because she caught the words 'smooth move' and 'baby brother.'

The brothers fell silent again.

Alice flipped through the notebook and couldn't believe what she'd found. There was page after page detailing people within the organization. Not only the legitimate front of Red Queen but criminal groups, politicians, actors, and anyone with a little power. DeeDee had been trying to find a way to take down Red Queen, like she said.

There were maps of the city and ways to get out. And names of people that might be able to help and who not to trust. Alice flipped to the last page, which DeeDee had been working on before she died. It was addressed to Alice.

> *Alice,*
>
> *I'm sorry for my part in the horrible things that have happened in your life. I know that only one will leave once they lock us in this room. I will do what I can to be sure it is you.*
>
> *There is no bomb. There is no city. None of this is real. Alice, you are trapped inside Dr. Turtle's lab. You and Kaleb are stuck inside your mind. Find a way out before it's too late.*
>
> *Marci*

Alice looked up at Marci, confused. *How had she written this in*

DeeDee's notebook? It didn't make sense. She looked over the page again, the letters rearranging, and the signed name no longer said Marci but DeeDee.

Alice sighed. She really needed to get some sleep. *Is any of the information useful? Or is it all mutterings of DeeDee's WonderLand-crazed mind? What am I going to do?*

She looked up at Kaleb, his head resting on the window, watching the world move past. *Will he ever forgive himself for letting me go into the room with DeeDee and Reid?*

Markus blurted out, "We didn't think they would hurt you. We had to play our parts to give us more time." He looked down at the grated floor and, in a voice that wasn't right, said. "We found you."

Kaleb glared at his brother. "What do you mean?"

The train clicked around a corner, reminding Alice they were close to their stop.

"Dr. Turtle is using you, the Reddings, and anyone that could be bought or made to disappear so he could keep doing his experiments in peace." The muscles around Marci's jaw tightened. "I have something he wants that once belonged to you and Alice."

Kaleb sat up straight. "Wait, what's going on? What do you mean?"

Alice looked down at their joined hands and at the bracelet made of liquid-filled beads. She knew that it had something to do with all of this. Turtle had asked her about it before he'd jumped out the window. She'd told Kaleb about the bracelet after Turtle jumped.

Alice looked at Marci and Markus, studying them. Something had changed about them in the last few seconds. Everything looked right, but the pain Marci had been fighting seemed to disappear. Something at the back of Alice's mind told her that right now was not the time to say too much.

For now, she needed to keep the bracelet and its contents a secret.

The garbled voice of the conductor sounded overhead. "Next stop salfkje station."

Alice stood, and the others followed. "Back in Red Queen, I found something Dr. Turtle wants. That's why he won't let me go."

"Where is it?" Marci asked.

"If we get out of here alive, I'll show you."

A knowing look moved across Kaleb's face. There was nothing to show, and Marci would know that. He clasped Alice's hand and led her toward the doors. His thumb glided across her wrist under the beaded bracelet, almost as if he had read her mind.

They stepped off the train, where a group of Bishops waited at the exit. Markus handed Kaleb a dark piece of fabric. Kaleb pulled Alice close to him, tying a black scarf with purple flowers around her neck, covering the bruises she knew marked her skin. Then she zipped up her jacket, mumbling something about Linc getting the wrong one.

"Donna," one of the Guards called out and started toward them.

Markus moved closer to Alice, his hand resting on what Alice knew was a gun. Kaleb, on the other side of her, still gripped her hand. That grip tightened as the Guard approached.

Alice's heart thumped in her ears.

The Guard that stopped in front of Alice looked vaguely familiar, but she couldn't place him. "Donna, it's so good to see you. Looks like normal life didn't stick," he said.

Stan. It seemed like a lifetime, not a few days since she saw him. She shrugged. "Guess not."

Stan looked at Alice and Kaleb's joined hands and back at the group of Guards checking armbands at the exit. "Star-crossed lovers?"

"What?" Alice asked.

Kaleb smiled but didn't say anything, his eyes fixed on the Guard at the exit.

Stan motioned to her and Kaleb. "Knight and Bishop."

"Something like that," Markus mumbled.

"Donna, always looking for trouble." Stan laughed. "Come on. I'll walk you out."

"Thanks."

Stan walked them through the checkpoint and into the street, away from prying eyes. He left them in the street next to an old, red truck with a book bag in the back.

"Donna?" Kaleb asked, his eyebrows lifted.

Alice knelt next to the front tire, hoping the hide-a-key was still there. "It seemed as good of a name as any." Her hand moved across the wheel well, feeling for the metal box. "When I picked it, I didn't know that memory loss wasn't forever."

Alice slid the box open and pulled the gold key from inside.

Kaleb helped Alice back to her feet. "Ready?"

Alice nodded. "Where's your brother and Marci?"

"They're not coming."

Why didn't they say goodbye?

Kaleb opened the driver's side door for Alice. "They don't feel right leaving their people here, especially now that Reid and DeeDee are gone. I give it twelve hours before the city falls into chaos."

She climbed into the truck and slid to the passenger side, knowing Kaleb needed a distraction. She tossed the keys to him and said, "That's a bit dramatic, don't you think?"

"Maybe." Not meeting her eyes, he moved to the driver's seat, adjusting it.

Whatever the reason for Markus not coming with them, Kaleb was leaving his family behind. A sad smile crossed his lips, breaking Alice's heart a little.

She reached out, squeezing his hand. He squeezed back before letting go to start the truck. "Sometimes we have to trust that everything is going to work out."

"What?"

"It's just something Marci said to me long ago."

He shrugged. "Nothing else to do."

They drove to the checkpoint. It wasn't far from Alice's apartment. With her and Kaleb's 'immune' status, they could pass without incident. Kaleb pulled the car over to the side of the road.

He turned to Alice and asked, "Now what?"

She wasn't sure. They had enough evidence to remove the Guard and clean WonderLand from the streets. Plus, they had the formula for whatever Linc and Tom released at the fountains. That would help those addicted to any drugs that had come from Red Queen. There was information from DeeDee's book: the organization within Red Queen and its leaders.

Alice slumped against the chair. She didn't have the energy to deal with that, not now. "Just drive."

Chapter 39

4 Years later...

Alice walked up the front steps of their house, grabbing the mail on her way in. A card attached to a small, paper-wrapped package addressed to Alice was the only thing in the box. She opened the card. A simple message was written on the card.

Welcome to the team.

Alice's phone rang, and she answered. Marci's voice hummed through the line. "Did you get it?"

"I did." Alice opened the front door, calling out to Kaleb. He didn't answer; the upstairs shower was running. Sitting on the couch, Alice slid her finger under the brown paper wrapped around the small box. Lifting the lid, Alice found a necklace with a small round charm that, at first glance, looked like a compass but was actually a clock striking midnight.

"Thank you," Alice said.

Marci laughed. "Now, it's time to earn it."

"You've located Dr. Turtle, then?" After Red Queen and everything in Salt City, Turtle was still the one loose end they hadn't taken care of.

"We found him working in one of the clinics set up by the new CEO of Red Queen. He's working under an alias. We've already got someone inside. All we need from you is information. I've sent the request to you. Have to run. See you later." Marci hung up without saying bye.

A bit frustrated, Alice opened her laptop and found the assignment. It wasn't much. The agent inside would contact her with any questions. She and Kaleb would be back up when the mission was near completion. "Not what I expected."

"What's not as you expected?" Kaleb asked from somewhere upstairs.

Alice smiled. "Talking to myself, but since you're eavesdropping, our next mission."

"Let me see," he called. The stairs creaked with his steps as he made his way down.

He greeted her, "You're in my seat."

Alice looked him over, staring at the rumpled black jeans topped with a black t-shirt. His blond hair was wet from the shower, the smell of aftershave hanging in the air, and a mischievous smile marked his lips.

She smiled at him.

The red cushioned chair she sat in scraped the hardwood floor when she stood. She examined the chair. First, looking at the seat, then the back, and even getting on her knees to look underneath. She pushed her short, brown hair behind her ears and smiled at Kaleb. "I don't see it. I've looked over every inch of this chair, and all I see is ALICE written in small black letters."

A smile touched the edge of his red lips. "Huh?" He reached behind him, pulling out the bug-eyed fluorescent pink sunglasses she thought she'd lost years ago. "You'll need these."

He handed her the bright pink sunglasses and stage-whispered, "invisible ink."

She took the glasses from him with a grin. "What are you up to?" she asked as she put the glasses on.

Kaleb shrugged.

Written on the chairback in Kaleb's curvy cursive were bright blue letters that read, **WILL YOU MARRY ME?**

Alice turned around to face Kaleb on one knee, a ring in his hand. Her breath caught in her chest. As much as she wanted to say yes, she knew something wasn't right.

Something's off. It's too perfect.

She looked past Kaleb's smiling face focusing on the room around them. The place they shared. A home that mimicked the color and design of the apartment she had in Salt City.

Huh, I never noticed that before.

"Alice?" Kaleb stood up, still clasping her hand in his.

"Uh..." He turned her around to face the light blue wall. "Do you see that?"

The wall flickered and she could have sworn she saw someone or something that didn't belong.

Am I dreaming?

Kaleb stood up and pulled Alice closer to him. *No, not a dream, something else.* She met his dark green eyes, and he was as confused as she was. They stood still, watching the wall as it faded in and out.

When it finally stopped flickering, Marci and Hank stood inside the wall, not next to it or in front of it, but inside it, as if they were a part of it and not at the same time. Their arms raised above their heads, pounding on the wall as their lips moved, bringing the sound of alarms buzzing with them.

Their lips formed words that Alice recognized but couldn't place.

Kaleb dropped her hand and walked toward the wall, his hands outstretched. She wanted to call out to him to tell him it wasn't safe. That they brought pain with them. The pain was already radiating through her back, down to her toes, and back up.

"Tsk tsk. You're asking the wrong question to satisfy an emotional need for resolution." Alice shook herself free of the words; they weren't hers.

They were Turtles.

He'd wanted her to stay.

To be trapped in this world.
You're only a sort of thing in his dream.
This isn't real.
Marci's words broke through the dream. "Wake up."

Alice blinked. The light blue apartment disappeared, replaced by a fan's spinning metal blades, their sharp edges highlighted by red flashing lights.

A cold weight settled inside her stomach.

An alarm somewhere behind her blared, causing her ears to ring. Alice moved her hands to her ears to block the noise. That's when she noticed the IV needle taped to her hand. She sat up, looking around the room, not believing what she saw.

Like the rows found in morgues, metal beds lined the walls of what looked like Dr. Turtle's lab. Her chest tightened, and her mind raced.

We got out.
I know we got out.
How am I back here?

She studied the room around her. Some of the beds were empty, but most were occupied with lumps of what could only be a person covered by a white sheet.

Rubbing her head, she tried to find her last tangible memory. Playing the images from the last moments of her life, overlooking what didn't fit.

There was a time jump.
More than one.

Visions of being trapped behind a wall in Salt City flooded her mind, resetting every time she or Kaleb found each other.

Marci... She wasn't part of it.
Marci was trying to find us, not the mind us but the physical bodies us.

The person that lay in the bed nearest Alice stirred. A low grunt could be heard between the thudding of the alarm that still screamed around them.

"Kaleb!" Alice stepped off the bed onto the cold floor, her legs unsteady beneath her, yanking the attached wires and IV free as she collapsed to the ground.

Her legs were unwilling to do their job. Alice crawled to his bed, calling his name with each agonizing movement.

Kaleb's hand hung over the edge of the bed, his fingers twitching at the mention of his name, propelling Alice forward. It took some time and a lot of effort, but Alice made it to Kaleb's bedside. Using the bed to pull herself up to a standing position, she shook Kaleb awake.

"Alice?" he said in a groggy voice. "What's—Why are we in Turtle's lab?"

Before she could answer, the doors behind her burst open, and people in hazmat suits flooded the room. One of them picked up a walkie-talkie, placing it against the plastic face mask.

"We have survivors."

Acknowledgments

Thank you to all my readers who have patiently waited for this sequel. When I started this book, I never imagined that we would be experiencing a pandemic. This book has changed so much because of that, and I hope for the better.

None of this would have been possible without the wonderful and talented women from my writing group, Stacy Wrytes, Emily Inouye Huey, Sarah Alva, Julie Hahn, and Apryl K.B. Lopez. If you have yet to read their stories, you totally should. They're awesome.

A special thanks to @jael_and_jenessa_reads, who had the uncanny knack for knowing when I need a reminder of why I need to finish this book.

Amanda Markus and Terri Daley, thank you for reading and commenting on my messy drafts. It made this book better for it.

Special thanks to Jade Fisher. Can you believe it's been 9 years since those early morning study sessions? Well, you studied, and I wrote. Now we get to be burnt out Elder Millenials trying to change the world in our own ways. The boaracorn would be so proud.

Thanks to everyone at Immortal Works Publishing who helped make this possible. I'm lucky to be part of such a marvelous and supportive group.

Some other amazing authors that help in so many ways are Ali Cross (Ali Archer), Rachel Huffmire, Cambria Williams, Holli Anderson/H.L. Anderson, Sabine Berlin, Staci Olsen, and Natalie Brianne. Thank you.

If you've read this far, you're awesome and now have a list of great authors to add to your TBR.

About the Author

Miranda Renae spent much of her childhood avoiding reading. One day her dad gave her a novel full of suspense and horror that she'd only seen in movies. Only better. From that day forward, she devoured the written word; no genre was safe. Miranda is a lover of both horror and romance–especially when the two collide. She spends her days weeding through paperwork. But at night, Miranda braves the dark world of her fears to build worlds of her own.

This has been an
Immortal Production